Under the Full Moon

SAMANTHA CROUCH

For my family, who always inspires me to do my best and of course, my sister, Lexi, who never fails to make me laugh. Also, for my two best friends, Blake and Allie, who will always be my own pack for as long as we live. There is nothing I wouldn't do for y'all. The Crovodds forever and always.

Allie

I used to be a girl who was all wolf. I was hot tempered, vicious, and stopped at nothing to get what I wanted.

He used to be a regular boy with no wolf. He was kind, caring, and always thought of me first.

We were alone, lost in an unknown world until we came face to face one day and our lives changed drastically. Sweet Home, Oregon had no idea what had hit them.

There were stories whispered around campfires, told from generation to generation about the wolves that used to roam these woods. They used to be regular old timber wolves but the stories changed and so did they. Werewolves were the subject of the stories and now hunters chased them out of their city. Apparently, there were no more wolves that howled at the moon, no more wolves running through the trees. That is until I came into town nine years ago.

I was young at the time, seventeen and not far from eighteen. I had friends and almost a family and I thought that nothing could go wrong. Now, I know how naïve I was for thinking that. Things could always get worse. It didn't matter who you were. I knew things were going to get ugly as soon as Jaxon Lochlan walked through the front doors of our tiny school. It was like everyone held their breath as he, a younger girl, and a girl our age stood in the doorway, the sun shining on them like a spotlight in a movie.

I stood at my locker, oblivious to the fascinating new kids that had captured everyone's attention. I was digging through my back pack trying to find my math worksheet when someone backed up into me. I toppled to the ground, my books and papers falling with me as the jock who had hit me walked away laughing. I puffed out a breath and pushed my long brown hair out of my face as I rolled onto my knees, collecting all the loose papers.

"Is this yours?" A new voice asked from above me and I looked up to see someone I had never seen before in Sweet Home, Oregon. The guy that was holding my paper out to me was probably six foot wearing a black t-shirt that wrapped around his muscles tightly. His skin was tan and his features were sharp. His eyes, chocolate brown, searched my face and his black hair was cropped short.

"Um, yeah, thanks." I said taking the paper out of his hand and then shutting my locker. I looked back at him one more time without any expression in my blue eyes and then walked to my first period class without another word.

If times were different, I would've stopped and talked to him a little more but everything was just too hard right now. I had just lost my father in Afghanistan. I was so close to him that, even when his face crossed my mind for half a second, it was like someone had ripped out my heart. So, I told myself that I would only focus on my schoolwork to keep my mind off of him. My best friend, Blake, had stayed by my side through everything and I was so happy to have a friend like her. I wasn't myself, that was for sure, and we barely hung out anymore besides school because I was always helping my mom with the horses and getting her through everything.

During my first period class, I was called down to the counselor's office. I dreaded the walk there, wondering if my mother had actually set me up for counseling or whether I was in trouble for something entirely different. I pushed open the glass doors of the office and found the counselor and one of the new kids standing there waiting for me. I halted abruptly and frowned, knowing exactly what I was going to have to do.

"Allison," Mrs. Rench greeted me with her usual prying smile that gave me goose bumps rushing up my arms. "This is our new student, Jaxon, would you please show him his classes?" her voice was too soft and silky for me to trust her completely and the look in her eyes made me take a step back.

"Sure," I ground out between gritted teeth. The last thing I wanted to do was show the new kid around and be hounded by thousands of swooning girls. But why was I so unsettled by Jaxon's presence?

Jaxon and I walked in silence as I stiffly pointed out his classes and he just nodded in response. I had to look behind me every few seconds to make sure he was still following me because his feet were light and soundless unlike mine that disrupted the quiet hallways. He was always there, though. But he was never looking at me. He was usually staring straight ahead like he didn't want to be there either. At times though, I would feel his gaze burning into the back of my head like he wanted me to turn around but when I did, he would look away. I held myself back from thrusting the schedule at him and yelling at him to do this himself. The soundlessness of his feet and the way I couldn't hear him made my blood run cold in my veins.

"And this is the lunch room." I said turning around to point to the cafeteria where kids were gathering for *A* lunch. "We both have *A* lunch so, you can either go find another place to sit with random people or you can sit with me and my friends." I said my voice tinged with irritation and I knew he could tell that I didn't want him to sit with me.

"Sure, I'll sit with you." He said flashing a smile that was meant to annoy me, which it did by the way, and then I stormed off with him right behind me.

By the time I slammed my tray down on the wooden table, I was red faced and so annoyed with Jaxon that I had to channel it into eating my gross lunch food. Jaxon sat down next to me without a word and for a few minutes we were the only two at the table. I was aware of the whispers that flowed from table to table about the two of us and I tried as hard as I could to shut them out. Out of the corner of my eye, I could see Jaxon smirking at the comments that were being made.

"What?" I snapped at him angrily which made his smile even wider. I looked away to pretend that butterflies weren't banging around in my stomach.

"You seem bothered by them." Jaxon observed the obvious and I rolled my eyes at him, looking at him like he was stupid.

"Of course I am bothered by them. I don't need any rumors going around." I said in a hard voice as I looked over to see Miles and Blake walking over to me with wide eyes. Blake looked like she was going to explode into girly screams.

“Hey, Al…” Blake said in a cautious voice as she came to sit across from me next to Miles whose green eyes were darting back and forth between Jaxon and me.

“Hey guys, this is Jaxon as you probably already know.” I said looking at Blake with narrowed eyes when I caught her staring at Jaxon. “I had to show him around.” I said and was watching Miles watching me.

I knew he had had a crush on me since we were little kids and I could see the jealousy in his green eyes as he looked at me. I averted my gaze and stared down at my half eaten sandwich. I laced my fingers together in my lap and stared at the clock, watching the hands strike in slow motion. I blew out a breath and ate slowly until I heard the bell and got out of the lunch room as quickly as possible.

I was only alone in the hallway for a few minutes before Blake and Miles walked up beside me, silently at first.

“So… is anything going on between you and Jaxon?” Blake asked, her shoulder length blonde hair bouncing in loose waves behind her.

No, I don’t have time for relationships with everything going on in my life.” I said running my fingers through my brown hair and thought about how much I would have rather been riding my horse instead of stepping through the hallways of high school.

Blake seemed to think about that for a moment but, before she could voice her thoughts, she had already walked through the door of her next classroom. Miles and I were alone, walking silently next to each other awkwardly.

“Allie,” He said in a soft, shaky voice. “Be careful around Jaxon.”

"I would never fall for a guy like that," I promised looking him in the eyes.

He smiled slightly, "I know, I just don't want you to get hurt." He said and, with that, disappeared into his classroom leaving me to think about what he had just said.

The bell signaling the end of the day rang, shrill and annoying against my ears and I quickly got out of there so that I could go hang out at the barn. I was walking home when I saw three people across the street, not looking at me but I had a feeling they knew I was there. It was Jaxon and his younger sister and his older sister who looked exactly like him. They all had deeply tanned skin, by blood, not from the sun and their hair was so black it looked blue in the sunlight. I watched them carefully. My eyes narrowed against the bright sun as I took all of them in but even when Jaxon turned his head to meet my eyes, I couldn't seem to look away. I smiled slightly, just a little twitch of my lips. Jaxon turned his head away and I saw him noticeably speed his walk up. The other two looked my way and then jogged to catch up to him, disappearing into the woods where I couldn't see them anymore. I rolled my eyes and then made my way to the barn where I could do my homework in peace.

I sat cross legged on a stack of hay bales with my textbook, pencil, and papers balanced on my knees. My horse, Ash, was watching me over my shoulder carefully, puffing breath onto my cheeks. He nudged me hard and I nearly fell off the stack of hay. I glared at Ash who just blinked at me through big brown eyes. I reached a hand up and stroked his dark grey face, his fur soft and smooth beneath my hand.

"Okay, you win." I said giving into Ash's wants and grabbing his bridle, deciding to go bareback out of laziness.

Ash's hoof beats thundered along the ground, the steady thumping filling my ears and matching my heartbeat that rose every second. The wind blew my hair back so that it swept across my shoulders. Hundreds of scents flooded my nostrils and the woods made me feel at home as Ash dodged in and out of trees. I pulled back on the reins and Ash slowed to a fast walk, his neck bobbing slowly up and down with each step he took. Ash and I entered a clearing with a big white house standing alone in the center of the field. Ash's ear pricked at the sounds inside the house when all fell silent for a few moments. Both Ash and I stared at the too quiet house when suddenly, there was the loudest crash, the sound piercing my eardrums. Ash's neigh rang out and his body raised, hooves cutting through the air, his eyes wild.

"Ash!" I screeched in fear as I felt myself being thrown backwards. I flew off his back, right underneath him, my back slamming against the ground and all the wind was knocked out of me. I curled in on myself as Ash leapt over me, trying hard to dodge me and missing me by half an inch.

He took off galloping across the field and then was gone in an instant, disappearing into the trees. I rolled over onto my stomach with a groan and pushed myself up off the ground. My rib cage hurt when I was back on my feet and I had to stand hunched over from the pain. I gritted my teeth and looked to the white house when the front door opened and a girl came running out. Her black hair was long and styled with spiral curls that flowed behind her like a cape. I gritted my teeth as I wrapped my arm around my rib cage that ached and cracked as I straightened my spine slowly.

"Oh my God, are you okay?" the girl asked when she reached me but I was focused on the two male and one girl figure standing on the porch watching me. I knew who the nearest one was, Jaxon Lochlan. My heart skipped a beat.

"Yeah," I grunted when I tried to take a step forward but there was no magic left in me. I stumbled and the girl caught me, wrapping an arm around my waist, she pulled my arm tight around her shoulders. “I can get home.” I protested when I felt the hairs on the back of my neck rise when I touched her. I tried to pull away but the girl wouldn’t let me.

“Stay until you are well enough to get home.” The girl said as she didn’t even struggle to carry half my weight across the wide open field.

“I have to find my horse.” I whispered as my head whipped back and forth, searching for any sign of Ash.

“I will go find him once you’re inside.” The girl said with a warm smile but for some reason my lips wouldn’t turn up in a returning grin.

Jaxon and the other male parted without saying anything but I felt their eyes boring holes into my body as Jaxon’s sister sat me down on the small couch in the living room. I crossed my arms over my chest, my mouth in a flat, hard line as I stared at the wall across from me. Number one: I hated being the center of attention and number two: there was something about the feeling of the house that made my skin crawl. I held back a whine that had wanted to escape my throat since I fell as the rest of the siblings made their way into the living room.

“I’m Erica by the way,” Jaxon’s sister said with a smile, gesturing to herself and then looking at her siblings standing beside Jaxon.

“I’m Katelyn,” The girl who I had seen with Jaxon the first day of school said with a silly smile on her face. She crossed her arms over her chest and grinned down at me with a curious look in her eyes.

“And I’m Terrence,” The last one said obviously the eldest of the siblings who towered above Jaxon and his sisters, all muscular and tan. His face was serious and I could tell he had been through a lot.

There was an awkward silence before I stood up. I had had enough of being treated like a puppy. "Thanks for helping me but, I need to find my horse." I said looking at Jaxon the whole time for some reason and then walked out the door.

I walked through the woods, my sneakers crunching on the leaves and I shoved my hands in my pockets. The forest was quiet and every sound pierced my eardrums as if it were one hundred times louder. I shuddered when a gust of wind washed over me, blowing my hair around my face. I paused when I was deep in the woods, looking around the trees with a little smile playing across my lips but when the memories hit, my lip curled into a snarl.

I could hear the heart beats like they were one. I could see the different bodies as if they were one. I chased after them, the feeling of freedom lighting up my golden eyes. The wind blew through our fur and I opened my mouth, tasting the air and all its freshness. I was a wolf. My silver paws struck the ground lightly when I carried myself as if I were running on a cloud. My alpha came to a halt after he had leapt up onto a rock. He lifted his head and howled and I let that sound vibrate through me as we galloped around him, letting our howls match his. I had been free my first few nights a wolf. But it never stayed like that.

I shivered and kept walking, away from the spot where the memories still lingered. I was a werewolf. I was born into a brutal werewolf pack that used the wolf inside them to kill people because they believed humans should've been eliminated. I was only a pup when they started teaching me their ways but I couldn't even kill a little bunny rabbit. I wanted to be like them and my pack mates so badly it hurt but deep down I had known what they stood for was wrong. So, when I turned eight years old, I ran. I ran as far and as fast as I could away from my alpha, my pack until I was wandering alone, a crazy omega with nowhere to go. Then a woman found me, my mother today, and she took me into her home as her daughter and my parents made me healthy again and taught me about God and what was wrong and right. I had started to believe in myself again. That was when I decided to never be the wolf again, to never know the pleasures of running under the full moon for as long as I lived. I pushed it down for eight years until this day. To help with keeping me hidden, I met a warlock named Spencer who had taught me how to push the wolf away so that it was buried so deep inside me that I couldn't feel it anymore. The potion that he made me drink all the time kept my scent hidden from others with my powers so that my old pack would never find me. I didn't want to know what they would do to me if I was discovered living with humans. I barely even had heightened senses, strength, or the power to heal quickly which made me sad when I thought about it but I usually pushed it out of my mind.

I caught Ash's scent in my flared nostrils and was about to move forward when I heard a crack from someone stepping on a stick. I whirled around, ready to attack but it was only Jaxon coming out of the woods with his usual serious face.

"You scared me." I said in a low, warning voice that portrayed no friendship. That guy still bothered me.

"Sorry," he said when he was standing in front of me. "You looked like you were ready to attack me." He didn't smile like I thought he was going too.

"You scared me." I said again with scrunched eyebrows and a semi-annoyed look on my face as I stared at him.

He crossed his arms over his chest, giving me a thoughtful look before he said to me, "You ran out of there pretty fast."

I gritted my teeth, "I don't like being the center of attention." I paused and then started walking in the opposite direction to where Ash's scent was strongest, "Now, if you'll excuse me I have to go find my horse."

I waited for him to completely disappear into the clearing before I started walking again, flaring my nostrils to use what was left of my wolf's enhanced senses. It wasn't much but it was still there. I found him standing in the middle of a clearing with his head down grazing like he was a wild horse. His dapple grey body was now darkened with sweat and dirt but he didn't seem to mind. He lifted his head and pricked his ears when he saw me, abandoning the patch of clovers he had been destroying and walking to meet me halfway.

I stroked his face gently, his eyes losing the wild glow, "Hey buddy, ready to go home?" I patted his neck and then swung up onto his back, nudging him forward until we were trotting home.

I didn't want to be mean to Jaxon, I thought, as I slowly put Ash's tack away. There was something about him that made me feel… unnerved and my blood rushed every time I was near him. I locked Ash's stall door and made my way back to the house, thinking about the Lochlan family. The sun was slowly setting over the horizon and I knew night was coming. It was my most hated but sometimes favorite part of the day. I remembered the days when I would look forward to running with my pack at night, free of human disturbances. Of course, if we did come across someone my alphas wouldn't hesitate to kill them.

I shook the memory out of my head and pushed open the screen door of my little house but froze when I saw my mom sitting at the kitchen table holding something in her shaking hand. I knew what it was the moment I stepped across the threshold. I squinted to get a better look at it realizing it was an old picture taken of my family in Florida on one of our past vacations. I had nearly forgotten about it. My dad was holding my little brother Dallas on his shoulders and I had my arms wrapped around his waist. Mom had been the one taking the picture because she didn't want to get wet. Tears sprang to my eyes at the memory which was a week before dad went back into the service. He had come home one more time recently before he went missing in action and still hadn't been found. We all presumed he was dead. I walked in on silent feet, wrapping my arms around mom from behind. She startled at my unknown presence but relaxed when she saw it was me, a girl whom she thought was harmless. She couldn't have been more wrong. I knelt down beside her chair, curling my fingers around hers and holding on tight.

"I miss him so much," Mom whispered in a barely audible voice. I gritted my teeth to keep from crying but it didn't work. Tears fell down my cheeks anyways but I quickly swiped them away.

"I know, we all do," I said in a soft, gentle voice that I hadn't used in so long. I could protect Dallas and mom so I had to try my hardest. "It's his birthday, isn't it?" I asked knowing how happy he always was when we would bring out the cake and sat around sharing stories and laughing. I held onto the memory in a death grip.

Mom nodded, mutely. I could tell she was remembering the same thing I was. "I know he would want me to be strong for the two of you but it's so hard when I don't even know if he's really gone. Couldn't he still be out there?" She asked looking down at me with the most hopeful expression on her face, making my gut twist.

"Mom," I said as tears fell down my face. She knew I was going to tell her that it was impossible for him to still be alive. They had sent tons of rescuers to find him and his troop which had gone missing. Part of me wanted to believe he was still out there somewhere but the other part, the human part, knew that it was false hope.

"I know, I know it's stupid to hope when I know that it's not possible," She said in a shaky voice making my heart break all over again.

"Don't blame yourself, I secretly hope also." I said and then squeezed her hand once before I went to visit Dallas who was most likely in the backyard.

Sure enough, he was sitting on one of the swings, slowly going back and forth but I could tell he wasn't having fun. His expression was somber and he was rubbing his fingers back and forth across something. When the sun glinted against the silver, I realized it was the cross necklace dad always wore. He had given it to Dal for his fourteenth birthday before he left.

"Hey," I said taking a seat in the swing next to him, gripping the ropes and playing with the grass underneath my bare feet.

Dal barely acknowledged me, he just kept staring at the cross lying in his open palm.

"You okay?" I asked even though I knew the answer by the tears in his eyes.

"Yeah, just thinking." He said then tucked the necklace back into his pocket. He was silent for a few seconds before he turned to me and said, "So, I heard there was a new kid in town."

I blinked, "Three actually, how'd you know about them?" I said raising an eyebrow at him but he just smiled at my expression. It was so good to see that.

"We live in a small town, word gets around quickly." He said and then looked straight ahead at the fence.

"Hmm, well they're interesting." I said in a thoughtful tone, making Dal look back at me with a strange expression.

"Why? Have you even met them?" He asked and I nodded.

"Yeah, Ash bucked me off and they helped me but I don't know… there's just something different about them." I said in a frustrated tone and he cocked his head at my voice.

"You need to learn to give people a chance, sis." He said shaking his head at me, his black hair flopping into his eyes.

"You should know by now that I never give people a chance," I said laughing but Dallas had a serious look on his face. I looked at my feet, knowing the question that was about to come out of Dal's mouth.

"Eight years ago, when mom found you, where had you come from?" As soon as the question left his lips, nerves racked my body. I hated lying to him like that, he was my best friend who I told everything to but I couldn't tell him about my past, not when it was so horrible. I bit my lip wanting to avoid the question with all my heart.

"Do we have to talk about this?" I asked him playing with the necklace around my neck like I did when I was nervous.

"C'mon Al, we deserve an answer. We've been asking for years." Dal said giving me a pleading look. I didn't want him to know who I really was and what I was capable of.

"Maybe in a few years. You're not old enough to know yet." I said and then stood up, walking out the back gate and digging for my keys in my pocket.

"Why? What happened that was so… terrible?" Dal asked running after me and falling into step beside me.

"It's… complicated, Dal." I said in a hard voice as I stared straight ahead.

“Ugh,” He sighed frustrated with me but then added, “Where are you going?” He asked following me out to my car and stopping when I hopped into the front seat.

“To get my medicine,” I said which was a total lie, I had to go visit Spencer to make me invisible to others around me.

“Can I come? It’s depressing around here.” Dallas said looking back at the house sadly. I pressed my lips together, thinking about it and then nodded and he hopped into the car beside me.

I pushed open the door to the small herbal/tea shop that Spencer and his family ran. I looked up when the little bell chimed, signaling a new customer. Spencer’s head whipped up from the sale he was in the process of making but his eyes went straight for Dallas who was inching inside behind me. I saw Spencer’s lips tighten before he went back to doing his work. His blonde hair fell into his eyes as he stared down at the cash register and finished helping the girl that was at the counter paying for whatever she was buying. Spencer was three years older than me and just like a brother except he was a warlock and not a werewolf. I waited at the back edges of the store with Dallas close behind me as his eyes darted around the small, herb infested shop that sometimes creeped me out too.

The woman turned and walked out the door, the bell chiming when she closed it softly behind her. I threw a small smile at Spencer who was looking at Dallas. I rolled my eyes at him.

“Hey,” I said snapping my fingers at him in annoyance, “Is it ready?”

“Oh, uh, yeah let me go look in the back.” Spencer said but before he disappeared into the back room he said, “Allie can I talk to you for a second?”

I looked back at Dallas, “You stay here and don’t mess with anything.” I told him but he just rolled his brown eyes at me.

"I'm not two years old, you know." Dallas said with a playful glare and I smiled at him.

"I know, it's just fun to pretend." I said ruffling his hair and he swatted my hand away, sticking his tongue out at me. I laughed as I followed Spencer into the back of the shop.

He was silent for a few minutes as he searched through the orders, finding mine and handing it to me. I clasped the tiny box in my hands, feeling the smooth surface of the blue wrapping paper that covered it. I gingerly pulled off the top, setting it down on a shelf and peering inside. I took a deep, shaky breath. The necklace that lay inside was going to help keep the wolf away, bury it even further down so that there was no chance of it coming back, no chance of my alphas finding me here.

"You're sure this will work?" I asked Spencer, knowing he hated it when I wasn't sure about one of his creations.

"Of course. I made it, didn't I?" He grinned at me and I rolled my eyes touching the small amber heart pendant that clung to a silver chain.

"You still have more of the potion, right?" He asked as he organized something on his shelf so that it was perfectly straight as usual.

"Yeah," I assured him because the potion hid my scent. "There's still a whole bottle left."

"Good, because we may have something to worry about." Spencer said and my heart skipped a beat, the blood flowing through my veins became loud in my ears.

"What happened?" I asked urgently, heat spreading across my body as fear washed over me.

“There was an attack in Ohio, ten completely torn apart and four missing. You know what that means,” Spencer said running his fingers through his hair in stress.

“They are turning people. They’re coming.” I said, my hands shaking so hard that Spencer had to take the box out of my hand. He pulled me into a tight embrace. I wrapped my arms around him and let his touch calm me, something that witches and warlocks had the power to do.

“As long as we keep you hidden, nothing bad will happen. I won’t let it.” He said and I smiled against his shirt, pulling away and taking the box in my hands.

“Thanks, Spencer. I don’t know what I’d do without you.” I said with a grateful smile but he shrugged.

“You would be surprised what you could accomplish on your own.” He said and then disappeared into his lair where he practiced his spells.

Dallas and I drove home in silence, the amber heart pendant resting lightly on my collarbone and the sky darkening around us. I still hated being outside after dark even though I knew the pack wasn’t here. I never knew what really lurked beyond the shadows. I gripped the wheel so tight that my knuckles turned white and my teeth were shut so tight I thought they would shatter.

“Allie?” Dal asked from the passenger seat when he saw my tense shoulders and the way I was about to kill the steering wheel.

His voice snapped me out of the thoughts of wolves and killing, “Yeah.” I asked blowing out a breath and running my fingers through my hair.

“Are you okay? You looked like you saw a ghost.” Dallas said and I blew out a breath seeing the worry in his eyes.

"I'm fine." I said the two words through gritted teeth as I stared out the windshield.

"Does this have something to do with your past?" He asked me making my muscles tighten at the question.

"No, just…" I was about to tell him to leave it when something dark darted into the road. I slammed on the brakes, squealing and pressing my hand against Dal's chest to keep him from hitting the dash board.

The car came to a squealing halt in front of the figure but the headlights illuminated the creature. I gasped when the silhouette took shape as a dark brown wolf with glinting yellow eyes that sparked in the shine of lights. The wolf stared at me for ten seconds before it lifted its lip, snarling and then disappearing into the woods. I let out a breath as my chest heaved up and down but the wolf was unfamiliar, not one of mine. It was probably just a regular wolf not what I dreaded most. I looked at Dallas who was staring wide eyed at the place the wolf had been standing.

That night, as I lay in bed I stared out my open window, the cool breeze washing over me. The moon was half full and as bright as a wolf's eyes against the night sky. I remembered the nights I would run as a wolf through the woods until I couldn't breathe and the cold winter air would burn my lungs. The feeling of my pack's fur brushing mine when we would all curl up and fall asleep next to each other, our cold noses pressed into each other's bodies. I pushed the memory out of my mind and then heard a rich, gleeful howl from deep in the woods somewhere. I sat straight up in bed, my hands gripping the windowsill urgently. My eyes found the part of the woods that it was coming from and they stayed there, wishing to see the wolf again, wishing I was out there like he was. But I knew I couldn't do that. They would find me and I wouldn't survive the punishment that they would bestow upon me.

The next morning I woke up to the sound of car tires crunching on the gravel driveway. I looked out my still open window to see a small black car pulling up to our house. I scrunched my eyebrows together and pulled the blankets back, my toes curling back when they touched the freezing hard wood floor. I pulled my hair back into a bun and shrugged on a big sweat shirt that hung to the middle of my thighs. I wore leggings that clung tight to my legs and made my way downstairs to find Dallas answering the door. My eyes widened when I saw the fourteen year old girl walking into the house. I knew her. She was Jaxon's sister… Katelyn.

"Hey, Kate," Dallas said with a huge smile on his face and I narrowed my eyes at his tone. Someone had a crush!

"Katelyn, hey." I greeted her and she turned to me with a smile on her tan face. Her black hair was slightly curled and flowing down her back. She looked exactly like her older sister.

"Allie, it's good to see you again." Katelyn said her voice formal and tight when she greeted me.

"You two know each other?" Dallas asked obviously confused by our little interaction.

"Uh, not really. Yesterday, Ash bucked me off and they helped me." I said folding my arms over my chest.

"Yeah, Jaxon's outside if you want to talk to him." Kate said jabbing her thumb behind her at the black car that was still parked outside. I nodded, shoving on my fuzzy boots and then heading onto the porch.

Jaxon was already getting out of his car when the screen door shut behind me. Mom must have been called to work early because her car wasn't there in the driveway. Jaxon walked up to me clad in a grey shirt, a leather jacket, and jeans. I studied him from where I stood shivering slightly from the cutting wind that the sweat shirt didn't shield me from.

"So, my brother and your sister?" I asked him when he took the first step onto the porch.

"That was my reaction." He said with a playful look in his dark brown eyes. I smiled slightly and he leaned against the post that held the porch up, his easy stance telling me he was at ease around me. I liked the fact that he wasn't acting like some superior alpha male. "You found your horse, right?"

I nodded, "Yeah, but let's not talk about that. It was embarrassing." I said laughing and he chuckled.

"At least you can ride a horse," he said his smile widening when mine did and for some reason butterflies flitted around in the pit of my stomach.

"It's not hard," I said challenge written all over my face and I knew he could see it too.

"I'll save both of us the pain of trying to teach me." Jaxon said making me laugh and I peeked inside the window behind me to see Dallas and Kate sitting on the couch watching the movie, Dal's arm wrapped around her shoulders. I smiled slightly at the sight of my brother finally happy. "Dallas will be good for Kate." His words made me look at him.

"And Kate will be good for Dal," I said looking down at my feet, "Ever since dad… died he hasn't been himself lately. I just want him to get better." I looked up to see Jaxon's eyes on me, something sparking in them as mine met his.

We stayed like that for few minutes, watching each other silently as if we were two alphas assessing each other. It was strange how much he reminded me of the wolves in my pack. The feeling was good and bad. I was the first one to look away, something that I did very rarely in my life because looking away meant submitting and I never gave up that easily.

The weekend passed with the same routine Sunday morning. Kate came over to hang out with Dallas and Jaxon came over to sit on the front porch with me. We mostly talked about our families and I found out that his parents had both died two years ago and their older brother Terrance was the legal guardian of the household. He told me they got in many fights, which were probably what had scared Ash the day I was bucked off. After a few seconds of hesitation, I told him my story except for the part about how I was found on the streets. I got choked up when I told him about dad but he rested his hand lightly on my arm, making my blood fizz and heating the spot his fingers touched.

I was not at all ready for Monday when it rolled around and I slowly got dressed for school, dreading having to go be social. I had hung out with Miles and Blake Saturday night which was a good way to get my mind off of the new attack that had occurred that afternoon. They were getting closer. I threw on a Michigan football t-shirt that my mom had passed down to me and some skinny jeans that fit snug around my hips. I touched my fingers to the amber necklace and grabbed the box of tea that was stored in my room that helped keep my scent away.

I made my way downstairs and mixed the tea with water, heating it up like it told me to. I poured it into a mug and Dallas and I walked to school, eager to get there and escape the freezing air. I lifted the tea to my lips and swallowed a big, bitter tasting gulp that made me scrunch up my nose and gag a little. I hated the taste of it and kept trying to tell Spencer to change the flavor but he said he didn't know how yet.

"What is that stuff?" Dallas asked when I had turned my head the other way to keep him from seeing my disgusted face. I finished off the mug and tucked it away into my back pack.

"Medicine, remember?" I told him as convincingly as I could but he didn't seem to buy it.

"What's it for?" He asked making my jaw tighten. I hated being questioned like that.

"It prevents a virus that I've had since I was a kid. I don't know all the details about it." I said that because the wolf was sort of a virus if you looked at it the right way.

I stepped into the parking lot, engulfed in teenagers, hormones, and music in half a second. I shouldered my back pack and wished that winter break was still here. We had just started school last week after a three week break. My eyes immediately found the Lochlans' where the three of them were walking out of the woods towards us. I saw Kate's brown eyes find Dal's within ten seconds of being outside and then Jaxon's met mine. My heart literally froze and I stood there like a deer in headlights with wide blue eyes and a slightly opened mouth. He didn't even smile when he looked at me and neither did I, it was like there was some sort of unspoken communication passing through us. I blinked and my heart was back to normal and I could feel my surroundings once again.

He sat down in the desk beside me and my hand clenched around the pencil I was holding, the lead poking into my skin. I could feel the heat rolling off of his body and it made every hair on my body stand up. What was with him? One minute, I could have a nice conversation with him and then the next I went crazy. My blood fizzed in my veins but there was something familiar about the feeling, something buried deep in my brain. The wolf. My blood fizzed when I was about to change. But why was that happening now? I wasn't going to change it was impossible because of the tea and necklace. A quiet whine escaped my lips, more animal than human. Jaxon looked over at me with a worried look on his face, only making the bile in my throat rise faster. Mr. Morris had already started talking but his voice was just like static in the background because all I could see was Jaxon. I squeezed my eyes shut when a wave of dizziness washed over me and knew I was about to see my breakfast again. My hand shot up in the air and I said through a rushed voice, "Can I go to the bathroom?"

Mr. Morris looked stunned at my urgency, "Sure." He said but before he could say anything else I was out of the room and sprinting down the hallway.

I burst through the bathroom door, thankful that no one was inside and leaned over a toilet, retching repeatedly. All the tea I had drunk that morning was out of my system and I could taste its lingering taste in my mouth. I groaned and crawled to the sink, using the edges to help pull me up. Looking in the mirror, I saw the dark circles under my eyes and my pale skin was lighter than usual. I gripped the edges of the sink, sweat rolling down my face as I stared at myself in the mirror. It was when I was about to leave that I saw my eyes flash gold, the color of the wolf's.

"No, no, no, no." I whined as tears rolled down my face. My eyes changing back and forth from gold to blue and when the colors stopped flashing they mixed to form a violent green color. I fell back against one of the stall doors. This couldn't be happening. I didn't want to be a wolf. Why wasn't it working?

A sharp pain cracked through my body, a strangled sound exploding from my throat as the crack racked my body. Another crack and I knew exactly what was going on. My chest rose and fell in deep, shuddering breaths and my body twisted, my spine making a horrible noise that made me want to puke again. My fingernails dug into my palms and I knew I had to get out of there before the transformation was completed.

I sprinted down the hallways as fast as I could, ignoring the office lady's protests as I pushed open the doors. I didn't realize I had left my bag in the class room until I was well across the street. I let myself be swallowed up by the woods. I collapsed on the cold ground when no one could see me and the aching in my bones had become a piercing pain, making me fall on my side and curl in on myself. I looked down at my hands when there was a stabbing pain in them and saw claws trying to replace my fingernails but they kept fading away. The wolf was trying to break through but all of Spencer's magic was still inside me, making it impossible for it to completely break the barriers. I knew the biggest reforming was about to come so I braced myself, tensing every muscle in my body and rolling onto my hands and knees. It came right on time.

When my rib cage tried to bow out, the loudest scream I could produce split from my throat. My voice faded back and forth between a murderous scream and a bloodthirsty roar. Tears rolled down my face but the wolf couldn't break through my barriers and it gave up eventually, leaving me huffing and puffing on the ground.

After about three minutes of trying to regain my composure, I rolled to my feet and tried to stay on them without wavering from my tired muscles that threatened to give out. I blew out a breath and dragged my feet across the ground as I made my way to Spencer's shop where hopefully I could get some answers. I pulled my jacket tight around me to hide the mud stains from rolling around on the ground but my face was probably a mess and people kept staring.

"Spencer," I sighed when I saw him working at the register. He looked up at me but when he saw the mud, his eyes were coated with worry.

"What happened?" He asked after he made sure there were no customers in the store.

"I… I was sitting in class and then I ran to the bathroom and threw up all the tea I had drunk that day. Then, I started changing. I went into the woods and was about to completely change when it all just stopped." I was panicked now and tears were streaming down my face as I told the story.

"The wolf is trying to break through the barrier that the necklace creates. Something is making that happen but I don't know what." Spencer was thoughtful. The look he got in his eyes when he was deep in thought had returned and I knew I needed to leave him alone for a little while so he could figure out what was happening to me.

I was walking home when I realized school was letting out. I didn't want to see anybody from that class but in Sweet Home, Oregon, everyone walked home from school. His scent hit me first, making my whole body tingle and I turned my head to see him walking with his siblings on the other side of the street. Our eyes met and I could see the worry clouding his chocolate brown eyes. I smiled slightly and gave a faint nod before he disappeared into the trees.

The next day brought on more fears as I hoped the wolf would stay back for the rest of my life. I couldn't afford to let it kill anymore. Spencer told me not to drink anymore of the tea because he was still trying to figure out what went wrong with the solution. Knowing Spencer, he was probably going to be holed up in his office for the next week trying to get everything just right.

I walked through the doors of the busy high school, the scents of people mixing together to cloud my senses. Only ten seconds went by before I was bombarded by the sound and smell of Miles and Blake who immediately fell into step beside me. The good thing was, they hadn't heard about what had happened yesterday which I was incredibly grateful for because I wasn't in the mood to explain it. Blake was already talking to Miles about something and I didn't seem to be a part of the conversation.

"… And I swear he smiled at me. Like it was a flirty smile too." Blake was practically jumping up and down in excitement at whatever she was talking about.

"I wouldn't read so much into it, Blake." Miles said from the other side of me, rolling his eyes jokingly.

I held up my hands, "Whoa, can ya'll catch me up? I'm lost."

"Okay, so yesterday I was in my history class and Chase Walker smiled at me." She was literally bouncing up and down in excitement but I just rolled my eyes at her in fake annoyance.

"It was just a smile, Blake. I'm with Miles on this one." I said with a smile nudging Miles in the rib cage with my elbow. He laughed quietly as we made our way down the hallway.

"Whatever, but when I get a boyfriend and you two are single, I'm going to be laughing at ya'll." Blake said crossing her arms and then she headed into her first period class. I saw Chase take the seat beside her and he indeed smiled at her in a flirty way.

"Well, maybe we were wrong." I said with a shrug as we moved past the class and I spotted someone very familiar.

Jaxon walked down the hallway towards me but I knew he was going to keep moving past me. His face was like stone, his eyes barely even moving but something was wrong. My wolf senses could smell it on him. He was anxious about something. The sharp tang filled my nostrils. I looked down and saw his fists clenching and unclenching when he walked by me. I paused and slowly grabbed his arm but he acted like I had come out of nowhere, spinning around as if ready to attack.

"Are you okay?" I asked him with narrow eyes and I could see his features being forced into a smile.

“Yeah, I’m fine.” Jaxon said nodding his head slightly but my eyes just narrowed more.

“Okay,” I said and when he started to turn away, I just grabbed his arm harder. I turned to Miles, “I’ll catch up to you later.” Miles glared at Jaxon and then moved on down the hallway.

Jaxon looked at me for a few seconds in silence; his mouth twitched at the corners, and then kept walking down the hallway. I growled quietly under my breath and he stopped, looking back at me. Was my growl that loud? I caught up to him, falling into step beside him.

“So, you’ve moved around a lot, right?” I asked looking up at him through curious eyes.

“Yeah, literally all over the place,” Jaxon cracked a smile, a small one, “Why do you want to know?” he said and I dodged someone, bumping into him and almost falling over. Instinctively, he grabbed my arm lightly to steady me. My skin seemed to ignite underneath his touch. Something stirred inside me.

I swallowed, “Uh, did you ever know anything about like… killings that happened anywhere?” I asked as I pictured the hunters of the pack ripping campers to shreds in the woods of London. I had been a part of that massacre.

Jaxon looked at me funny but his expression was guarded. His heart beat sped up. He was nervous about something. “Every once in a while there would be a strange killing by animals like a cougar or something but they could never find the animal.”

I bit my lip, tossing the information around in my head. “Okay, thanks.” I said when the bell rang and was about to sprint to my class but Jaxon grabbed my arm. It felt like the wolf inside of me started awake. I turned to him slowly.

“Why do you want to know?” he asked his mouth in a flat, hard line that made me think it was a touchy subject.

“I’m doing this report for one of my classes. I just needed an opinion.” I said with a convincing smile and then made my way to my class but I found myself thinking about the woods. I knew exactly what tomorrow night was.

Lunch came around and everyone filed into the crowded cafeteria where the scents were overpowering. My amber necklace felt heavier on my collarbone and the sounds practically burned my ears. I gritted my teeth and tried to put on a friendly smile when I slammed my tray down on the table.

“Whoa, are you okay?” Blake asked when she saw my face and my eyes flitted to Chase who was sitting next to her.

“I’m fine,” I sighed readjusting my smile to be more convincing, “Just failed a math test and my mom is going to kill me.” I lied but froze when Jaxon’s scent filled my nostrils.

“Hey Allie,” Jaxon’s sister, Erica Lochlan, said in a cheery voice as she set her tray down on the right side of me. Jaxon quietly took the seat on my left side.

“Hey,” I said but kept my gaze on Jaxon who was staring down at his food and not eating it.

“So,” Blake said interrupting the awkward moments of silence, “My birthday party is tomorrow night at my house. It’s going to be awesome. You,” she pointed to me, “are required to come because you’re my best friend. Erica and Jaxon can choose if they want to.” She was beaming and I couldn’t help but smile at the sight of my best friend so happy.

But tomorrow was the full moon and that was the night I hunted for clues about the whereabouts of my old pack. The wolf was strongest on those nights because werewolves drew their power from the full moon. My wolf never came out completely but it was right underneath my skin, lurking beneath the surface. Secretly, I had a stash of guns loaded with silver bullets hidden in the basement which I took out every night just in case I ran into any unwanted creatures. I realized I hadn't spoken for a while so I cleared my throat and said, "Yeah, I'll be there. What time?"

"Eight o'clock sharp. Don't be late." Blake said and I laughed at the way her eyebrow arched as if she were my mother.

"I won't." I said and, right before I was about to get up, Erica said something that made my heart race.

"Be careful, it's a full moon tomorrow night." Erica laughed and that was all I heard as the siblings disappeared down the hallway.

The school day passed and night came. It was always my least and most favorite time in my life because I was reminded of what I used to be. I walked home with the cold winter wind biting at my cheeks and realized I made the mistake of forgetting my sweater at home before I left that morning. I wrapped my arms around myself and rubbed them to get the goose bumps to go away. Someone came up behind me.

"Need a jacket?" Jaxon asked handing me his black sweatshirt. I hesitated but then took it gratefully, pulling it over my head.

"Thanks," I sighed crossing my arms and snuggling against the soft cotton, "I was in a hurry this morning. I love winter." I smiled and looked up at the cloudy sky.

"So," He said running his fingers through his hair and then clearing his throat, "Terrance wants to have you and your brother over for dinner tonight? Are you guys free?" I could hear his heart beat speeding up and I couldn't help but smile that I made him nervous.

“Yeah, we’ll be there.” I promised him and then he crossed the street to join Erica and Katelyn who smiled at me. I was about to yell at Jaxon that I forgot to give him his sweatshirt back but when I looked up, there was no trace of him except for his scent, fresh rain in the forest.

I pushed open the screen door of my house, breathing in the scents that made me think of home which was something I never had before I came here. I found Dallas at the kitchen table doing his homework in deep conversation. I set my bag down beside him and he looked up, smiling at me for a second before going back to his homework.

“Where’s mom?” I asked him as I grabbed an apple from the fridge and bit into it.

“Downstairs meeting with people from her work,” Dal said nodding his head towards the basement door where I indeed heard voices but I couldn’t make out what they were saying.

“Well, you and I have dinner plans tonight with the Lochlans. So get dressed, we are going in a few hours.” I said patting him on the shoulder before heading up the old wooden stairs.

“I’m a guy it doesn’t take me five hours to get dressed.” Dallas said laughing quietly.

“But, you do have a girlfriend so you have to look like you put effort into it,” I yelled down the stairs at him before I shut the bathroom door so that I could shower.

I got dressed into leggings, a soft sweater that went to mid-thigh, and tall brown boots that went up to my knees. I swiped on some mascara and a thin line of black eye liner which was very rare for me. My hair hung in loose curls down to the middle of my back and I made my way to the first floor where I saw Dallas ready to go.

"You look handsome." I smiled jokingly at him as I practically skipped down the staircase.

"And I can't remember the last time you got dressed up and looked happy about it." Dal said as we made our way to the car, not bothering to say bye to mom because she was still holed up in the basement doing who knew what.

I pulled up in front of the giant white house that stood alone in the middle of the blank field. For some reason, there was something comforting about it but also unsettling. I put my car in park and Dallas and I got out slowly, my heart beat racing when I smelled Jaxon inside. We made our way across the field and as soon as I stepped onto the porch, Terrence opened the door. I jumped a little at the quickness of it.

"Oh, hi." I said awkwardly with a smile on my face. I was sure my cheeks were bright red not only from the cold but also from my nerves.

"Come on in," He said with a welcoming smile and a glint in his eyes that made me glance over his right shoulder, a sign of submission. Why was I submitting to him?

Everyone was sitting around the table, Jaxon to my right and Dallas was across from me next to Katelyn who were deep in conversation. Katelyn laughed at something Dal said and I smiled at the way she leaned into him.

"Allie," Terrence said bringing Dal and Katelyn's attention back to the table, "How long have you lived here?"

"Since I was eight," I said instinctively looking at Dallas who knew I hated talking about my past, "Before that I moved around a lot." I shrugged taking a sip of my water.

“Any particularly interesting places?” Erica asked and at first I thought she was being pushy but when I saw the smile on her face I knew it was a sincere question.

“I was born in London…Ohio…” I said watching Dallas when I saw his head snap up at the sound of my past, “But, we only lived there for a year before we had to leave. We had… financial issues.” I lied because the real reason was that my pack had killed too many people and we were going to be figured out sooner or later.

“That’s a shame,” Katelyn said surprising me by the sound of her voice, “London sounds like it might have been a beautiful place.” Her white teeth contrasted brightly against her tan skin.

“Did you hear it’s going to snow tomorrow?” Erica said reclining in the white chair and taking a sip of her glass of water.

My jaw tightened. It was nearly impossible to track a scent when there was fresh snow on the ground. “I like the cold weather but snow…” I shook my head and smirked.

“C’mon everyone loves snow.” Jaxon said with a smile and I laughed quietly.

“Not me,” I said crossing my arms over my chest. I was about to say something when there was an alarm sound on the TV. I practically leapt out of my chair, ready to attack what was coming.

“What’s going on?” Dallas asked as we made our way into the living room.

I sat beside Jaxon on one of the couches, leaning forward in anticipation as Terrence turned up the TV. A news lady appeared on the screen, thin as a twig with short blonde hair. She was holding a microphone the size of her hand. She was standing in front of a place that was blocked off with police tape.

"Our reports are saying that the group of friends was out camping in a small Kentucky town when in the middle of the night something attacked, killing everyone but Athena Matherson the eight year old girl who went missing. FBI is saying that they found wolf hairs and bite marks on the people, giving us the suspicion that it was a pack of rabid wolves that committed this crime."

My mouth had gone dry and my heart was racing like it did before the change. My fingernails dug into my palm until I was sure they had cut into my skin because I knew where that eight year old girl went. She was bitten by my alphas and turned into a werewolf like me. They were in Kentucky on their way to Oregon and picking up some human souvenirs on their way. I ran my fingers through my curly hair and then stood up, ignoring Dallas calling my name. I pulled open the front door and stepped out into the cold air, closing my eyes and breathing in the scents of rain and snow. I walked slowly over to the swinging bench and sat down crossing my arms, thinking about what was going to happen to me if they found me.

"Hey," Jaxon said walking up to me and taking the seat beside me. I smiled at him sadly, liking the way his body warmed mine against the cool winter air. "Pretty gruesome stuff, huh?"

"Yeah," I sighed shrugging and leaned my head on Jaxon's shoulder instinctively. I didn't realize I did it until his muscles tensed and my breath froze in my throat. I was about to pull away but then hesitantly, he put his arm around my shoulders. I closed my eyes and listened to his heart beat that relaxed me until I was almost asleep.

Almost as if he didn't realize it, his fingers drew slow circles on my upper arm. The wolf crawled to the surface at Jaxon's touch but I didn't fight it. It felt good. He said quietly, "I just don't want them to come here."

I lifted my head from his shoulder to look at him, "Haven't you heard the legends of the wolves?" I asked smiling at him out of the corner of my eyes. He shook his head, smirking at me. "Well, last time they spotted a pack of wolves was fifty years ago but multiple packs used to roam these woods. The hunters chased them off though," I said looking out over the dark woods that had turned into a place where monsters hid.

Jaxon shifted beside me, sitting forward and removing his arm from around my shoulders. It made me feel like he pulled a part of my body with him. The wolf inside me snarled at his retreat. I narrowed my eyes at him and leaned forward, resting my chin in my hands.

"It's just a story but some people…" I let out a breath and rolled my eyes, "Some people in this town dedicate their lives to finding those wolves again."

Jaxon turned to look at me and I faced him when he said, "Do you believe in the wolves?" His voice was low and we were sitting so close together that I could feel his breath on my rosy cheeks.

I swallowed, my brain clouded by Jaxon's scent. My wolf wanted him closer, to feel his touch on my cold skin. I looked at him in silence, my eyes searching his face for any sign of what his next move was. But I couldn't read him like I could other people.

I remembered his question, "I don't know," I said glancing down at my hands that were folded in my lap, "Maybe I do."

"You know you're different than most girls," Jaxon said and my eyes met his in a heartbeat.

"Is that a good thing or a bad thing?" I said one corner of my lips lifting in a teasing smirk. He smiled and the butterflies in my stomach bat their wings harder.

"All good," he whispered when his hand came up to brush a piece of hair behind my ear. His fingers whispered across my cheeks and came to caress it gently.

My hand slid up to rest on his chest, right where his heart was so that I could feel it underneath my fingertips. My lips parted when he leaned forward, resting his forehead against mine, heating my whole body. Our lips were about to touch when someone's voice filled my ears.

"Allie!" Dallas called and I snapped my head up, away from Jaxon. I felt something tug at my insides. Dal was walking towards us and I could sense the waves of nervousness all the way across the field from him. He made it to the porch with a red nose and cold cheeks, "We have to go. Mom called and she is freaking out about the attack."

"I'll be there in a second." I said and he darted inside to say his goodbyes.

"You'd better get going." Jaxon said his voice riddled with disappointment. I swallowed hard and played with the ring on my finger.

"Yeah," I sighed and then added, "You're going to Blake's party, right?"

Jaxon smiled, making the butterflies go nuts, "Yeah, can I pick you up at seven forty five?"

I was beaming with overwhelming joy, "Yeah, that'd be great." I said nodding, "I'll see you tomorrow."

I walked down to my car but couldn't help thinking about what would've happened if Dal hadn't interrupted us. Jaxon was going to kiss me. I guessed the unsettling feeling that I got around him was because I liked him and so did my wolf. *So did my wolf,* I thought to myself and turned around to see if Jaxon was still standing there but the porch was empty. That was why I had almost changed that day at school. Jaxon made the wolf come out because she was attracted to him and wanted to protect him. But with my pack getting closer and adding more wolves, could I afford to risk being with Jaxon? Even though I could barely stand being away from him? I grumbled underneath my breath and I pulled open my car door, jumping into the seat and blasting the heater to warm my freezing limbs.

That night, I sat up in bed and looked out my open window with my knees pulled up to my chest and my arms wrapped around them. I rested my chin atop my knees and breathed in the cold air that stung my lungs but I liked the way it felt. I thought about Jaxon and the way his body warmed mine when his arm rested lightly on my shoulders. I sighed, a smile playing across my lips and I glanced at the moon that would be full tomorrow night. I stared out over the woods that covered Oregon like the fur on a wolf's body during the winter. There was a knock at my door and I glanced at the clock. It was around 1:00 in the morning. I closed my eyes and breathed in the scent of the person on the other side of the door. Dal's scent flowed into my nostrils.

"Come in," I said in a quiet voice so that I wouldn't wake up mom. The door knob twisted and Dallas came in with a strange look on his face.

"Did I wake you up?" He said when he sat down at the edge of my bed. There was definitely something bothering him because Dallas didn't like to stay up late.

"No," I sighed turning so that I was facing him, "I've been awake for hours. Are you okay?" He was looking at his fingers and everywhere in the room except me.

"Yeah," Dal lied and I narrowed my eyes at him, "I just want to talk to you about two things."

"Shoot," I said grinning at him but he was nervous about something.

"Are you and Jaxon…?" He didn't have to finish the question. I knew exactly what he meant.

I shook my head, "I don't know…maybe?" I said glancing out the window at the moon that seemed to be getting bigger by the second and imposing on our conversation. "Why do you want to know?"

"Because I'm dating Kate and I really like her and if something bad happened between you and Jaxon then it could drive Kate and I apart and I don't want that to happen…" Dallas drifted off from his rambling which he usually did when he was either mad or upset about something. I understood where he was coming from though. If I were him, I would've said the same thing.

"Dal," I said resting my hand on his knee, "I can promise you that I'll never let my problems become your problems, okay?" I said and he nodded. I wrapped my hand back around my knees and smiled at him, "Besides, knowing me, it probably won't work out."

"Yeah, that was the other thing and I know you don't like to talk about your past but you lived in London?" Dallas asked looking sincerely interested which I didn't understand.

"Yeah, but only for a year, besides it was Ohio not England. It was nothing special. Then, I moved about one hundred other places before we came here and was orphaned." I said playing with a thread on the end of my blanket. I wasn't necessarily sad about being orphaned but at the time I had been so lonely it was like someone carved a hole in my chest.

"Well," Dallas said and I noticed the drowsiness that riddled his voice, "That was the most information I've ever gotten out of you." Dal laughed quietly and rubbed his eyes. I smiled at him when he lay back on the bed, closing his eyes.

His chest moved up and down slowly and soon he was quietly snoring, stretched out so that he took up the entire bottom half of my bed. I gently brushed his hair back from his eyes and then curled up into a tiny ball at the top of my bed, closing my eyes and thinking immediately about Jaxon.

The next day was the full moon or The Night of The Wolf as Lydia, my alpha and mother, used to call it. I stood in front of the full length mirror that hung on the door in my room as I fastened the tiny clasp of my amber necklace. Dallas had left my room in the morning without waking me up which was surprising because I had tossed and turned all night, plagued with dreams about the days I ran with the pack. I woke up from the dreams in a cold sweat. My mind was somewhere else entirely as I walked downstairs for breakfast.

"Hey mom," I said when I saw her reading the newspaper at the dinner table but she was barely able to stay awake. "You okay?" I asked grabbing my back pack and checking the chore schedule that was on the wall, realizing it was my day to muck the stalls after school.

"Yeah, just tired." She sighed taking a sip of her coffee. Mom was a hard working lawyer who didn't stop at anything when she was on a case.

"Who were those people here last night?" I asked shouldering my back pack again and fingering my amber necklace. "They were here pretty late."

"Just some people from the office," She said rubbing her eyes and I pressed my lips together, "There's another girl missing. She's around sixteen. The family is frantic trying to find her but she left absolutely no trail of where she was going." Mom said her fist clenching in frustration.

"Was she treated badly at home or something? Why'd she run away?" I asked fully interested in the case now. If I knew something about her, maybe I could help bring her home.

"She was bullied at school pretty badly is what they later found out but she doesn't want to be found." Mom sighed and then Dallas walked down and she didn't share any more information about the case.

It was Friday. The kids were pent up with energy that was about ready to explode with weekend excitement. I wasn't at all ready for the weekend or the night that came when school was over. My fingers twitched at my side anxiously as I made my way down the hallway. When Blake tapped my shoulder, I nearly jumped three feet in the air.

"Whoa, sorry to scare you." Blake said laughing and I smiled nervously at her. "So, I heard that you went to dinner at the Lochlans. How'd that go?" Blake asked with a sing song voice and I knew she thought something had happened.

"Well, it was all good until the news came on and then we went outside and were sitting on the bench. He was so close to kissing me until my mom called and interrupted it." I said feeling like a total girl in that instant and I had to admit it felt kind of good.

"What? No way," Blake said stopping me and grabbing both my arms, "This is legendary. Allie likes a guy. Is this real life?" I glared at her jokingly and she laughed, trotting into her classroom.

Jaxon wasn't at school that day and for some reason it gave me the chills. I didn't know what he was doing but he was probably just sick or something like that. After school, my Spanish teacher made me stay after for tutoring. Why he wanted me to stay after on Friday I did not know but I was forced to stay there with him. I drummed my fingers on the desk and glanced at the clock for the hundredth time in the last hour and when the clock struck 4:30, I sprinted out the door.

The sun was setting which meant the moon would be at its peak soon enough and every werewolf would be awake. I sprinted up the stairs after school, throwing my backpack on the table. I had had to stay after for tutoring meaning the moon was closer and I needed time to prepare. I shut the bedroom door, locking it firmly behind me and pulled my shirt over my head, changing into a black tank top, leather jacket, black jeans, and tall lace up boots. I let my hair fall loose around my shoulders and bent down, my fingers running over my floorboards until I found the place where it opened. My eyes rested on the glinting bow and arrows and guns that lay in piles underneath my wood floors. I pulled on my black leather gloves as I loaded silver bullets laced with wolfsbane, something that would kill a werewolf the size of Mt. Everest. By the time I was prepared to leave with my bow and gun strapped to my belt, it was nearly dark out. My phone buzzed and I answered it, "Hello?"

It was Blake, "You are going to be here, right? Because I'm freaking out right now."

Crap, I thought to myself when I remembered that tonight was also my best friend's seventeenth birthday party. I had to make an excuse that I was going to be late, "I'm going to be late. I have some things to take care of."

"Seriously?!?" Blake sounded angry on the other line and a twinge of guilt hit my stomach.

"I'm sorry, it's really important. I'll be there as soon as I can." I said and before she could argue, I hung up the phone. The good thing was, mom knew that I was going to be at Blake's house for pretty much the entire night so I just had to pretend that was what I was doing.

I didn't realize my mom and brother were downstairs until I was on the very top step. I froze when I heard them talking and growled lightly underneath my breath. I turned on the heel of my boot and dashed back into my bedroom, pushing open the window and jumping onto the roof. I stood on the roof with the wind blowing my long hair behind me and every scent filling my nostrils. The moon was probably an hour away from its full strength but already I could feel the pull and it made me want to cry out in joy. Instead, I ran off the roof, doing a front flip just for the fun of it, and landing on my feet perfectly. I gave a quiet, giddy laugh and sprinted across the street into the woods on the other side.

I paused at the edge of the woods and took in the darkness that surrounded me. I still had pretty good night vision but it was darker than usual and it made me nervous. I shifted the bag of arrows on my back and gripped the bow that fit perfectly in my hand. When I was younger, my dad gave me a choice of weapons to train me. I picked the bow and arrow and I trained, competing in competitions and winning all of them until he disappeared. Now, I just do it in my free time, to take my mind off of things.

I took off running. The wind dragged its fingers through my hair as I sprinted, dodging trees and leaping over ditches. The feeling of freedom was unlike anything I had felt in a long time. I pushed my legs faster and they pounded the ground as silent as a rabbit when spotted by prey. I growled and lowered my head and shoulders until I was barreling through the woods, missing a tree by half a second. That was when I heard it.

There was a crack in the trees, so low that I thought I was imagining it at first. I froze, reaching back for an arrow and notching it firmly. There was a threatening growl, low and menacing that made butterflies flick in my stomach. I stretched the bow back and in the dark, three figures took shape in the shadows. Three wolves surrounded me, low to the ground and baring their teeth at me. I spun in a circle to see one in front of me and two behind me. The male in front of me was the alpha for sure because he was the one that stood straight up, staring at me.

The black wolf took a step towards me, his red eyes bright with predatory rage. I tried to keep my hands from shaking as I stared the wolf in the eyes and was reminded of my past. I knew that the wolves behind me were getting closer and I could feel their breath on my legs.

"Get away!" I yelled at them, adding a snarl for good measure. The wolf didn't even blink, it just snarled even louder. I pulled the bow back and aimed at the alpha, letting the arrow fly and it lodged itself into the alphas shoulder. He yelped but I missed his heart, maybe because I didn't want to hit him.

When I realized I had just made him angrier, I threw the bow to the side and ripped the amber necklace off and chucked it to the side. I was about to summon the wolf for the first time in a long time when gun shots filled the air. I yelped like the wolves and closed my eyes, instinctively ducking and I realized tears poured from my eyes. When everything was silent except for the pouring rain, I leapt up grabbing my gun and pointing it at whoever had fired the shots.

His hair was plastered to his forehead from the rain and his brown eyes looked brighter than usual. Jaxon Lochlan stepped out of the trees with a gun at his side and a serious look on his face. When I saw him, I dropped my gun and broke down in tears, running into his arms. He held me tight against him and he stroked my hair like I was a child. I buried my face in the crook of his neck and shivered as the air turned colder and the rain got heavier.

Jaxon pulled away and shrugged out of his jacket, making me realize I had taken mine off when I was running, and he draped it around my shoulders, "Come on, it's cold out here." Jaxon said quietly and I nodded, wiping tears from my cheeks that just blended in with the rain.

I was still shaking from the nerves when we entered Jaxon's big warm house and I couldn't keep the flash backs of killing people as a wolf from my mind. New tears fell down my cheeks as I took a seat on the couch, pulling my knees up to my chest and hugging them close as I silently cried. I flashed back to a night when I was six years old.

Mom and I crouched low in the bushes, her silver fur brushing against mine that was identical to hers. We feasted our eyes on a camp ground where about ten tents were set up and teenagers were hanging out inside them. Mom was teaching me how to hunt a massive group of people. Her voice was inside my head and she told me to go. I did what she told me like I always did.

I leapt from the trees and clawed my way into the tents one after another, ripping into the flesh of people as they screamed and blood dripped down my throat.

"Allie?" Jaxon asked and I flinched, coming back into reality. He handed me a warm mug of hot chocolate and sat on the couch beside me. I turned so that I was facing him with my legs tucked underneath me.

"How'd you know where I was?" I asked over the rim of the mug that warmed my freezing palms. Jaxon avoided my gaze and talked to the floor.

"I was supposed to pick you up for the party at 7:45," He said looking at me and I bit my lip, feeling bad instantly, "I saw you leaving and followed you."

"Mmm…" I smiled laughing lightly, "Stalker much?" Jaxon laughed, his shoulders shaking slightly. I set the mug down on the coffee table and my fingers went to my collarbone but my necklace wasn't there anymore. I panicked at the loss of it because I didn't know if just the tea would hold back the wolf.

"What were you doing out there with a bow and a gun?" Jaxon asked his lips twitched into a small smile but I blinked at him.

"Practice," I said shrugging, "It works better at night in the woods so that the cops aren't suspicious." I smiled at him, jumping when there was a flash of lightning out of the corner of my eye. I blew out a shaky breath and looked up at the ceiling, blinking back tears.

"Hey, come here." He said pulling me against him, tucking my head under his chin as I leaned on his chest. "Are you okay?" The way he held me, it felt like we had been dating for years rather than just meeting. Could I allow myself to get so close to someone when I could have to leave at a second's notice? But, it felt so good to lean against his body and actually feel safe for once. I didn't want to lose that feeling.

"Yeah, I'm fine." I said pulling away reluctantly and resuming my original position. "We don't really know much about each other. Tell me about yourself." I felt like an idiot asking him to tell me about himself but I needed to know more. It was rare that I let anyone get that close to me like I let Jaxon.

"Okay," He said shifting uncomfortably and I heard his heart beat jump. He obviously didn't like questions. "When I was younger, my parents did…" he paused, searching for words, "Something that pissed the CIA and FBI off. They never told us what they did and then one day our parents shoved us in a closet but… but we saw everything." Jaxon didn't meet my eyes and it was hard to see him in the unlit house except for when there were flashes of lightning. His hands were lightly shaking and I carefully wrapped my fingers around his, keeping them still. He swallowed and then continued the story, "They took them and I remember them saying something about finding us but they never did and just like that my parents were gone and we never saw them again."

There was another flash of lightning and I could see the shine in his eyes when he looked at me. I was completely frozen in fear and astonishment. I couldn't remember the last time somebody opened up to me like that. To be honest, it scared me. I wanted to comfort him, to rest my head on his chest where it felt safe, but something kept only my hand on his. The deal I made with myself when I first ran away was that I wouldn't get close to anyone because I could have to leave in a matter of seconds. It was easier just not to care about anyone like I was beginning to care about Jaxon. I looked away from him and ran my fingers through my wet hair which was starting to get curly from the rain. I swallowed and looked out the window; the moon was perfectly in view and bathing the two of us in vanilla twilight.

"I… I can't imagine what that was like for you." I said taking my hand back and resting it in my lap, "I'm so sorry." My voice dropped to a whisper and I thought about when that soldier came to my house and told me my adopted dad was assumed dead.

"Terrence takes good care of us, even if we are a little difficult sometimes." Jaxon laughed and I was relieved to see the smile on his face. He was about to say something when my phone rang in my pocket.

I answered it, "Hello?" By the noise in the background I knew exactly who it was.

"Where in the world are you?" Blake's voice rang on the other side, ridded with anger, "You were supposed to be here two hours ago!" she had to shout over the noise and I held the phone away from my ear, werewolf ears were sensitive.

How could I have forgotten? My best friend's birthday party and I was sitting here, soaking wet, and talking to a guy who I barely knew. "Oh my god, Blake I'm so sorry. I… this thing is taking longer than I thought." I lied but I was afraid Blake would see through my alibi. I was right.

"You're a terrible liar, Allie." Blake's voice cracked on the other line, "Where and what are you doing that's so important?" She asked and I clenched my jaw, not sure what to say.

Jaxon's front door opened and Terrence, Kate, and Erica walked in laughing about something. Jaxon said, "Guys, shut up." A little too loudly. I glared at him with wide eyes.

"Who was that?" Blake asked and I scolded myself for not remembering my best friend's birthday. "Are you with Jaxon?"

"Yeah kind of." I said hesitantly and I heard her puff out a breath in annoyance.

There was a muffled voice on the other side, Miles said, "Where is she?"

Blake covered the phone but I could still hear her, "She's with Jaxon."

"Look, I'm sorry. There was just something I had to… to take care of." I whispered looking up to see the whole family watching me from different spots in the room. Terrence was leaning against the wall in a dark corner where I could only see his eyes. Kate and Erica were on the floor sitting cross legged.

"Okay, whatever Allie. I'll see you at school Monday." Blake snapped and hung up the phone before I could say anything else.

I sighed in anger when I hung up my phone and shoved it in my pocket, standing up and handing Jaxon his leather jacket. "I have to go. I possibly just lost a friend." I said sadly with a tad bit of anger lacing my words. I paused before I opened the door, "Thanks for… everything." I said and then disappeared into the night.

I walked through the woods, retracing my scent so that I could find my weapons and necklace that I had dropped out of pure terror. I wrapped my arms around myself and I found the spot where the wolves had tried to attack me. I grabbed my leather jacket and pulled it on, shivering at the memory of the wolves' bright eyes and salivating jaws. I swallowed hard and picked up my bow and arrows then lastly my gun which was buried underneath some leaves. I scoured the ground for my necklace, pushing aside clumps of leaves but I couldn't find the bright little pendant anywhere. I knew I threw it around here somewhere but without that necklace, the pull of the moon was going to have a bigger effect on me than ever before.

I searched some more, even making my way a few yards in case adrenaline had kicked in and I threw it harder than I meant to. Something was off though. I couldn't have thrown it that far, I thought to myself. Panic gripped my chest and I glanced up at the moon that was now at its peak and when I felt the tug in my stomach, I knew I was going to have a problem. The pain felt like a hand gripping around my heart and squeezing with all its might. I fell to my knees and groaned as the blood rushed in my ears and nearly deafened me. There was a stinging pain in my fingertips and I brought my hand close to my face so that I could see it clearly.

"This can't be happening." I snarled in a voice that wasn't human at all. Where my fingernails should've been, black claws stuck out, sharper than a thousand knives. My head ached and my rib cage felt like it was on fire but the sound of voices filled my head. I looked up, my gold eyes glinting in the dark and scrambled quickly behind a tree. I sat on the ground with my back pressed against the scratchy trunk that dug into my arms. I listened carefully to the new voices.

"She said the radar picked up the wolves in this spot." One man snapped at somebody else and I noticed the annoyance in his voice. He obviously thought that he was better than whoever told him where the wolves were.

"Well, they obviously aren't." A woman sighed, "Didn't you hear the gun shots? Someone got here before us, Dale." The woman said in a hard voice and I heard her gun click into the holster.

"You can tell the boss that. She scares me when she's angry." Dale said in a low voice as if he were afraid that the boss would over hear them.

"You're such a baby sometimes." The woman said and I heard her feet rustle in the leaves as she stalked off into the night.

They are looking for me.

Run.

And so I did.

Jaxon

As soon as Allie left the house I spun on my siblings, bursting with anger and irritation at their carelessness. I snarled at Terrence who raised his eyebrows calmly in surprise but he didn't move from where he casually leaned against the wall.

"Are you insane? You could've killed her!" I yelled at him pointing my finger accusingly at his chest. Terrence looked evenly back at me, his place in the household keeping me from attacking him.

"No, but you are." He said as if he were saying *Hey what's up?* The blood in my veins surged forward like water blocked by a dam. I fought to keep my temper in check, something that had always been hard for me.

"And why is that?" I responded.

"Because you brought her here and you let her get close. We can't afford to do that, little brother. There are some things in life that people like us can't have." Terrence said and I thought I heard a tiny but of… longing? I took a tiny step back, looking at the ground instead of into his eyes, "Some things we can't change."

That was the end of that conversation. Terrence left the room and went upstairs to go to sleep. I glanced at Erica and Kate who were cross legged on the ground, ran my fingers through my hair, and then marched upstairs to my room where I could crash into bed and pretend like today never happened.

The night probably got five degrees colder within the next hour. I woke up shivering, feeling the cold all the way in my bones. The full moon bathed my bedroom in pale, silver light and the cold winter air burned my lungs. I immediately thought that the heater must've turned off in the middle of the night which got me to thinking if any of the others had woken up too. My nose had been the only part of me sticking out of the blankets, making it feel like an ice cube when I lightly touched it. It was too cold. *Dangerously cold.* I threw the blankets back slowly, regretting it when the air bit at me. I pulled a hoodie over my head and then made my way upstairs to see Terrence already up looking at the thermostat on the wall.

"What's wrong with it?" I asked trying to ignore the shivering in my bones.

"How am I supposed to know?" Terrence snapped. I knew it was the cold that was aggravating him so I tried not to take it personally. I couldn't help but wonder though if he was also angry about me bringing Allie over.

"Look, man. I'm sorry about what happened last night. I shouldn't have blamed you guys because I was almost a part of that. But we have to be more careful. You heard what I said about the legends. People still believe." I said and saw my reasoning dawn on his face as he considered my words. He looked steadily at me, his eyes the only part of him saying that I was right.

"Yeah, we'll be more careful. Why weren't you out there with us?" Terrence asked noting the way I was shivering as the pull of the cold made me want to run through the woods, over the bumpy terrain that could only be navigated by a wolf. Like me.

"I was supposed to pick Allie up for the party," I held up a hand before he could say anything, "I know, I know. I can't get too close to her." Terrence pressed his lips together in careful agreement like he didn't want to actually say it. "What about Kate and Dallas?"

"They're younger, still oblivious. There's something about Allie…" Terrence drifted off, looking back at the thermostat instead of at me.

"What? You don't trust her?" I asked bringing his brown eyes back to mine and holding them there with a blazing gaze.

"I…" He was about to say something when his body shuddered, the smell of the wolf suddenly panging the air like a sword. I gritted my teeth as a wave of nausea rolled over me, knowing what that meant, I opened the front door. The cold winter air washed over me like water and I felt the familiar tug in my gut. I looked at the clock, 3 o'clock in the morning.

Behind me Terrence, groaned, low but loud, and crumpled to the floor. In an instant, a black as night wolf took his place with piercing red eyes and teeth as sharp as daggers. The wolf that was Terrence snarled at me before he dashed outside into the night, blending in with the shadows that the trees cast. I sighed, giving in and dropped to the ground, completing the painless transformation of becoming a wolf. I wasn't me anymore instead strong muscles rippled underneath thick brown fur and gold eyes darted around the house. Terrence's howl pulled me back and my ears pricked forward.

Alpha. Pack. Run.

And so I did.

Allie

That night I crawled into my window and collapsed on my bed, tears streaming down my face as I pulled the covers around me, not bothering to take my dirty, wet clothes off. I squeezed my eyes shut and silently cursed myself a hundred times for being so stupid. What was I thinking? I never broke promises. I didn't hurt people. *I'm not my mother.* My hands fisted around the blankets and I cried. Blake was my best friend and I had probably just lost her. Not because of that night, which was a big part, but also because I hadn't been completely there ever since dad died. My mind was always somewhere else in the world. Miles was probably furious with me also, considering he was the one who warned me to stay away from Jaxon in the first place.

I fell asleep a little while after that, hating myself for doing what I did to Blake. I roused slightly when I heard a rich howl pierce the still night and a pang of fear twisted my gut. I didn't go back to sleep after that.

Jaxon wasn't at school on Monday which struck me as odd because I had seen him only last night. I tried not to read too much into it, maybe he was sick or something from being out in the rain last night when it was so cold. I hadn't seen Blake yet which was a good and bad thing. She was probably avoiding me but I had to find her and apologize for what happened last night. I couldn't lose anyone else. Then I spotted her.

"Blake!" I yelled from all the way across the hallway when I saw her. Her head snapped in my direction and a look of betrayal crossed her face before she started shoving past people frantically to get away from me. I did the same and eventually caught up to her after bumping into everyone. She started running down an empty hallway and I felt like a wolf chasing a rabbit. I wrapped my hand around her upper arm and she jerked to a halt, spinning around to glare daggers at me.

"I don't want to talk to you." Blake said in a low voice that betrayed the look of pure anger on her freckled face.

"Then don't talk, listen." I pleaded and when I was sure she wasn't going to run away, I let go of her. "Look, I'm so sorry about Friday night. I was stupid and I have no idea how I could've forgotten my best friend's birthday party. You have a right to be angry with me and I'm sorry I haven't been a good friend lately. It's just with my dad dying and… everything else going on… I can't lose you too." she looked back at me with sad eyes and I knew she didn't accept my apology even before she said it.

"Sorry, Allie but you're right. I do have the right to be angry with you." She said and then turned down the hallway, walking out of sight. I growled under my breath and retreated down the hallway, walking into my classroom and pretending that the other half of me wasn't walking down the hall.

My day just went downhill from there and the sky darkened with the oncoming snow that the forecasters promised. The bitter coldness made me grouchier and so did the fact that Miles was also avoiding me, angry that I ignored what he had told me about Jaxon. So, I kept my head low and my mouth shut all day, noticing that Erica and Kate weren't at school either. That couldn't have been a coincidence, I thought to myself.

A slow, boring week passed without any sign of new killings from my pack which I was grateful for but it also made me wary. What were they planning? Mom was still working hard on the case of the missing girl which was getting nowhere, making me think mom wasn't seeing the bigger picture. *Stop being so paranoid.* I had to stop thinking that everything linked back to my past. Jaxon had come to school after that first day but he was staying away from me too and I had never felt so utterly alone in the world. *You deserve it, this is how it should be.* The little nagging voice in my head was right. There was no stopping fate and this was my fate. After school every day, I would go home and do my homework outside in Ash's pasture while he peacefully grazed in the green grass.

Friday rolled around like water in a calm ocean right before a storm. The snow had melted away but the air stayed frigid and for some reason I found it comforting considering that was how I felt inside. The sky, darkened with winter clouds, loomed above me as I leaned against the white picket fence, reading my book and listening to Ash's steady breathing as he grazed quietly in front of me. I smoothed my fingers along the edges as my eyes moved over the words. The story was about some sort of murder mystery that wasn't particularly interesting to me but it was a way to keep my mind off of everything.

The day grew darker and my eyes strained against the dim light as I tried to finish the last few pages. I hated the ending. Turned out the boyfriend was the true killer. I closed the book angrily and threw it on the grass, picking it back up, and standing up so that I could go visit Spencer who I hadn't seen in a while. I poked my head inside the house, grabbed my keys off the wall, and then jumped into my car as a few rain drops started to fall.

I passed by the Lochlan's house and felt a pang of need and want. I hadn't heard Jaxon's voice in what felt like years and it slowly ate away at my insides. What was it with him? How could someone make me feel this way? It was like I needed to touch him and hear his voice fill my head. But I knew it was better this way. We weren't meant for each other. If he didn't want me, he didn't want me. I would just have to live with that. I turned on the radio and kept driving, hoping to drown out my thoughts as if they were words. But the song just made me angrier.

Something always brings me back to you

It never takes too long

No matter what I say or do I'll still feel you here till the moment I'm gone.

I turned the song off. Tears blurred my vision but I wiped them away angrily, realizing that I had driven way past Spencer's shop. I was probably twenty minutes in the wrong direction. I had no idea where I was and it was pitched black outside, the only light was from the street lamps that hung lazily over the wet pavement. Rain blurred my windshield, forcing me to turn on the wipers so that I could see clearly. The sound lulled me almost to sleep but the anger and sadness that burned through me was too great to relax completely. I slowed down, trying to figure out where I was because I never really left the safety of my little town before. I turned down an alley that was lined with apartments but it was even darker and it didn't necessarily look like a very *safe* neighborhood to be in at night all alone. I was about to back out when I saw a very familiar shape walking away. Anger and desire surged through me, battling like two angry alpha wolves as the person moved under a street lamp and became Jaxon.

I didn't care who saw me anymore and I slammed my foot on the gas, speeding down the quiet alley and braking when I came up next to him. He startled and tried to walk faster either because he thought I was going to kidnap him or he really didn't want to talk to me. I was out of the car in less than a second, practically drowning in the pouring rain. I blinked the water away and glared daggers at Jaxon's back.

"Jaxon!" I yelled disturbing the peace but not caring one bit. He stopped but he didn't turn around. He cocked his head to the side, listening to me. "What the heck is wrong with you?!? You've been avoiding me for a week and I don't even know what I did wrong!" I started crying but this time didn't bother to wipe the tears away, "I have no one right now! And it's bad enough that Blake and Miles hate me, I don't need you hating me also! At least I know what I did to them!" I paused in my yelling to swat angrily at my wet hair, "Well, here I am stumbling blindly in the dark trying to figure out what the heck I did wrong and you won't even tell me!"

I saw him slightly duck his head in shame. I wasn't quite done yet. My voice rose.

"Jaxon Lochlan, running away from your problems is not…" And he kissed me. He turned around so fast, grabbed both sides of my face, and crushed his lips to mine. At first I was so stunned that I just stood there frozen but then I let him force my lips open and I slid my arms around his neck, bringing his face closer to mine as if we could melt into each other. I stood on my tip toes, running my fingers through his wet hair and I let the sunshine spread through me despite the dark night. I opened my mouth and kissed him with all the desperation and longing of the past couple of days that had been eating up my insides. His mouth was gentle on mine but I could still feel the urgency as his hands slid down my back and pulled me closer to him, close enough to hear the hammering of his heart and mine together. I had never felt more alive and I knew this was what home felt like. He pulled away to look at me, his forehead resting against mine and I could practically see the spark in his brown eyes.

With a shaky hand, I reached up and traced his jawline with my pointer finger and his eyes fluttered shut at my delicate touch. When he looked back up at me, his face was apologetic.

"I'm sorry," His voice was shaky as he trailed his fingers down my arm, lacing his fingers through mine, "About the last couple of days." I could barely think straight and I had to fight the desire to get my next words out.

"That kind of made up for it," I whispered and then he kissed me again and I was lost in him.

Jaxon. Jaxon. Jaxon.

I fell into bed that night as if I were floating on a cloud. A giddy laugh escaped my lips and for some reason, I had to fight back the urge to howl in excitement. I replayed the moment over and over again, the way his hands made my whole body tingle, the way his lips felt against mine, and how I fit perfectly into his arms. There was nothing that could compare to how I felt when I was with him. I fell asleep still feeling his touch on my skin. A wolf howled in the distance, happy and free. Exactly how I would've howled if I were still a wolf.

As soon as I woke up the next morning, I reached for my phone to call Blake. I had almost finished dialing her number when I realized that we still weren't talking so I had to keep my excitement penned up inside me. I swallowed my disappointment and went to brush my teeth after throwing on a big sweatshirt and leggings to keep me warm in the cold house. I heard Dallas walking down the stairs sluggishly as I dragged my toothbrush across my teeth. I braided my hair to the side and then headed downstairs to say good morning to my early bird family.

"Hey guys," I said rubbing the sleep out of my eyes as I poured orange juice into a cup. I realized in surprise that I still didn't have my amber necklace on because someone had stolen it.

"Where did you go so late last night?" Dal asked from where he was leaning against the counter eating an apple very loudly. I looked at him and when he saw my cheeks flush, his smile got wide and taunting, "Jaxon, huh? You hear that mom? Allie's finally got a boyfriend." We both laughed and looked at mom who was leaned over some documents.

"Yeah, that's nice honey." She said in a detached voice and went back to work. I looked at Dal and rolled my eyes in annoyance.

The problem with mom's and my relationship was that we didn't really get each other. I was more of a daddy's girl. When dad died though, she threw her grief into her work and barely acknowledged Dal and I, making me think we were tied too close to dad and looking at us was painful. I sighed and looked at Dallas jingling my keys at him.

"Want to go for coffee?" I asked slipping on fuzzy boots.

"Do you even have to ask?" He said laughing and we trotted out the front door, leaving mom alone inside to do her work.

I recognized Blake's car immediately as we drove into the lot and parked up at the front. I hesitated before I got out, seeing her in line through the windows. She was with Chase and Miles, her fingers laced through Chase's and she gave him a peck on the cheek. When did they happen? Sadness gripped my heart as I realized how bad I missed my best friend.

"You and Blake still not talking?" Dal asked when he followed my gaze to where the three of them were in line.

"No," I swallowed hard, "Can we go somewhere else?" I asked about to plug the keys back into the ignition but Dallas grabbed them out of my hand, shoving them in his pocket.

"Running away from your problems is not a good trait, Allie." He said and my eyes widened when I realized that was exactly what I had told Jaxon. Dallas was right.

"Fine, you win. Let's go." I growled and pushed open the car door, preparing myself to walk into a war zone without any armor.

The delicious smells of coffee and pastries blasted my nostrils when I pushed open the glass doors and I tried to concentrate on that instead of Blake in front of me. But she noticed me in a heartbeat. For an awkward moment, we locked eyes and she was the first one to look away and then Miles was the one holding my gaze. His lips twitched into a tiny smile and just those tiny movements made the rain cloud hovering above me lighten a fraction. Dallas nudged me forward and I glared at him but he just pushed me a little more. I frowned at him but made my way to where Blake and Miles were waiting in line. I tapped her on the shoulder.

"Hey, can the three of us talk for a second?" I asked watching the hesitation on her face but when she nodded, relief washed over me and I felt like I could breathe. *So far, so good.*

We found an empty table at the back of the shop and sat down in awkward silence for a few minutes before I broke the glass.

"This silence feels like the time when we first went out together," I observed and smirked at the memory of the first time we had hung out outside of school when I first moved here. Blake and Miles both laughed quietly at the memory. "Why are we mad at each other?"

Blake looked at me with a sad expression in her eyes. She sighed and ran her fingers through her hair, "I don't know, to be honest. It was kind of a stupid fight. Will you forgive me?"

"Of course," I said unable to keep the tears out of my eyes when we got up from the table and wrapped our arms around each other.

Dallas and Chase joined us around the tiny table and it was just like old times. We made fun of each other and joked around, laughing until our stomachs hurt. One time Miles almost spit his coffee out at me when we were making fun of Mrs. Jin, a weird teacher at our school.

I dropped Dallas off at home and decided to go for a ride in the woods and maybe, "accidently" walk by Jaxon's house. I was too lazy to actually put on a saddle so I just slipped on Ash's bridle and swung up onto his bare back, no helmet. Hopefully, I wouldn't fall off or I would get seriously hurt but I didn't care because I would heal eventually.

Ash and I galloped through the woods, weaving through the trees and jumping over fallen logs. I nudged Ash with the heel of my Sperry and he leapt forward, lengthening his stride until we were flying through the woods at incredible speeds. My hair flew behind me like a cape and I raised my face to the sun that poked through the trees. After about ten minutes of galloping, I slowed Ash to a walk and we moved aimlessly over the ground.

"Hey," Someone said off to my left and I squealed in fear. Ash made the same noise I did and was about to lift off the ground but Jaxon grabbed his reins and held him down.

"Goodness," I laughed lightly as I slid off of Ash's back, "This is the second time you've scared my horse." I walked over to Jaxon and slid my arms around his neck, breathing in his scent.

Jaxon laughed, his shoulders shaking lightly, "I think he hates me." He said quietly, resting his forehead against mine.

"Only a little," I laughed and then kissed him, brushing my lips against his. Ash nudged my back impatiently, pushing me into Jaxon but his arms were there to steady me and I laughed.

Ash followed us as we walked hand and hand through the woods. I had spent many years training him to follow me everywhere I went. We walked through the part of the woods where the wolves had attacked me all those nights ago on the full moon, shuddering at the memory. Jaxon squeezed my hand and looked down at me.

"God, that freaked me out." I laughed nervously and rested my head on his shoulder. "I don't think I ever thanked you for saving me." I turned him towards me and pressed my lips to his. "So, thank you."

"Anytime," He said pressing his lips to my temple and then added, "Just please don't make a habit of it." He laughed and I rolled my eyes at him.

We walked in silence for a few minutes, Ash's hooves on the ground the only sounds in the quiet forest. Birds chirped, hidden in the trees and somewhere in the distance a squirrel chittered angrily at something. The morning air was cold and I was slightly shivering underneath my jacket. For some reason, I remembered a day a long time ago when I was a wolf.

I leapt down a hill with all the power of a wolf and was suddenly joined by two more wolves, both pure white and one with gold eyes and one with piercing blue ones. My best friends, Khione and her twin brother Jason, galloped next to me as we leapt like bunnies through the snow. My silver fur glittered wonderfully against the white background. I snapped at Jason playfully and he leapt at me, wrestling me to the ground while Khione barked and whined at us. I kicked Jason off of me and we kept running back to the cave where the rest of the pack was waiting for us.

I blinked out of the memory, wondering why I was thinking of that at a moment like this. But I remembered that amazing, careless day like it was yesterday. We arrived at the clearing where Jaxon's house was but I still couldn't bring myself out of the memory completely, not until I heard Jaxon groan.

"Are you okay?" I asked when he leaned over, clutching his stomach and groaning again.

"Yeah," he gritted his teeth and I slid my arms around his shoulders to help him walk, "I'm fine." I had to hold almost all of his weight but with some werewolf strength it wasn't too difficult.

Jaxon

The pain in my gut gnawed at me as the wolf tried to break through because of the cold. I couldn't shift in front of Allie or she would probably run away screaming. As we slowly walked across the field, Allie supported all my weight without any problem at all.

"This is a problem," Allie grunted as she stepped up onto the porch and hauled me up with her. "What's wrong with you?" there was a sharp pain in my shoulder and I realized her fingernails dug into my shoulders, drawing little pinpricks of blood. I ignored the stinging because she was helping me not turn into a wolf.

Terrence came to the door, opening it before Allie even had to knock and the look he gave me was pure fury when he realized what was happening. He growled under his breath and I shot him a pleading look.

"You, get inside, now." Terrence growled pointing behind him angrily and then shoving me inside. I stayed near the door to monitor Terrence's exchange with Allie. "You can leave now. We have this under control. Thanks." He started to close the front door but Allie held up her hand, slamming her palm against the wood.

"Don't you dare slam this door in my face," She snarled staring right into Terrence's brown eyes, something that a person with any sense would never do. She narrowed her eyes, lowering her eyebrows and grinding her teeth together.

Terrence shoved the door to get it to close but Allie pushed it harder, stepping an inch across the threshold. The muscles in Terrence's shoulders tightened when she barged inside, a look of triumph on her face. As she walked by Terrence, she rammed her shoulder into him for good measure and my muscles bunched, ready to intervene if his alpha instincts took over. He just watched her walk away with wide, bewildered eyes at her unusual boldness. When the door clicked shut, she paused and smirked before helping me sit down on the couch.

The pain subsided when I sank into the couch and I folded my arms across my chest, pressing them against my stomach to keep the throbbing away. I watched Allie; the soft skin just above the waistband of her jeans seemed to glow. I pulled my gaze away and realized she wasn't sitting down next to me like I thought she was going to. Instead, she stood almost in front of me with both hands on her hips and every muscle in her body tensed like they were about to snap. Terrence was walking to the kitchen and the whole way there, the two of them didn't take their eyes off of each other. When Terrence disappeared into the kitchen to talk to Erica who was making lunch, Allie's shoulders relaxed and she fell onto the couch next to me and casually threw both her legs across mine.

Her scent drove me crazy, jasmine and citrus, not helping the fact that I had almost turned into a wolf a few minutes ago. She rested her forehead in the crook of my neck and I gently kissed the top of her head, rubbing my fingers up and down her arm.

"You're good at making Terrence angry." Erica's voice came from the entrance to the kitchen where she was standing, wearing an apron and holding a very big cutting knife. Allie lifted her head, looking warily at the knife in Erica's hand and then smiling at her. She threw her legs over the side of the couch and stood up. It felt like she took a part of me with her as she walked towards Erica.

“Thanks,” She said twisting her hair into a high pony tail instead of the low braid she had had it in before. Somehow the bare skin of her neck made the wolf stir in my stomach. “It’s kind of a talent of mine. Need help with lunch?” She asked and then both girls disappeared into the kitchen, chatting animatedly about girl stuff that I drowned out.

Terrence appeared out of the kitchen and looked at me through half lidded eyes but his expression was slightly amused. I stood up, watching my brother carefully to see what he did next.

“I like your girlfriend,” He said and then grabbed his coat, walking out the front door.

I laughed and joined Erica and Allie in the kitchen where they were finishing lunch.

Allie

“You guys are seriously bad at cooking.” Monica laughed covered in flour and chocolate. She threw a puff at me and I ducked, screaming like a girl and swatting at the cloud.

Khione swooped in from where she had been perched on top of the refrigerator and dipped her finger in the mix, licking her fingers despite Monica’s protests. Monica frowned, crossing her arms and flicking her blonde hair over her shoulder. Rachel was sitting casually on the counter, watching us intently and combing her fingers through her thick blonde hair.

“Salem is going to kill us when he comes home to find his cottage destroyed, you guys.” I said glancing at Emma and Lindsey who didn’t seem to care at all what we were doing.

“There are some things that are just inevitable.” Rachel chimed in and I smiled at her, flashing gold eyes before I helped her clean up the mess that Khione made from spilling the brownie mix.

The sounds of our laughter echoed through the empty house.

"Allie? Are you okay?" Jaxon's voice brought me back into his kitchen and I realized I was staring out the window with my hand on the mixer that was still buzzing in the bowl of brownie mix.

I choked back a sob and looked down at the mix, stirring it slowly. "Uh, yeah, sorry. What's next?" I asked plastering a smile on my face.

"Okay, so we have to pour that," Erica pointed to the bowl, "in this pan and then we can put it in the oven." She said and with my mind still in the memory, I lifted the mixer out of the bowl without turning it off.

Liquid brownie exploded out of the bowl and splattered on the walls of the kitchen. I squealed as my whole body was covered in thick chocolate and I ducked to avoid getting the gist of the batter but my hair turned sticky. When I opened my eyes and looked up, the once white kitchen was now covered in splotches of an unattractive brown color.

"Omigod!" I said covering my mouth with both my hands, trying to keep from laughing when I saw Jaxon and Erica covered in it also. At first Erica looked stunned but then she and Jaxon burst out laughing and so I let my pent up laughs come out too.

Jaxon came up behind me and wrapped his arms around my waist and I tilted my chin up to his face. His eyes sparked and I pressed my lips to his, tasting the sweetness of the brownies and feeling the electricity all the way to my bones. Erica blasted the radio just then and my favorite pop song came on. I made a squeaking noise and danced away from Jaxon who looked at me with a bright predatory gaze in his eyes. I spun Erica around with both of us laughing and brownie batter flinging from the ends of our hair as I swayed my hips to the music. Hands in the air, Erica and I sang loudly until our throats hurt. Jaxon watched us the whole time, his eyes on me as I let down my hair, literally, and danced around the kitchen until I was out of breath.

"What happened in here?" Kate asked when she walked in, holding hands with Dallas who had wide eyes.

"Brownie mishap," Jaxon said looking pointedly at me as I wiped the remnants from his cheek and licked it off my finger.

I raised my hand, "Guilty as charged." I tried to focus on talking to my brother but Jaxon's fingers trailing down my arm made my head spin and I felt heat spread through my cheeks.

"Why is Ash outside grazing?" Dallas asked and I raised my eyebrows in surprise.

"Oh crap, I completely forgot about him." I laughed, still giddy from dancing and kissing Jaxon.

"Mom wants us home anyways," Dal said, my spirits dropping when I realized how much I felt at home here and that I was going to have to leave, "Says she has some sort of announcement."

I rolled my eyes and started grabbing paper towels to help clean my mess up. Jaxon rubbed my back and I leaned into his touch.

"You don't have to clean up. I'll do it." He whispered, his breath cool against my cheek and I shivered, kissing him on the cheek before going back to cleaning the floor. He puffed out a breath, laughing quietly, and then all of us worked to get the floor and walls sparkling again.

Dallas and I walked home, Ash trailing behind us and we laughed the whole time as I told him the story of the exploding brownies. We walked slowly, not wanting to waste a minute in the perfect weather that seemed to reflect my mood. I couldn't remember the last time I had had so much fun in one day since I left the pack.

Sure, my definition of fun was different back then but it had been a long time since I felt normal. We stepped into the driveway, disturbing the gentle quietness of the barn and I fell silent as if I could save the peace.

I sensed someone new in the house as soon as my foot hit the gravel driveway. I furrowed my eyebrows in confusion as I tried to recognize the scent but it was hard to tell because it was mixed with mom's familiar honey and raspberry smell. I narrowed my eyes at the closed front door and cautiously walked inside. When I pushed open the front door, I was taken aback by the presence of a man probably in his late thirties standing beside my mom. He was muscular but at least two feet taller than mom and ten times scarier. His face was cleanly shaven and his thick black hair was cropped short so that he looked like he was from the military. He had piercing dark brown almost black eyes that made every hair on the back of my neck stand on end as he tried to force his stone features into a tight smile.

I took a hesitant step back and crossed my arms over my chest, protecting myself from this man's creepy smile.

"Allie, Dallas," Mom said breaking the awkward silence but I didn't dare take my eyes off of the mysterious military guy. "This is Oliver. He is one of the officers that I worked with a long time ago and is being transferred from New York to Oregon." She laid her hand on his arm and I sensed something more than just work partners. I bristled at the contact. "He's going to be staying in the guest bedroom for a couple of weeks while his house is being built."

My breath froze. *He was going to do what?* I fought back the urge to snarl at my mom for just throwing this information on us. I narrowed my eyes but then tried to force my features into a smile like Oliver had done when we walked in. I didn't think he really liked the thought of living under the same roof as two children who were pretty wrecked on the inside from the loss of their father.

I took a deep breath through my nose, "Well, then we'd better get to know each other." I unfolded my arms and was surprised at the look of relief on mom's face. I was pretty sure she thought I was going to throw a punch at the guy. Newfound annoyance spread through me and the house suddenly felt too small. "But, starting tomorrow, I'm going over to Blake's tonight."

Before she could protest I was up the stairs and calling Blake in half a second. When Blake told me that I could stay at her house, I packed my things as quickly as I could and then drove into her neighborhood which was much more populated than mine. Dallas had dashed out of the house too, finding sanctuary at one of his friend's houses.

As soon as Blake swung the door open, I blew off the steam that was building up inside of me like a volcano. "Ugh, I am so pissed!" I snarled, pushing into her house and slamming my backpack on the counter in her kitchen.

Blake came in with wide astonished eyes and looked at me, "Okay, what happened?" She grabbed a bag of potato chips from the pantry and placed them in front of me. I grabbed one and munched on it angrily before I swallowed and told her what happened.

"Since dad died she's been so distant and throwing herself into her work," I ranted angrily, pacing the kitchen and flinging my hands everywhere, "And now she just brings in some scary military guy who is going to live with us! What the heck is that about? Ugh!" I snarled at no one in particular and felt Blake's eyes on me as I babbled on and on.

"Whoa, calm down Al. I think we need to have a girl's night. We need to relax, talk about boys, and just have fun. Something we haven't done in a long time." Blake said opening the freezer and getting something out. When she turned around, I saw that she was holding two pints of Oreo ice cream.

My frown turned into a wide smile and I clapped my hands together, "You're the best friend ever!" I squealed and took the pint of freezing deliciousness when we headed upstairs to watch sappy romance movies.

Blake and I sat cross legged on the floor, leaning our backs against the couch and swallowing spoonful after spoonful of ice cream until we had finished three movies. When the credits of Dear John rolled across the screen, Blake flicked off the TV and turned to face me, licking her spoon before talking to me.

"So, you and Jaxon?" She asked smiling brightly at me, "Anything happen?" She knew exactly what had happened between us but she wanted me to say it.

I ducked my head and laughed quietly, "Here's what happened." I said and relayed everything to her down to the second I had come to her house.

I woke up with a massive headache and an aching stomach like I was suffering an ice cream hangover or something. Blake was sprawled on the couch, her arm hanging over the side and I was curled on the floor as if I were sleeping in my wolf form. There was a shrill ringing in my ears, making me cringe but when Blake mumbled at me to turn it off; I realized it was just my cellphone ringing. I crawled to where it was lying on the other side of the room, my bones cracking and my muscles were as stiff as cardboard. I stretched them out and pressed the answer button without looking at the caller ID.

"Hello?" I mumbled sounding like there was cotton balls stuffed in my mouth.

"Allie, shut up…" Blake groaned, turning away from me and falling back asleep. I rolled my eyes and moved into the bathroom where I wouldn't disturb her.

“Hey,” Jaxon’s voice came from the other line and I smiled, heat spreading across my cheeks as his voice filled me with sunshine.

“Hi, what’s up?” I asked trying to wipe the grogginess out of my voice without any luck. I glanced in the mirror and raised my eyebrows in surprise when I saw my reflection. I looked like a mess.

“Did I wake you?” He asked.

“No, Blake and I just stayed up way too late last night watching movies.” I laughed lightly, finding myself listening to the background noises also. Everything was quiet except for distant voices humming. It was probably Erica and Kate in the kitchen doing something.

“Nice,” he chuckled quietly and then he dragged in a long rugged breath. He sounded nervous, like he was going to tell me something that wasn’t good news. I swallowed my nerves, keeping my breathing steady and light. He said softly, “Terrence and I are leaving for a couple of days to visit… some relatives who are sick. Erica and Kate are staying at the house until we get back.”

I forced the whine that was crawling up my throat back down and collected my voice so that I didn’t sound like a disappointed, obsessed girlfriend. “Oh, um when are you leaving and how long?” I asked combing my fingers through my hair as I heard Blake moving around the game room and made my way out there to start packing my clothes.

“Tomorrow morning we have to leave and at most only two days so I’ll be back by Tuesday.” He said in a matter of fact voice and the words only made me wish that he wasn’t leaving. Even if it was for two days. I held the phone between my ear and shoulder as I bent down the shove my jeans and t shirt into the back pack I had brought the day before.

"Oh," I sighed and dragged my fingers through my hair. For some reason, I couldn't think of anything else to say because I was too afraid of sounding like a clingy girl. I had never had a boyfriend before and werewolf mates acted differently. They were supposed to be clingy.

"Can we hang out today before I leave?" He finally asked and I let out a breath of relief that I was sure he heard on the other line. I was right and he laughed, "What, did you think I wouldn't want to hang out with my girlfriend before I left?"

Blake saw me blush and she raised her eyebrows with a smirk. I smiled at her and then laughed lightly, "Yeah, pick me up in two hours?"

"See you soon," He said and then hung up, leaving me with sparks crawling up my spine at the mere sound of his smooth voice.

After some squealing time with Blake and obsessing over Jaxon, I drove home with my windows rolled down and my Yankees baseball cap pulled down over my flowing brown hair. I cranked the radio up (country music) and rolled down my window, singing my favorite song *I Love You Forever* by: Jewel. My voice rose above hers, pure and for once I sounded innocent but deep down I knew there was so much blood on my hands that there was no bare spot. I sighed, taking in the scene of the peaceful woods that passed by me too quickly and I found myself only wishing that I could be passing those trees on four feet. I swallowed back the desire and turned my eyes away from the enigmatic woods, pulling into my driveway.

Voices drifted to my ears from inside the kitchen so I didn't get out of my car right away, listening closely I waited until the conversation rose again. Oliver's deep voice hit my ears first and I gritted my teeth to keep from growling in anger.

"Aren't you going to tell Allie and Dallas about us?" He asked quietly though my sensitive werewolf ears caught every word and hung onto them.

"Not until they get used to you staying here," Mom said in a voice I had never really heard her use before, except when she was talking to dad. That time a growl did escape from my lips when my brain put together what was going on. *They were dating.*

Scorching white hot anger coursed through my veins and everything was coated in a ghastly red color. How could mom do this to dad? It's only been a couple of months and she's already moving on. *Or maybe it's time for you to move on.* No, no I wasn't going to move on. I didn't even know Oliver and the vibe that I was getting wasn't a good one. And I trusted my instincts with my life. My hands curled into fists, my fingernails making little crescents on my palm as I tried to restrain from marching in there and screaming at my mother. She had no right to ignore us for all those months and then all of the sudden come back showing off her new boyfriend. I swallowed the bitter taste in my mouth, dragged in a ragged breath, and then marched inside.

As soon as I pushed open the front door, mom and Oliver stopped talking and stared right at me. Squirming under their gazes, my eyes found the floor and I started to head to the stairs but my cleared her throat like she wanted me to say something.

"Allie?"

"What?" I accidentally snapped at her.

"We are having family day today so no going out." She said when I had turned back around to head back upstairs. I froze and spun around so fast my hair actually hurt my face.

"No, I'm hanging out with Jaxon today." I said calmly as I battled with the teenage girl instincts that were raging inside of me.

“Well, please cancel because you are staying home today.” She said not even bothering to look at me as she kept her eyes on the newspaper that was in front of her.

“Since when do you get to tell me what to do?” I snarled and noted the way Oliver’s dark eyebrows rose slightly at my tone.

“I am your mother and you will not go out today. Cancel your plans and get dressed. We are going to lunch,” mom said and I knew I couldn’t say anything else to get her to change her mind so I spun on my heel and darted upstairs.

I dialed Jaxon’s number and he answered on the first ring. “Hello?”

“Hey, so change of plans. I can’t get out of my house. My mom wants to try to have a family day, which is dumb because that hasn’t happened in like seven years.” there was a long silence on the other line and I heard Terrence’s voice in the background.

Terrence said angrily, “No, we are going in the morning.”

Jaxon growled but then said calmly, “What about later tonight? I know a really cool place we can go for like an hour or two before I leave.”

I glanced at my closed bedroom door and smiled just at the thought of spending time with Jaxon where everything was carefree and I could actually be myself, well mostly myself. “Yeah, I can meet you in the woods at eight? I have to sneak out.” Butterflies danced in my stomach to a new unfamiliar beat. I had never snuck out before against my mother’s wishes. She never used to control me so I never went against her.

“I’ll see you in the woods tonight then,” he said and I knew he was smiling. I hung up with the feeling of triumph radiating through my body.

In two hours, I was showered, dressed, and driving in the backseat of mom's car with Dallas who looked equally annoyed to be here. Mom and Oliver were in the front of the car, talking about random things that I didn't bother to listen to because I was so irritated. The only thing that kept me from jumping out the window was seeing Jaxon in only a few hours and I was dying to know what he had planned. I aimlessly played on my phone as we drove and tuned out the entire world until we pulled into the parking lot of a fancy restaurant. So that was why mom made me wear a freaking dress and heels.

The waiter sat us down a little too enthusiastically for my taste and I picked up a menu, holding it up so that it covered my face. I fidgeted uncomfortably in my dress that clung tightly to the curves of my body. Why we were here for lunch, I did not know and I really did not care. I just wanted this day over with as soon as possible. I glanced at Dallas and he seemed to be trying to burn a hole through the brick wall with his eyes. I smirked at his expression.

"Allie, put down that menu and engage in conversation." She said as if she were some rich woman obsessed with manners. I mentally rolled my eyes at her but deliberately lowered the menu. I plastered a stupid smile on my face and tried to keep the annoyance out of my expression.

"So," I said folding my elbows on the table and looking at Oliver, "How did y'all meet, exactly?" I tried to at least feign interest in them but even I knew I sounded fake.

Oliver obviously didn't see it because he said, "We've been friends for a long time and then I was transferred here from New York." The way he looked at mom just then made my heart cry out in pain because that was the same look dad gave her right before he left.

"Wow," I said unable to find words and I didn't really trust my voice to say a whole sentence without crying.

Dallas saved me from awkward silence, “Anything cool that you have been working on lately?” He asked and I smiled. Dal always loved to know about that kind of stuff.

Oliver hesitated and that one nervous swallow told me that he indeed was working on something cool and mom knew about it too. She glanced up at him for half a second before taking a sudden interest in her soda. “Uh, nothing really. Things are slow out here which is a good thing for the community. It means there’s not a lot of crime. That’s something you don’t see everywhere.”

“So, you guys aren’t studying the recent wolf attacks?” Dallas asked and my breath froze in my throat though I quickly forced it out evenly. I ran my fingers through my straight brown hair and studied Oliver’s expression.

“Nah, that’s not our job considering they haven’t come here yet.” He said and to myself I thought, *Oh, they will be.*

Lunch went on for another two hours and by the end of the day I was ready to pull my hair out. I didn’t want to be sitting at the table with someone who was lying about what they were studying because the wolves were definitely on Oliver’s list just like they were on mine. After that, Oliver brought us to some museum that was also for rich people, making me think that Oliver was indeed rich and sooner or later we wouldn’t be living in the tiny house we live in now. Mom adored him. I could see it every time she laughed and looked at him. My feet were killing me by the time we were done walking around the giant museum which made my head hurt looking at all the art that meant nothing to me.

We pulled into the driveway at seven o’clock after a long day of acting like I didn’t muck horse stalls for the fun of it. I dashed inside after telling mom that I didn’t feel good and quickly changed into jeans and a t shirt, grabbing Jaxon’s sweatshirt that I still hadn’t returned to him. Mom and Oliver were still awake downstairs but

Dallas had closed himself in his room shortly after I did. I was home free. I slid open my window, stepped out onto the roof, and jumped.

Jaxon

I leaned against the tree as I waited for Allie's slender figure to melt out of the shadows. The cold bit at my nose but I made sure that I wore two sweatshirts so that I wouldn't shift on accident. Darkness touched the forest with magical fingers, making everything shine from the moonlight. I shoved my hands deeper in my pockets and looked up at the stars that peeked out of the full canopy.

I didn't want to leave with Terrence tomorrow morning. We were going on a hunting trip, shifting in the woods and then running across the country to try and find any signs of the pack of psychotic wolves that liked to use their strength for weapons of destruction. There was no way that we would be able to take the entire pack with just the two of us. But if we could challenge the alphas then maybe we could take over the pack and teach them our ways. We would have to pretend to be regular wolves just like them.

"Hey," Allie breathed, closer to me than I thought and I jumped slightly at the sound. She laughed lightly when I turned to face her and a smile creeped across my face.

"The car's parked on the street." I said holding out my hand for her and she took it, lacing her fingers through mine. They fit perfectly.

I turned the key into the ignition and the car roared to life, warming us instantly. Allie curled her legs up to her chest and hugged them tightly, trying to get warm after being out in the bitter cold. Her nose and cheeks were rosy, something I found adorable, from the wind and her wide blue eyes looked like ice compared to her brown hair. She looked at me and smiled, making my heart beat faster when

I closed my fingers around hers and rubbed my thumb across her cold hand.

We drove in comfortable silence; the only thing that I could hear was her steady breathing beside me. She was stiff though, making me think something had happened during family day and I wanted to ask her about it but something was holding me back from prying. I asked her anyways.

"How was family day?" I asked with a smile and she looked over at me with a playful glare on her face.

"Horrible," She said the one word like it left a bitter taste in her mouth, "I actually had to dress up, go to a fancy restaurant, and then a freaking art museum. Like who does that?" She threw her free hand up in the air and I laughed.

"Uh, normal girls would love that sort of thing." I teased and she looked at me with the same fake glare.

Allie narrowed her eyes at me jokingly, "Well, I'm not like other girls, am I?" she was right. Allie Jennings was nothing like other girls and that was why I liked her so much.

"Of course not," I leaned over to kiss her but she pointed to the windshield.

"Eyes on the road, Lochlan, or we'll both go down." She laughed and I sighed turning my eyes back to the road but she quickly pecked me on the cheek and leaned her head against my shoulder.

"So, where are we going?" She asked after a few more minutes of silence.

"It's a surprise." I smiled looking at her out of the corner of my eyes and I saw the look of annoyance on her face.

"C'mon," Allie laughed, "Please tell me, I hate surprises."

“Well, since you say it like that,” I paused, “No.”

Allie glared at me from where she rested her head on my shoulder so I wrapped my arms around her and pulled her closer to me. She scooted to the middle seat of my car, resting her cold forehead in the crook of my neck. Jasmine and citrus flowed into my nostrils and it took all of my control not to kiss her right then.

I pulled into the clearing, bracing Allie for the bump of the curb that we had to drive over and laughing when she made a cute little squeak. I parked in the center of the large field and we both got out, going around to the front of the car. I remembered coming here once before as a wolf when we first moved to Oregon and admiring the way the stars shined brighter than the ones near the city. There was the one bad thing about being a werewolf though. I couldn’t remember some things when I shifted back into human form. Of course there were exceptions but only the important things to my wolf came with me to my human mind. I guessed the wolf really loved this place.

Allie must’ve too because she hopped onto the hood of the car and leaned back on the windshield, her face tilted towards the sky. A tiny gasp escaped her lips when she took in the view and I jumped onto the hood beside her, leaning back so that we were lying beside each other. It was strange to think that when I first met this girl, every instinct of mine told me to stay away from her but now they were screaming to get closer. Allie shifted so that her head was resting on my chest and the wolf inside of me shivered at her feather like touch.

“It’s so pretty,” She whispered lightly her breath visible even in the darkness. I smiled, glad that she liked what I had planned for her. Allie lifted her face to mine and I reached down, our lips meeting and the darkness was replaced with light.

She accepted my kiss, opening her mouth and grabbing a fistful of my hair as she brought my face closer to hers. I sat up slowly so that I could cup her face in my hands as our lips moved together like we were made for each other. The only thing I could smell, feel, taste, and hear was Allie and she was all I wanted in my life. If I could've paused that moment and lived in it for the rest of my life, I would've been perfectly happy.

She pulled away a few inches so that she could look at me and the sparks in her blue eyes made me melt even more. Her face was serious as she ran her fingers through the hair at the back of my neck. She whispered softly, "Do you have to go tomorrow?" *No, I don't.* That was what I wanted to say but I knew I had to put an end to those rabid wolves that were tearing up the country.

"Yeah," I was surprised by how ragged my voice sounded but Allie's eyes took on a triumphant look like she was happy that she could do that to me.

"What am I going to do without you?" She laughed lightly and then kissed me again and we were swallowed in the darkness as the night plowed through.

After I dropped Allie off across the street so her mom wouldn't see, I opened the front door to hear Erica and Kate yelling at Terrence. They wanted to go with us but we needed someone here in case things didn't go as planned. Erica and Kate knew that Terrence would win the argument because he was the alpha but it was still funny to watch them try. I glided right by them and into the kitchen where I could somewhat be in peace. I looked out the window and was, for some reason, reminded of a strange night in my past.

My eight year old legs stretched to keep up with mom and dad who were walking ahead of Erica, Kate, Terrence, and me. Dad's hand enveloped mine and he dragged me along, his arm stiff and his mouth pulled into a tight line. I didn't know what was happening but I was amazed at all the shiny, breakable lab equipment that was scattered around the room on the different tables with men and women in lab coats working behind them. I remembered one woman looked sadly at me as I walked by but I didn't know why she looked so sad. But, for some reason, I held onto that women's face as we walked by and I remembered smiling at the little girl that peeked out from behind her legs as I passed by. The girl watched me with a mature, serious face despite her young age and her wide blue eyes held my brown ones the whole way there. We didn't wave at each other or say anything but I could tell she was interested in me, though she didn't know what I was doing there and why. I also remembered wanting to reach out and touch the soft curls of chocolate hair that spilled around her shoulders. I wanted to see that girl again as soon as we turned the corner into the testing room where my whole life changed.

The men in white coats were buzzing around the big warehouse type room that we had entered and Terrence's hand tightened on mine, his fear stirring mine. There were six tables set up around the room evenly spaced from each other with multiple wires dangling near them. I hated needles and my eyes widened at the site of so many of them. The scientist people separated me and my family, tying us down to the tables not gently at all. I struggled like my life depended on it but they struck me with a needle and I was out like a light.

When I opened my eyes the next time, they had altered my DNA and turned me into a werewolf.

Terrence's footsteps brought me out of the memory and I watched him warily as he made his way towards me, resting his giant hand on my shoulder heavily. The corners of his mouth twitched into a tiny smile.

"Better get some sleep, we have to head out early tomorrow morning if we want to make it back by Wednesday." He said and his comforting hand left my shoulder and I was alone in the kitchen with the little girl's apprehensive face etched into the back of my eyelids.

Sleep didn't come easy to me that night because all I could think about was the little girl peeking out from behind the woman's legs as I walked by her. Her blue eyes, brown hair, damaged gaze. Only one name came to mine when I thought about those words. Allie Jennings. I sat straight up in bed, my heart racing and forehead sweating. I knew Allie was familiar when we first met but I didn't think it could go that far back into my past. Then, the woman who was with her must've been her adopted mom, who was also lying to her about what she did because Allie said that she was a lawyer. *In her spare time, maybe.* She created me, turned me into that monster that I never wanted to become and now I was in love with her daughter. *Did I just say I was in love with her? No, no, no I couldn't be in love with her. Not when my secret could hurt her even more than if I was normal.*

With those thoughts in my head, Terrence and I left before dawn that morning. We didn't have to bring anything with us because as soon as we stepped outside, we leapt into our wolf forms and took off, yipping and snapping at each other through the woods. Terrence leapt over me as I barked playfully, snapping at his tail and lengthening my stride to catch up to him as we disappeared into the thick woods.

Allie

Jaxon left the next morning and as soon as I opened my eyes I could physically feel his absence. A small whine escaped my throat that sounded more animal then human, making me realize that maybe the wolf felt more strongly towards Jaxon than just the simple craving for his touch. The slight anxiety that tainted my limbs told me Jaxon was more than just a high school romance. I doubted he felt the same way because my feelings were mine and a wolf's mixed together, forcing them to be stronger than normal.

I got dressed for school as quick as I could and ran out of the house before mom could resume her yelling. She had caught me sneaking in my window last night when she came to check to see if I was feeling better. All I could remember though, was the way Oliver stood back and watched me with his arms crossed firmly over his chest and a hard, accusing look in his nearly black eyes. I decided that I never wanted to see that look ever again.

Dallas and I drove to school in silence as usual because I wasn't really a morning person and he knew that. As I pulled into the parking lot, I braced myself for the longing that would consume me when I wouldn't see Jaxon's rusty old car across the lot. I parked and we hopped out but even as I told myself not to, my eyes scanned the lot and landed on the car that sat alone. Instead of Jaxon getting out of it, though, it was Erica and Kate and the disappointment consumed me.

Lunch came around slowly and quietly, I placed my tray down on the table across from Blake, Miles, and Chase who were chatting animatedly. I swirled my straw in my water and gritted my teeth in annoyance. Why did I feel so… lost without Jaxon beside me? I didn't need him that much, did I? My teeth ground together at the thought of me having to depend on someone like that. It was completely against my nature and for all my life I depended on myself and myself only because no one else cared about me. Maybe that was it. I wasn't used to having someone care so much about me.

"Al? You okay?" Blake's voice snapped me out of my thoughts and I looked up, startled by the sound.

"Yeah, I'm fine. Just still getting used to Oliver being at my house." I lied even though it was partly true but I wasn't as worried about that problem.

"Mmm… how's that coming along?" Miles asked even though I didn't remember telling that information to him. I looked to Blake and she gave me a guilty smile and shrug.

"It's… definitely a work in progress. He still creeps me out." I said imagining his black, bottomless eyes that stared through me.

"Why?" Chase asked which surprised me because he never really talked when I was around. I stared at him for a few seconds in shock before speaking my mind.

"I don't know… but my instincts are telling me not to trust him." I said raising my eyebrows to prove my point.

"They're just instincts. If your mom trusts him then you should too." Miles said but everything he said went against what a werewolf stood for.

"They're not just instincts. I have spent every day of my life trusting them and I am not about to stop now." I said blood rushing to my cheeks when I realized I was practically leaned across the table as if I were going to attack him or something.

Erica slammed her tray down red faced, saving Miles from answering me though I saw the look of shock on his face. Erica growled, "Why did I have to have two brothers? Wasn't a sister enough?"

"Whoa," I said smiling at her, "What'd they do this time?"

"They wouldn't let us come on the trip. They said we had to stay behind as if we were children. Just because of a little family feud doesn't mean I don't want to go to New York." She complained throwing her hands in the air in exasperation.

"Family feud?" Blake asked between bites of her sandwich. Erica looked at her for a second before answering.

"Yeah, Kate and I have this thing that happened a long time ago with our aunt and I wanted to get past it but she obviously doesn't. I swear adults act more like teenagers every day." Erica said but my breathing stopped when I heard her heart beat faster at the word aunt. Only one thing came to my mind. Erica Lochlan had just lied to me which meant that she was hiding something about the trip. It also meant that Jaxon lied to me too but I was too caught up in him that I didn't listen for it. I let my guard down and I was not okay with that.

Biting back a snarl, I abruptly stood up from the table, "I just remembered I have to… go talk to a teacher about something. See you guys later." I said hoping my face didn't betray me as I hefted my backpack onto my shoulder and then headed out into the hallway.

I whipped my phone out of my back pocket angrily and before I knew what I was going to say to him, I dialed Jaxon's number with hasty precision. The phone rang once.

Four times.

Seven times.

Voicemail.

I snarled in annoyance and nearly crushed my phone in my fist. Where was Jaxon? I looked down the hallway towards my next class and then to where the front door was, leading into the outside world where maybe I could find some answers. My fingers tightened around the strap of my bag as I bounced the consequences around in my head. My mom was bound to find out because the school would call her. Then I would have to see the venomous gaze of Oliver when she yelled at me. But school really didn't seem appetizing that day.

Just before I was about to turn the corner to leave the school, two voices floated towards my ears and I recognized them immediately. I froze where I was and listened closely.

"They can handle themselves, Kate." Erica said in a clipped, annoyed tone. Kate was in ninth grade but we were all in the same building so the freshmen and juniors were allowed to mix.

Kate huffed, "What if they get hurt? We can't protect them when they are so far away, Erica."

"Terrence won't let anything happen to Jaxon and they are both powerful. We don't have anything to worry about. If they aren't back in two days then we will go after them." Erica said and then I heard her footsteps coming towards me. I silently ducked into the bathroom, waited for her to pass, and then dashed out of the school. I had something to figure out.

The air, cool and crisp, washed over my pale skin as I sprinted through the woods towards my destination. I had abandoned my backpack and other belongings under a fallen tree that I used as a marker to find my way around. My combat boots pounded the leafy ground but they were silent and didn't disturb the peace of the woods. I could feel the wolf crawling to the surface as the trees beside me blurred faster, my feet barely touching the ground any more. I had the sudden urge to leap forward onto my hands and feet, becoming something more powerful than a mere human. I had the urge to be a wolf again.

That thought made me stop dead in my tracks, the red and orange leaves spraying up behind me and my hair flying forward into my eyes. I swatted it away in annoyance and stared at the sky above me, blinking at the bright sun. I couldn't want that, not when the pack was quiet because that meant they were getting closer to me. I knew how they worked because I used to be one of them and I hunted in the same way, just like my mother taught me. My fingers touched my bare collarbone where I expected to feel the heavy amber necklace but it was gone and newfound fear gripped my stomach with cold hands. I needed to see Spencer about getting a new necklace if I was going to succeed in staying hidden.

My eyes locked on the horizon ahead of me where I could see the big white house standing alone on the hill. I gritted my teeth, tested the air with flared nostrils, and then surged forward until I was standing on the front porch. I slipped on black gloves to cover any traces of me being there and then tested the doorknob. It turned swiftly to the right and the front door swung open. *Really? Didn't Erica know how to lock doors?* I stepped across the threshold, immediately cringing when the floor creaked even though no one was home. The house felt colder than the last time I had been here like without Terrence and Jaxon, everything was different. I quietly closed the front door behind me, my eyes darting around the room as Erica and Kate's conversation ran through my head over and over again.

What if they get hurt?

We can't protect them.

They are both powerful.

What did that mean? Where did Jaxon and Terrence go that could mean they might not come back? But most importantly, what was so horrible that Jaxon had to lie to me about it? Questions with no answers clouded my senses, forcing me to stop and collect myself before I resumed my search. Something was going on and I needed to know about it before I lost any more people that I loved.

I searched for over an hour, nothing pertaining to the conversation I had overheard in the hallway. I *had* to find something. I wouldn't be able to live with myself if Jaxon got hurt and I had had the chance to do something about it. I made my way upstairs and into Terrence's room which was clean and orderly unlike the others. I carefully picked my way through the room and to the desk that was pushed up against the wall in the corner. Unlike the clean room, the desk was trashed with paperwork spilling onto the floor around it. I grabbed the first folder I saw and opened it slowly. My breath caught at what I saw.

Written in bold letters was the name: **Mary Jennings- Head Scientist**

Mom? I didn't understand the rest of the writing on the pages since it was all too scientific for my taste. I held it close to my face and narrowed my eyes as if I could force the words to make sense to me. There were a bunch of confusing graphs and equations typed neatly in rows but there was no point in me trying to figure this out. Female voices rang in my ears as Erica and Kate neared the house. I cursed under my breath and folded the paper up, stuffing it in my pocket. My head whipped from side to side, trying to figure out how to get out of here without being seen. I was upstairs which meant getting down would be impossible unless they were blind. The only option left was the window. I bit my lip, nerves bouncing around in my stomach because the last time I jumped out a window I was with Khione and I was still a werewolf. Then the footsteps started coming up the stairs. I shrugged my shoulders and thought to myself, *Well here goes nothing.* I peeled open the window but there was no roof to make my fall lower. I crouched on the sill and then jumped.

Jaxon

Terrence and I had been trotting along rocky terrain for what felt like years but had only been a couple of hours. By then, we were in a different state but my wolf brain didn't really seem to care. All I wanted was for that pack of psychotic wolves to pay for what they did. Then, I wanted to get home to Allie. She was all that I could think about. Her daring blue eyes, silky brown hair, and soft lips. I shook my head and pushed my legs faster as if I could run away from the thoughts. I couldn't be thinking of her when I had an important job to do. I leapt onto a hill, watching Terrence gallop below me. I barked at him playfully but all he did was flick a black ear towards me and kept galloping ahead. I lifted my lip, snarling slightly at Terrence's seriousness as I leapt down the side of the hill and landed beside my alpha. He snapped at me, half playful and half annoyed. I danced away from him, a high pitched yip coming from my mouth. Thunder rumbled above us as we picked up our pace because rain washed out scents and that was the only thing that was leading us to the pack.

Rain suddenly poured down on us as if we had walked straight into a tsunami. Terrence snarled in annoyance as the water clung to my fur and weighed practically my whole body down, making it hard for me to keep the same pace.

Terrence's deep voice echoed in my mind, *You smell like a wet dog.*

I am a wet dog so, what's your excuse? I thought back to him, pinning my ears jokingly but Terrence just quickened his step.

Just keep going, Jaxon. Terrence thought in a hard voice but I did what he said and galloped ahead of him just to keep things interesting.

Something heavy and powerful blindsided me, sending me flying across the woods and into a tree. The air whooshed out of me all at once and my lungs worked overtime to get new air inside them. I gagged and coughed. When I lifted my head, my eyes focused on a pure white wolf with ice blue eyes and her teeth peeled back over sharp fangs. She was of medium build but there was so much muscle underneath her snow white fur that it rippled as she got ready to pounce. Uh oh. Terrence leapt forward to intercept her but this wolf obviously had been in many fights before because she faked her attack, darted under Terrence as he jumped, and came after me with all the ferocity of a professional killer. I scrambled away from her as she dug her claws into my shoulders and rode me like a horse. I snapped at her but only caught air between my teeth so I bucked around and eventually Terrence ripped her away, his teeth tearing into her flesh and staining her once pure fur crimson. She went after Terrence then with ferocious precision and her teeth came inches away from snapping his windpipe. Blood flowing the claw marks in my shoulders, I charged the wolf and we met with wide open mouths.

Teeth clicked together, saliva flung everywhere, and I locked my jaws around the wolf's front leg. She refused to yelp or show any weakness as the sickening crunch of bones filled my ears. She wasn't at all trying to save her leg because she writhed and twisted out of my grip, swiping her claws across my cheek and nearly blinding me. She was about to come at me again, when an ear piercing gunshot filled the air and my head whipped towards the sound. When no other sounds followed it, I looked back to the white she-wolf but the only thing she left behind was a small trail of blood.

What the heck just happened? I asked Terrence who was staring in bewilderment at the trees where the wolf had disappeared.

She was an omega. Most likely kicked out of her own pack for being a psychotic lunatic… Terrence thought his loud voice tinged with scorn inside my head as I saw his red eyes assessing my wounds.

I'll heal in a couple of hours or so. We just need to find a place to rest because there is no way I am taking on two alphas like this. I thought as a tiny whine escaped my throat which was sore from growling that much.

The cabin is only a few miles north. We should get there soon if we go now. Terrence thought and with one last glance at the little puddle of blood on the ground, we walked steadily towards the cabin.

Allie

Okay, lesson of the day: Never, ever under any circumstances jump out of a huge two story window. As soon as I landed on the cold, hard ground I realized that. I tried to land with my knees bent like I was taught but even that couldn't keep the sickening crack of my ankle bone from shattering the air. I bit the inside of my cheek to keep from screaming in agony as I rolled forward to come up on one knee. I dug my fingers into the ground to prepare myself for the pain and then I half sprinted/ half limped back towards the barn where I could properly figure out what those charts and graphs meant.

I made my way into the barn instead of my house because I knew my ankle would heal faster than a normal human's and I didn't need mom asking any suspicious questions. Hobbling towards the hay loft, I climbed the ladder with only one foot and then settled comfortably on the blankets I kept up there. Everything was quiet and the sun was dying beneath the horizon, forcing me to turn on the lantern for light. I untied my combat boots and wrenched it off of my left foot which was so swollen it was probably the size of a bowling ball. Bruises already colored my skin, turning my foot an ugly blue. I gritted my teeth in agony as I moved my face closer to examine the damage I had inflicted upon myself. It obviously wasn't intentionally but I was the one who had jumped from the window. Propping it up on a bucket, I grabbed the piece of paper from my pocket which was now slightly crumpled but it survived the jump.

Taking a deep breath, I unfolded it and smoothed it out on my lap, trying to get the ridges out. My breath came out in short gasps as I tried to figure out what I was reading even though I had the feeling it wasn't anything good.

Mary Jennings- Head Scientist

S.L.C Lab Corporation

Time of tests: 8:00 A.M.

Day 1 Results:

Annie Lochlan: Aggression, uncontrollable shifting.

Dan Lochlan: Enhanced hearing but no control

Terrence Lochlan: Stronger, faster but uncontrollable

Kate Lochlan: Shifting but within control possibly because of her young age.

Erica Lochlan: Incredibly fast but lacks strength

My breath caught in my throat as I read the last line and I had to swipe at my eyes as tears blurred my vision.

Jaxon Lochlan: stronger, faster, more developed than the others but at most ten times more territorial.

Shifting. Aggression. Strength. Speed. Only one word came to my mind and my breath whooshed out of me as I said, "Werewolves." My fist closed around the paper as white hot rage surged through every ounce of me. My arm swung back and I chucked the paper over the side of the railing and angrily I shoved my aching foot back into my shoe, the rage masking the pain that shot through me. How could he not tell me? How could I not know? When his stomach was hurting that one day it was because of the change and I had been too naïve to believe that my life could get worse. I fell to the ground as sobs racked my body and the scream I had pent up inside me for so long, clawed its way out, tasting the fresh air. The horses neighed angrily at the shrill sound of my voice but I didn't care. I was going to find Erica and if she wasn't going to talk then I would hunt down Jaxon and force him to tell me the truth because I wanted to hear it come from his mouth. As sobs racked my body, I climbed down the ladder, turned around, and almost smacked right into somebody.

"Allie?" the girl in front of me said urgently and with wide eyes I took her in. She was tall and lean but still muscular for a girl with swirling blonde hair that fell to her hips and looked dirty and dull. The skin and muscle on one of her arms was torn and nearly shredded, making me suspect it was probably broken too. Blood also dripped from multiple cuts on her face and four claw marks across her chest.

I looked into her wide blue eyes and both excitement and horror clung to me as I said, "Khione?"

Tears welled up in my pack mate's eyes and soon we were both sobbing. We clung to each other as if she was my life force and hugging my best friend made me feel whole again because she always understood the way I felt towards my mother. Khione smelled strongly of blood and the wolf which made me ache with longing but also gag at the metallic scent.

We pulled away and I looked at her, finding myself noticing every detail that was different about her since the last time I saw her when I was eight. Obviously she was taller but everything about her face was different. Gone was the look of freedom and happiness that we both had once. In its place was the fierce look of many years of secretly hating what was going on and slowly watching the people she loved turn more and more into my mother. I knew that look because it was something I carried around with me for much too long.

"I can't believe I found you." Khione said as the tears flowed faster down her cheeks, making me think that something more had happened when I was gone.

"What are you doing here?" I asked measuring the look of hurt on her face but I couldn't let the others find me.

"I couldn't take it anymore." She sobbed as her canines lengthened into fangs. Something had happened while I was gone, "They killed so many people and every time I followed them, it made me want to be the one that died. I realized that wasn't what being a werewolf meant. Lydia and Marcus abused their power and I was sick of having to kill for the fun of it. And then Jason…" Khione sucked in a devastated breath at the sound of her brother's name. Fear gripped my chest. I loved Jason too, he was practically my brother. Khione said quietly, "Jason got out of control and he tried to challenge Marcus. I mean who does that? Marcus…" I knew what she was going to say. My hand flew to cover my mouth and all the anger I had towards Jaxon a few minutes ago was now channeled towards Marcus and Lydia. *I can't even call them mom and dad.*

"Oh, God I hate them so much. Khione, I am so sorry." I said as I watched her heart break all over again. My friend, her brother was another victim of my parents.

"I'm done. I don't want to be a part of a pack anymore." She whispered with so much helplessness and vulnerability that I almost didn't recognize her.

"Then you don't have to." I said even though I knew an omega wolf would eventually go insane. "You can stay with me. I have… methods to hiding from Lydia and Marcus." I looked over my shoulder to make sure mom, Oliver, or Dallas hadn't heard me screaming before.

"Please. We have to stop them. They are going to keep killing." Khione pleaded but every instinct in my body told me to gather an army and then let them come to us.

"Let them come to us." I said seeing the short flash of anger in her eyes. I said calmly, "In the meantime, you can stay here. I will just tell my mom that you were my foster sister who ran away like I did. She'll believe me." I promised a little guiltily because my mom had always been good to me but I was just throwing that away.

Khione nodded but she looked outside the barn towards the house as if it were a giant, slimy monster waiting to eat us both. I grabbed her arm and we climbed the ladder to the hay loft, sitting down on the blankets in comfortable silence. Again, I studied her and realized that her torn up arm was slowly starting to heal along with the rest of the claw marks on her body.

"What happened to you?" I asked her as the last of her wounds faded into gruesome white scars.

"I was hungry and the pack was getting closer. I went… crazy and attacked two wolves. One was an alpha." She said in a shaky voice and the anger from before surged through me as I put the puzzle pieces together.

"That was my… boyfriend and his older brother." I snarled through gritted teeth and a look of amusement spread across her scarred face.

"What'd he do to piss you off?" Khione asked with a little laugh and I turned my glare on her but she just kept smiling.

"He made me believe that he was just a regular human." I said looking at my fingers that were laced in my lap, "I don't trust werewolves at all. He lied to me for so long. Since the moment we met, he lied to me." I stabbed my finger to my collarbone in anger.

"Did you tell him that you were also a werewolf?" Khione asked and I sucked in a breath when the truth in her words rolled over me like a storm.

"I… no… I haven't told him but technically I'm not a werewolf anymore so I have nothing to hide." I shrugged but then I realized I had just told her I was completely defenseless. My whole body tensed as I was consumed with the overwhelming feeling that Khione was here to hurt me.

"Whoa, back up. What do you mean you aren't a werewolf anymore?" She asked with wide blue eyes that were full of shock and… fear?

"I mean I can't shift anymore." I said but comprehension was nowhere on her face so I added, "When I came here, all I wanted to do was get away from my old life and I didn't want to be a wolf anymore. So, I found this warlock who," I chuckled, "hated me at first but I convinced him to help me. He gave me this weird tea stuff that masks my scent from other wolves and an amber necklace that stops me from shifting. Therefore, I am not a werewolf anymore." I finished my story and ran my fingers through my windblown brown hair.

"Allie, you're a werewolf. It's in your blood. You can't just shut down that part of yourself. That's like… that's like a real wolf never hunting again and living in a hole for the rest of its life." Khione pointed out in a hard voice. She was sitting in front of me now with clenched fists as she tried to convince me that my choice was a bad one.

"I don't care. I will never be that… animal ever again. I would rather die than shift again." I said but Khione raised one thin blonde eyebrow as if she thought I was just over exaggerating, "I'm not kidding. If one day I shift again, I will kill myself before anyone else gets hurt."

Khione's jaw clenched in frustration and I could see the flare of fierce anger in her eyes. It was the same look she got in her eyes right before we would fight back when we were little. My muscles tensed and carefully we assessed each other. Then her hand cracked against my cheek.

"How dare you say you are going to kill yourself?!?" She screamed at me but I wasn't the type of girl that would just let Khione hit me. Before she could say anything else, I body slammed her and we both went tumbling over the edge of the loft.

We both screamed as Khione landed on top of me and I was sucked into a big pile of hay. I snarled at her and crawled out of the hay into the isle of the barn. Khione leapt out and slammed her shoulder into my chest but I knew she was holding back even though she wanted to pound me. She stood over me, tall and menacing as I sat on the ground, looking up at her with challenge and fear.

“You can’t leave me alone!! Not when I have lost everything!” She screamed at me with blazing blue eyes and her finger jabbing the air in front of me.

“I can’t let anyone else get hurt because of me!” I yelled right back at her which only made the trembling in her limbs even more violent.

I leapt up and before I could lunge at her, voices came from the outside of the barn. “Allie?” Mom called as she rushed into the barn and grabbed me, locking my arms behind my back.

“Let me go!” I snarled and pulled my arms out of her grip, fearing the shock on her face at my own strength. Khione’s eyes were no longer filled with anger. Instead they were bright with strange curiosity.

“What’s going on in here?” Dallas asked coming up beside me with Oliver behind him.

“Just a small misunderstanding,” Khione said her eyes locked on Dallas when he laced his fingers protectively through mine.

“A small misunderstanding? The whole neighborhood could hear you two screaming.” Mom said throwing her hands up in the air with red cheeks, obviously embarrassed that I wasn’t a lady like her. Then she looked at Khione for real, “Hold on, who are you exactly?”

Khione glanced at me nervously so I said, “This is Khione. She came from the same foster home as me. She ran away and came to find me.” I let go of Dallas’s hand and grabbed Khione’s, letting her know that I was sorry we fought. But I still wasn’t sure which one of us was right.

“Nice to meet you.” Khione said holding out a shaking hand and looking over my mom’s shoulder as she shook her hand. It was a sign of submission.

"I remember when Allie came here so if you need a place to stay, you are welcome to stay here." Mom said and relief washed through me, happy that I could protect my best friend from the horrors of the pack.

"Thank you so much." Khione said the gratefulness in her tone pinching my stomach with nasty fingers.

"All I have to do is talk to a judge and get your parents to sign you over. Will that be a problem?" Mom asked in her lawyer voice and I tightened my fingers around Khione's.

"I don't have parents." She said in a hard tone that made her Australian accent seem stronger and even though I didn't know much about how Khione came to the pack (she didn't like to talk about it), I still felt sad for her.

"What about foster parents?" Mom asked then made a gesture for us to follow her into the house.

With the question still hanging in the air, we crowded around the tiny kitchen table inside my small house that would always be tainted with painful memories. It seemed my whole life was like that. Khione sat in the chair beside me but I couldn't help but notice the slight shaking in her fingers as she fiddled with her rings. I smiled at the rings that she still wore though. We would collect rings from every place that we ever lived in and we never took them off, except I did when I came here and I shoved all of them in my drawer upstairs, locking them away. I pulled my gaze away from her hands and turned back to mom.

"So, your foster parents?" She asked again, snapping Khione's attention back to the table.

"They kicked me out." She simply said with a strangely calm look on her face when she raised it.

“Why?” Mom asked receiving a glare from me and I saw Dal watching Khione with skepticism and curiosity.

“I don’t know.” Khione snapped but when she realized her tone, she recoiled and said, “I’m sorry.”

“It’s okay. I can’t imagine what this is like for you.” Mom said with a sympathetic smile but knowing Khione that would just make her madder. Mom added, “All I need to do is talk to a judge about making me your legal guardian and so that you can go to school. You do want to stay here, right?” Khione’s eyes widened and she nodded eagerly. Mom smiled before she pulled out a whole bunch of paper’s and went to work on making Khione my sister once again.

The moon came alive and shined brightly in the sky as Khione and I settled in for the night in my room. Khione slept on a mattress on the ground beside my bed but before we went to sleep, both of us climbed out onto the roof and watched the stars. Khione leaned back with her arms behind her head and I sat cross legged beside her. The wind gently brushed against my cheeks and the sweet scents of the country filled my nostrils, making me feel at home. I ran my fingers aimlessly through the ends of my hair and looked out over the woods where I imagined Jaxon as a wolf running through the trees. I flashed back to a night that seemed many years ago.

Dal and I had been driving home from Spencer’s when I first got my amber necklace. Dallas had started asking me questions about why I was so freaked out about the killings when out of nowhere a dark brown wolf with glinting yellow eyes jumped out of nowhere. I knew those eyes. They were Jaxon’s.

I shivered and blinked out of the memory but all I could remember was Erica and Kate’s words in the hallway.

They can handle themselves.

What if they get hurt?

We can't protect them.

If they aren't back in two days then we will go after them.

Who were Terrence and Jaxon going after? I didn't know if I could get used to Jaxon being a werewolf. Not when I spent nine years hating them and blaming them for ruining my childhood. I was prepared for the time it would take to get used to Jaxon turning into a wolf when the temperature dropped. I just couldn't tell him about me, not yet. I had to make sure he wasn't like the other wolves.

"I wonder what Monica and Rachel are doing right now." Khione said out of the blue in a soft, fragile voice. I glanced down at her and saw the stars reflected in her eyes.

"Why didn't they come with you?" I asked her though I was afraid to break the silent night with my voice.

"They were afraid. I didn't even bother trying to convince Emma, Lindsey, and Alexa. They still practically worship Marcus and Lydia." Khione said, "Once they realize I will never get caught then maybe they will join us in this little rebellion."

I smiled at her and that was when I knew that I could once again trust Khione with my life. I was going to put my rings back on and I was going to be me again.

"Okay, so Jaxon is… a different kind of werewolf," I started, "He wasn't born one like we were. Their DNA was genetically altered… by my mother." I said and watched as Khione's eyes got wider with shock.

"You're kidding me?"

"No, I found the lab sheet in Jaxon's house and the head scientist was my mom. I always knew she was hiding something but I wasn't sure what. Wait…" my mind worked over time as I put the pieces together.

She said the radar picked up the wolves in this spot.

Didn't you hear the gun shots?

She scares me when she's angry.

Everything clicked. "That night in the woods! Those hunters worked for my mom. The notes said that the wolves were out of control so to cover her tracks she is trying to completely wipe them out." I exclaimed in anger and excitement. I pinched the bridge of my nose when realization set in, "My mom is trying to kill me, you, my boyfriend, and his whole family."

"Well, then we need to do everything in our power to stop her." Khione said and when she saw the flash of protectiveness across my face she added, "I don't mean killing her. I mean convincing her that we aren't bad and protecting Jaxon and his family. They are one of us whether you like it or not and wolves protect their own kind."

Khione's words set in as we settled into our beds for the night and I lay looking out the open window like I did every night. I realized that maybe being a wolf wasn't as bad as I thought. Maybe it was something that was going to save the people I cared about. Maybe it was going to save me. My eyes wouldn't close as my thoughts swirled viciously inside my head, pounding against my skull and forming a massive headache. All I could think about was Jaxon, what he was hunting, and if they were in trouble. I wanted to go find them. I needed to. But something held me back.

My eyes were finally about to close when a rich howl burst the silent night like fragile glass. Khione and I sat straight up in our beds and scrambled to my open window towards the sound. It came from the Lochlan's house. Another howl joined it and Erica and Kate's voices filled the air with a peaceful, hopeful song. There was no response from their brothers at first but then a few seconds later, two very faint howls whispered in the wind, barely audible against my ears. The strange thing was that I could pick out Jaxon's voice and I held onto that sound until I fell asleep that night. I dreamt terrifying things.

I was in a dark room but I couldn't see the walls and my senses told me they stretched on for miles. The air was dank and moist as I breathed it into my lungs, my eyes straining against the dim light. Oxygen would only hold out for a few more minutes and I tried to keep the chilling grip of panic away from my chest. I spun around and around, desperately trying to find a way out but when I spun to my left, a familiar face was staring at me. The woman looked like me with spiraling brown hair and piercing blue eyes. She wore a delicate white gown but crimson, metallic blood streaked all down the front of her shirt, covering her hands and collarbone area. Lydia stared at me with a devilish smile on her face and I screamed when I saw her white teeth stained bright red from blood.

"Don't be scared, darling." She said in a silky smooth voice, "This was you. It still is you. Don't think you can run away from your destiny, sweetheart. It's impossible to outrun it." She snarled viciously and I closed my eyes as I readied myself for her attack. But when I opened them again I was alone in the dark room.

My breathing was loud and heavy, echoing in the never ending hallways. I called out desperately over and over until my throat was sore and my nails had drawn blood from my palms. Footsteps came from behind me and I whirled around, ready to attack. But Jaxon's face was illuminated under the tiny lamp.

"Jaxon," I breathed in relief and I was about to run to him but he took a step back.

He said in a stiff, pleading voice, "Allie, help me." then his whole body tensed and Jaxon was no longer Jaxon. He was Marcus, Marcus with bloodstained fangs and piercing red eyes.

My scream pierced the room until my whole body shuddered.

My eyes snapped open and my body shot straight up in bed with a tiny shriek that was nothing compared to the scream that busted out of my throat in my dream. Tears were falling down my cheeks like a water fall but I couldn't stop the shivering that rattled my bones. The desperate look in Jaxon's eyes was still etched on the backs on my eyelids as I tried to fall back asleep. *It was just a dream. It was just a dream.* Jaxon was okay and he would be home in two days. Then we would sort out the whole werewolf thing and our lives would go back to normal, well as normal as dating a werewolf could be.

Deciding I couldn't go back to sleep right away, I threw the blankets away from my sweaty body, stepped around Khione's sleeping form, and then made my way downstairs on shaky legs. The house was eerily quiet; the only sound was the floorboards creaking underneath my feet as I made my way towards the fridge. The light from the refrigerator washed over me as I opened the metal door and grabbed the milk carton. Too lazy to actually pour it into a cup, I popped open the tab and lifted it to my lips when I heard a crash in the basement. Every muscle in my body froze as I stared at the door that was always closed and forbidden by my mother to enter. I swallowed the fear that engulfed me and gently set the carton down before grabbing a giant knife out of the drawer.

Gripping the knife firmly in my sweaty palm, I held it up and out in front of me for easy access. Hushed voices arose from down the stairs as I wrapped my fingers around the cold metal doorknob. Soundlessly, I turned it and made my way down the steps with the stealth of a werewolf. My fingers found the light switch and I readied my knife. I flicked it on.

"Mom?" I asked in a not so quiet voice when I saw many people gathered around a wooden table covered in maps and weapons.

My mother was standing at the head of the table, holding a scary looking crossbow in her hand.

She froze when she saw me, lowering the bow and setting it on the table, my teeth grinded together as I walked forward into the room. I recognized the scents of Dale and the other woman from the night in the woods when they were searching for the wolves. My eyes widened as once again my brain had to put together the puzzle pieces.

"You're hunting the wolves?" I asked in astonishment even though I partly already knew that answer. For some reason, seeing my mom holding a weapon was even freakier than learning my boyfriend and I were secretly the same species.

"It's not like that." She said but it was like she couldn't explain herself to me. As if I haven't judged her before.

"I know what it's like mom." I growled angrily, "And I know that you turned innocent people into *werewolves.*" At the last word her eyes grew to the size of baseballs.

Mom's face turned into a white sheet of shock as my words froze the air around us. The hunters' fingers gripped the cold weapons that stuck out against the white plaster walls of the basement. My hand shook slightly as if there was a tiny earthquake deep in my bones and I found my fingers tightening around the hilt of my knife. My mom was the one hunting Jaxon and I had to do everything in my power to protect him and his family, for my sake and his.

Anger surged through me and I was forced to close my eyes to calm myself. A white room flashed behind my eyelids, tables scattered around the depressing tile floor full of test tubes and other scientific things that I couldn't even begin to name. Men and women, dressed in long lab coats, worked diligently behind the stainless steel tables and I was there. Holding onto mom's legs and staring into the brown eyes of someone very familiar as he walked past me holding his mom's hand.

"You took me there didn't you?" I asked in a shaky voice when my eyes snapped back open.

All she could was nod; words didn't come from her mouth. I tried not to sweat nervously under the curious but angry glares of the hunters with twitchy trigger fingers. Carefully, I lay the knife down on the stool beside me and schooled my features into something calmer. I couldn't tell her that I wanted to protect the wolves. Well, one set of wolves. A light bulb brightened in my head and I tried to keep the smile off of my face. If I could pull this plan off, I would have the hunters, Khione, Spencer, and Terrence's pack on my side against the pack that would continue to terrorize my home.

Mom started to say sorry but I interrupted her with a hard, determined voice, "I want you to teach me how to fight them." I was surprised when my shoulders straightened in confidence and the courageous gleam in my blue eyes was something I had always had but in that moment it was magnified.

"Are you sure?" Mom asked, "This… isn't easy." She said as the rest of the members nodded their agreement with smirks or unwavering hard glares.

I took a deep breath as I smiled slyly and grabbed the knife off the stool, shaking it at the group, "You'd be surprised at what I'm capable of." With a wink, I left the basement for the hunters to discuss their plans.

Mom went to work before the sun even came up the next day and thankfully, I had gotten about two hours of sleep before I had to get up for school. Immediately, I told Khione what had happened last night and of course she tried to convince me to shift if I wanted to fight the wolves. I told her, no, there was no way. The benefit of mom getting to work so early was that she took care of Khione living with us and got her enrolled in school. For once, I appreciated her being so engrossed in her work.

The funny thing was, as soon as Khione walked in the school, every guy froze like deer in headlights and I swore I saw a string of drool fall out of their open mouths. There was also the fact that every girl froze too, green with envy as they took her in. Khione was stunning compared to every other girl and I thought they knew it too. She was all long legs, tan skin, and swirling blonde hair but she had no idea that she was beautiful. I played with the rings on my fingers as we walked side by side down the hallway, passing starry eyed boy and catty girl. She was only an inch or two taller than me but beat me by far in beauty points.

Three classes went by and Jaxon wasn't in any of them. I tried to concentrate on something besides the fear and worry that consumed me as I pushed through the classes. Something was wrong. I was sure of it by now and I desperately needed to do something about it. When the bell rang for lunch, I met up with Khione in the hallway who couldn't keep the smile off her face as she told me all about her classes and the people in them. My heart beat faster at the sight of my best friend's happiness and I wondered how she did it, how she managed to still be happy even though she lost so much. I wanted to ask her that someday.

Miles, Chase, and Blake were already sitting at the table but there was no sign of Erica and Kate. *They are looking for Jaxon.* Khione walked apprehensively beside me, her boots clicking on the tile as we neared the table. My friends looked up and I couldn't help but notice the widening of Miles's eyes as he watched Khione take the seat across from him. I tried to hide my smirk as the once chatty group fell into silence.

“Guys, this is Khione. She’s my sister.” I said smiling at her out of the corner of my eye and watching the shock morph my friend’s faces. “Khione, this is Blake, Chase, and Miles.”

Blake was the first one to get over her initial shock, “Since when do you have a sister?” Miles was still staring dreamily at Khione though I didn’t think she noticed.

“I was in the same foster home as Allie when we were little,” Khione said, “Then she moved away and they kicked me out a few days ago so I found her again and her mom adopted me.” I began to realize that Khione was an exceptionally good liar because her heart beat didn’t waver once.

“Oh,” Blake said but I could practically smell the jealousy in the air. I would have to deal with that later. Right now, my fear for Jaxon was getting stronger by the minute and my heart raced as if it were in a race against a cheetah.

Khione noticed it too because as soon as I mentally acknowledged my fear, her eyebrows scrunched together in confusion and she dipped her head towards me, listening. I gave her a tiny smile, trying to convince her that I was okay but of course she knew me better than that. I was about to make small talk when my phone vibrated repeatedly in my back pocket. *Please be Jaxon. Please be Jaxon.* When I looked at the caller I.D. and saw Erica’s name on my screen, my heart skipped a beat. I answered it.

“Allie?” her voice was frantic and her breath came in short gasps.

“What’s wrong? Are you okay?” I responded in an equally worried tone but it was the voice in the background that made tears spill down my cheeks.

Jaxon’s voice was muffled and full of pain in the background when he said, “Erica, stop. Don’t… don’t drag her into this.” I could hear the sound of movement but it faltered and Jaxon cried out in pain.

"Allie, we need help. We…" her voice stopped, making me believe she was listening to someone coming. "Hurry, we are in an abandoned church about an hour out of…" there was a smash and the line went dead.

"No, no, no." I whispered to myself as I shoved my phone in my pocket and abruptly stood up from the table, motioning for Khione to follow me out of the cafeteria. I ignored Blake and Miles calling my name because I needed Khione's wolf sense to help track them down and this wasn't the job for humans.

We drove home furiously and way above the speed limit but luckily the cops weren't out that afternoon or they were asleep in their cars. I told Khione everything that Erica had said on the phone even though she hadn't gotten the chance to answer because something bad had happened. I also knew that Jaxon was hurt and I needed to do something about it. No matter what the cost was, I was going to make whoever hurt them pay for it.

The good thing was that mom or Oliver weren't home which meant I could freely come and go without getting stopped and questioned. The second I pulled into my driveway, Khione and I were out of the car and bolting up the stairs and into my room. Khione didn't need weapons so she changed into more suitable clothing like I did and watched as I loaded the arrows into the quiver and strapped a gun to my belt. Khione knew Jaxon's scent thanks to the sweatshirt that I still hadn't returned to him so we sprinted out the front door and I hopped into my truck, pure adrenaline coursing through my veins as I watched with envy as Khione shifted into a snow white wolf and took off into the woods. She stayed close to the edge so that I could follow her without any problems. I drove as fast as I could without drawing any attention to myself because I didn't think a girl loaded with weapons would go over well with the cops.

Erica had said the abandoned church they were in was an hour away from something. I just didn't know what that something was. That was the bad news. The good news was that Khione was one of the best trackers in the pack so I was almost positive that she would find them in time. She had to. The sun was still high in the blue sky but everywhere I looked I saw blood, the blood of Jason, my father, and Jaxon's. *He isn't dead, stop thinking about that.* My knuckles turned white as I gripped the steering wheel tighter and glanced out my window, watching Khione with her nose to the ground hunting the people I cared about. The clock struck higher and higher until I was sure we were too late. But when it reached 1:03, Khione stopped where she was and barked at me.

Slamming my foot on the brake, I parked my car on the side of the road as a quick getaway for us to use. Clad in all leather, I gripped my bow in a shaky right hand and followed Khione's white form up the hill to where a halfway burned down church stood proudly with the sun shining on it like a spotlight. All my thoughts were focused on finding Jaxon but I knew that if I rushed in there with nothing but impulse on my side, things would get ugly real fast. So, when we got to the front door of the church and I indicated the voices were coming from the basement, I swung open the wooden door that barely clung to its hinges and let Khione slide in first.

I notched an arrow and aimed it in front of me, pulling the string tight in case of any surprises. My hands were no longer shaking, the fear no longer consumed me because in its place were pure strength and undying love. I could do this. I could make it through the fight against my pack. I could get used to the fact that my mom was a werewolf hunter. And most importantly, I could look past the fact that Jaxon was a werewolf. My fingers tightened on the string as Khione and I descended down the wobbly staircase with nothing but our senses guiding us.

The dank air was nearly suffocating as my lungs struggled to take it in. Sweat beaded in small clumps on my upper lip and forehead as I counted each step I walked down just in case we needed to get out of here quickly.

Seventeen.

Eighteen.

Nineteen.

My foot hit the basement floor with a loud creak but the voices didn't quiet and I picked out at least five of them. Five men to be exact. How were we going to beat five men who were most likely ten times the size of me and twice as armed? I tried to keep my hands from shaking as realization dawned on me which felt more like a bus falling on my head than anything. If I had to defend myself, then that meant I would have to kill. *This was you. It still is you.* Lydia's voice from my dream echoed through my mind as Khione stopped just around the corner and pricked her ears up. I listened too. *Don't think you can run away from destiny, sweetheart.*

Deep, bored voices came from the other side of the wall, "Steve, I really don't want to hear about your love life. Let's just silently wait for them to get here."

"They are still over an hour away, are we just gonna sit here in silence."

"Might as well." And their voices were quiet but they were the only two engaged in conversation. Several pairs of lungs breathed in and out evenly.

From what I could hear, the men were sitting and standing in front of a door that was located at the complete other side of the room, guarding it with various types of guns. On the other side of the door were Jaxon and the others. I listened carefully for voices on the other side and was able to hear their whispers. I didn't have time to worry about the fact that my hearing was getting stronger.

"Jaxon, we have to do something. We can't just sit here." Erica snarled in a whisper which somehow made her sound even more intimidating. Khione's muscles twitched as she glanced back at me and then listened to more of the conversation.

Jaxon made a low groaning sound that twisted my gut, "I have to sit here. There is a bullet in my arm and it hurts."

"I know but..." Erica was interrupted by Terrence's alpha voice.

"Both of you knock it off. Knowing Allie, she will be here soon to rescue you so we just need to wait them out." He said and I tried not to take offense to his assumption even though it was true because I had gotten there in an hour.

Their voices went silent and Khione's blue eyes found mine, a silent agreement on both our faces. It was time to get them out. As if we had planned it out before, Khione sprang from her hiding place with a bloodthirsty snarl, rousing the men as they raised their weapons in a heartbeat and opened fire. Khione was fast for a wolf though, and she easily dodged in and out of the pews to avoid getting hit. When the first man let out a terrified scream and fell abruptly silent, I knew Khione's teeth had struck and now it was my turn to do what I had been made to do. I rolled behind a pew and came up on one knee, already letting an arrow fly at the nearest burly man. The arrow lodged itself deep in his shoulder and the man fell, disappearing behind a table. I cursed myself for purposely aiming higher than the heart. I let loose three more arrows, but none of them were lethal because I was restraining myself without realizing it. Turned out, there were way more than five men but Khione had no problem with them. She took them out one by one as if they were a set of dominoes.

I tried to keep my eyes off the blood and I held my breath to keep the metallic scent out of my nostrils. But even doing that, didn't keep the rolling nausea out of my stomach for very long. At one point, my arrow went straight through a man's stomach and I knew his heart had stopped beating. Blood spurted like a waterfall from the wound and since he was only a foot away from me, I was also drenched in it. A sob escaped my throat as I realized what I had just done and I doubled over, clutching my stomach and puking up all my lunch from that day. Tears fell down my cheeks as I stared at the man's lifeless body but I didn't have time to freak out because a big fist grabbed my arm, tossing me like a ragdoll across the room. My back cracked against the wall and a high pitched scream of pain whooshed out of my throat. Before I could move, the man was there and he carelessly ripped the quiver of arrows of my shoulder and threw it only a few feet away but my bow was nowhere to be seen.

Khione's snarls filled my head and as I stared at the man that was holding me by the arm, I knew he wasn't going to make my death fast. Slowly, his fist closed around my throat, cutting off my air when he pinned me against the wall. My feet reached for the ground but it suddenly wasn't there and everything turned red like the blood that covered my body from the man I killed. *Breathe. Breathe, Allie, breathe.* I wheezed until my stomach hurt but already I could feel the world tilting, spinning, and darkening. *Don't lose. You can't lose this. Think of Dallas, mom, Khione, Blake and Miles. They need you.* Anger surged through me as I stared back at the man with nothing but defiance in my blue eyes. My gums ached and fangs replaced my canines as the wolf finally broke through the barrier. I could breathe again. I bit down on the man's hand so hard that he was forced to drop me, and I crumpled to the ground, leaping out of his way before he could grab me again. I crawled like an animal towards my quiver but I could hear his footsteps right behind me, deep and loud as my hand tightened around an arrow. He grabbed me around the waist but before he could hurt me anymore, I spun with the speed of a warrior and plunged the arrow deep into his chest

Warm, crimson blood coated my hands like water as the man's hands went limp and he crumpled to the ground. No more sounds came from the men or Khione but I knew she was alive. The men weren't so lucky. The man that had captured me looked at the ceiling with glassy eyes as his heart came to a stop. I couldn't get away from the scent or the sight of it. No matter where I looked, all I saw was blood and none of it was mine like it should've been.

Jaxon

Chaos erupted like a volcano outside the metal cell we were locked in. Guns fired, men screamed, and a wolf snarled? None of us could decipher what was happening on the other side but people were dying and we were locked in a freaking closet, powerless because the door wouldn't open. Then after ten minutes of fighting, I had heard a scream that I would always recognize. Allie's voice was on the other side and I couldn't do anything. The scream was short though and then I couldn't hear her anymore. Pure terror washed over me as I strained against the pain in my shoulder from the bullet to hear her voice again. She couldn't be dead, not when I had so much to explain to her, to tell her how I felt. *No, she isn't dead. She's still out there and she needs your help.*

Everything went deadly silent and I glanced at Kate in fear. Her eyes were bright gold as she fought to hold back the wolf. There was no sound except for two pairs of lungs gasping in air, Allie and someone else. Allie was in the center of the room towards the wall but the other person in the room was closer to us but was this unknown being a friend or a foe.

"Allie!" a girl's voice rang out from the person closest to us. The smell of blood was everywhere in the air and it nearly choked me. "Allie!" She screamed again but there was no reply, only Allie's quickened breathing made me believe she was still alive.

Just then there was a rattling sound at our door and it shook violently as if the girl was trying to tug it off its hinges. Turned out she was. With the strength of anything but a human, she pried the door off and we were face to face with a tall, blonde girl, covered in blood but I knew it wasn't her own. Her blue eyes found mine in a heartbeat and they filled with worry when she glanced over her shoulder quickly.

"She needs your help." She said in an Australian accent as she once again looked over her shoulder to where Allie sat with her back pin straight against the wall, her knees pulled tight to her chest, and her body slowly rocking back and forth.

Her blue eyes were frozen on something ahead of her and I realized it was the body of a man with an arrow protruding from his heart. She held a bow in her hand. Allie was covered in someone else's blood and I knew she had risked her sanity to save my life. I didn't want that for her. I didn't want her to have blood on her hands like I did.

"Allie," I breathed in relief when I saw that she was okay. I struggled to stand, holding my wounded arm with the other one and slowly I made my way to where she was sitting, tears rolling silently down her cheeks.

She was whispering something over and over again, "I am not my mother. I am not my mother." I didn't know what she meant but I quietly knelt down in front of her and pried the bow from her fingers.

"Allie?" I asked quietly and her eyes seemed to refocus on the present as she took me in. Her breathing quickened and the silent sobs were now noisy and heartbreaking. She threw her arms around my neck and I hugged her close, ignoring the scorching pain in my arm and pulling her onto my lap.

Her whole body was ice cold as if she had gone swimming in the lake during the winter. Shivers ran through her, making me hold her closer to my chest to calm her down and make her feel safe. That was my job. I pressed my lips to the top of her head but was met by the metallic scent of blood that clung to her skin and it took all of my power not to cringe away from her. I could feel the heavy gazes of my siblings and the unknown blonde girl on me as I whispered soothing things into Allie's ear. Her fingers curled tightly into the hair at the back of my neck as if she were afraid she was going to slip away at any moment.

"I can't believe I did that. Why did I do that?" She asked me, her voice muffled against the fabric of my shirt. I shifted her carefully so that I could see her face.

"Did what?" I asked in a voice that I wasn't sure she could hear but she did and her jaw clenched.

"I killed two men. The others I just wounded but I actually killed them." her voice was desperate when she looked over at the man with blood spilling out of the hole that went straight through his body.

I didn't know what to say. Yes, she had killed them when she could've just wounded them. I didn't even know what to think. Ever since I killed a scientist a long time ago, I learned control and I never killed anyone ever again. So, with Allie sitting here, telling me she killed two people, my mind went utterly blank. The whole time I was thinking, I didn't realize that Allie had gone completely still in my arms. She stared at me with a stone cold gaze that made me feel like she wasn't looking at me on the outside but the inside. Only one hand was around my neck now and the other was reaching for something by her belt.

Faster than a werewolf, Allie whipped out a shiny gun, rolled away from me, and jumped up. The gun was aimed straight at my chest. The blonde girl was at her side in minutes, baring sharpened canines with snarls rolling into the air. There was something dark in Allie's gaze as she stared at me, the gun in her hands unwavering. My pack was suddenly beside me but none of them gave away the fact that we too had fangs and claws. I put my hands slowly up in surrender. What happened to her? There was no fear in her eyes, only the scary look of defiance.

"You could've told me you were a werewolf." She said in a deadly cold voice that made a shiver run up my spine. *Werewolf.* How did she find out? Words didn't come to my mind as I stared incredulously at her smoldering face.

"Why didn't you tell me?" She asked again, tightening her hand on the gun but it had started to shake and I knew she wouldn't shoot me. She just wanted me to know that she was that angry

"How did you know?" were the only words that forced their way out of my mouth which only made her eyebrows lower more.

"Because I was there! I just didn't realize it was you. My mom was the one who changed you." Allie said in a shaky voice. She sounded so fragile. I wanted to go to her and wrap my arms around her but there was still a gun aimed at my chest.

Beside me, Erica spoke up, "No, you broke into our house and stole the lab sheet from Terrence's room and then jumped out a *window*." The look on Allie's face was absolute surprise.

"You did what?" I asked her but she wasn't looking at me and I was relieved to see the black, shiny weapon back in her belt. She slowly picked up her bow and arrows, slinging them onto her back.

"How did you know?" She repeated my question but aimed it at Erica who smirked arrogantly with her arms crossed over her chest. The pain in my arm grew stronger by the minute but I knew we needed answers.

“For future references, gloves don’t hide all of your scent.” Erica said with a sassy wink that caused Allie to growl.

“Plus, I kind of saw you jump.” Kate added quietly like she was afraid to be noticed.

Before either one of us could answer, the sound of tires crushing grass filled our ears and our eyes widened in fear. More people were coming, possibly reinforcements. We had to get out before we were trapped inside and possibly killed.

“We have to get out of here.” The blonde werewolf said as she looked over her shoulder and then over mine and I had a feeling I knew what she was thinking. There were no doors down in the basement and if we went up the stairs, we would be blown to bits within seconds so therefore the tiny window peeking just above ground was our only option. I glanced at Allie whose legs were shaking slightly either from exhaustion or fear, I couldn’t tell. The blonde wolf wrapped her fingers around Allie’s upper arm and tugged her forward as the rest of us jogged towards the back wall where hopefully escape wasn’t inevitable.

Terrence smashed his fist through the glass as if it was paper and he helped Kate squeeze through the window without any problem at all. I forced Allie to go through next, though she still wouldn’t look at me and that wrenched my stomach more than the pain in my arm did. The rest of the girls got through easily and I deliberately heard the safety on Allie’s gun click. Terrence forced me to go next though I was hesitant because footsteps sounded on the floor above us.

“Go, Jaxon. I’ll be right behind you.” Terrence said and I looked back at him one more time before I squeezed my broad shoulders through the tiny window.

Sure enough Terrence came out right behind me. Voices rose from where we had come from and we looked at each other with wide eyes. Terrence mouthed the word, *go,* and we took off running at a dead sprint towards Allie's truck that was parked out on the side of the road. Terrence, Erica, and Kate piled into the back seats of the truck, the blonde wolf got into the driver's seat, I got into the middle, and Allie was to my right, still silent.

"Over there!" a woman yelled from where the abandoned church stood alone and the girl slammed her foot on the gas, sending us flying down the road.

Gun shots filled the air like firecrackers and before we knew it, we were being shot at, the bullets hitting the car with a piercing ringing sound. The girl drove as fast as the car would go and her knuckles stayed white as she gripped the wheel.

"Khione, drive." Allie snarled leaning across me, receiving a glare from Khione but she definitely *drove*.

"They aren't going to stop chasing us! We are dead!" Khione yelled as she looked in her review mirrors with a horrified look.

"Not if I have anything to do with it!" Allie yelled back with the same ferocious gaze in her eyes and she unbuckled her seat belt, grabbing her bow and arrow. I grabbed her arm with my good one before she could stand up on the seat.

"What are you doing?" I snarled at her but her eyes were unwavering.

"Protecting you," she said before she rolled down the window, stood up on the seat, and leaned out with her elbow against the roof of the car so that she was halfway shielded.

Allie

Red hot anger surged through me as I climbed halfway out the window and aimed at the two black SUVs trailing behind us. My truck wouldn't hold out for much longer if they kept up their insane speed. There was a man leaning out the window, pointing a small gun at me but he was waiting for me to do something first.

Jaxon's a werewolf.

I let an arrow fly.

He didn't tell you.

It flew through the air.

You are the only human left.

It lodged itself into the man's throat.

Time is up.

Three more arrows flew and wounded the two drivers, sending them and their cars flying over the guardrail. Something feral burned inside of me as I gazed out at the empty road from where I leaned out the window. I didn't want to have to face Jaxon or Khione and explain to them that I willingly killed five men. The bad thing was, I didn't hate myself for doing it. *It's because you have a good reason,* I thought to myself as I climbed back into the car without looking at Jaxon though I knew he was my reason. The car was deadly silent except for the thrum of the tires on the road. Khione had to do a U-turn to actually make it back to Jaxon's house. There was no way we were going home drenched in blood and loaded with weapons. I glared out the window at the familiar woods that zoomed by me and I remembered when the man had me pinned against the wall. Fangs had saved my life. Fangs that I had wanted to get rid of but somehow they came when I needed them. A giddy feeling buzzed in my stomach at the remembrance of the change I had felt only minutes ago.

After an awkward, silent hour of looking anywhere but at each other, Khione parked on the street in front of the Lochlan's house. I got out slowly and turned around just in time to see Jaxon get out and crumple to the ground. My breath whooshed out of me as Terrence and I rushed to him in fear. His skin was almost as pale as Khione's hair and when I looked down at his arm where he got shot, it took all of my willpower not to barf. Where the bullet hole was, puss and blood bubbled from it which was the nastiest part but fear gripped me when I saw the three dark blue lines traveling up his arm, clawing towards his heart.

"That's poison. If you don't get it out…" Khione started but I glared at her to be quiet. We didn't need any more negativity.

Despite my hesitation on whether I forgave him or not, I bent down and wrapped his arms around my shoulder and mine around his waist. Terrence's eyebrows lifted when he saw me being able to carry Jaxon by myself. I tried to pretend like I was struggling but when Jaxon nearly fainted again, I didn't care who saw me and I trudged up to the porch and kicked open the door.

I was about to lay him on the couch when Erica burst in, "No, no, no not on the couch!" I ignored her of course and lay him gently on the couch. Erica let out an exasperated breath but complied.

"Okay, we need to get this out. The longer it stays in…" I drifted off and looked at Jaxon's closed eyes and pale face. I pressed my hand to his forehead and was met by scorching flames.

"We need a knife or something." Kate said but a knife wouldn't be able to grab the bullet from the crook of his elbow.

I looked at Khione, "A knife won't be able to grab the bullet." She understood what I meant and she clenched her fist together. When her fingers snapped open, long claws replaced her nails.

"Then we have to do it the old fashioned way." Khione said and wrapped one hand around his arm to hold it still. Jaxon's eyes flew open at a stranger's touch and even though he was nearly dying, he registered what she was going to do.

Wrenching away from her, he pulled his arm from her grasp but was trapped by the back of the couch and me when I was forced to straddle his stomach. That was when I knew the full power of werewolf strength. Jaxon fought hard but it was only halfhearted because it was easy for me to pin him once again to the couch. Feelings of betrayal and love battled inside of me as I reached a shaky hand towards him, resting it lightly on his hot, pale cheek.

"Get ready," Khione said with a long breath and she tightened her fingers around his arm. Jaxon thrashed again, nearly hitting me in the face with his other arm. I grabbed his wrist and pinned it down to his side. Khione looked at me, "Give him something to focus on." She said though I could barely hear her over Jaxon and Terrence's growls.

"Like what?" I asked but she wasn't paying me any attention. All of it was focused on Jaxon's arm where the blue line was at his shoulder. A tear fell down my cheek and I knew what I had to do. What I really needed and wanted to do was kiss him.

So I did. I held both sides of his scorching face gently but urgently and pressed my lips to his. He went completely stiff at first but when his eyes opened gold and he realized it was me, his mouth softened against mine. I was startled at the feeling it awakened deep inside me. No longer did the out of control feeling plague my mind. I was me. I heard Erica snicker off to my right but it was only a tiny sound in the back of my mind because all that mattered was that Jaxon was here with me. We were safe for the most part and hopefully my secret wouldn't get in the way. I reached my hand up to tuck a piece of my hair behind my ear that had fallen in front of me impatiently, never breaking contact. This was what it was supposed to feel like.

Finally, I had to come up for air at some point. I pulled away with a sharp gasp of air, my eyes flying open to see that we were in the room alone. The others were down in the basement, there voices just a slight buzzing static in the back of my head. Awkwardly, I realized I was still straddling Jaxon, realizing how that must've looked to the others and concluding why they gave us some alone time. I moved off of the couch and perched on my knees on the floor beside it. Jaxon looked at me with smoldering gold eyes, the heat in them telling me I was much more important to him than I thought. My lips lifted at the corners when I reached out and trailed my finger down his jawline.

"Are you okay?" I asked hoping he wouldn't be angry with me for pointing a gun at him since the moment was over.

He grimaced when he tried to sit up but he forced a nod, "Yeah, but that doesn't matter. You had me really worried, Allie." He said in a painfully gentle tone that made tears well up in my eyes. I didn't want to cry though. I had done enough crying.

"I'm fine," I said the two words but even I didn't believe them.

He raised his eyebrows at me and said, "Liar."

My finger still traced his jaw lightly. It was almost mesmerizing. "Well, it is a shock to learn that my boyfriend is a werewolf." I shrugged though it was a total lie.

"Who was that werewolf that helped you?" He asked protectively and I smiled at his tone. Now that I knew what he was, I could actually see the wolf inside him, even though his gold eyes had turned to their usual warm, chocolate brown.

"My best friend, Khione. She saved me when I was really little and we've been friends ever since. I hung out with other wolves a lot when I lived in foster home after foster home." I told him in the most convincing way I could. I laced my fingers through his and he rubbed his thumb across the back of my hand. My muscles felt as heavy as bowling balls and the realization of how tired I was dawned on me quickly.

“You look tired,” he whispered as I leaned my head against his chest from where I sat on the floor. It felt so good just to be near him and breathe in his woodsy scent. My whole body ached from rolling, being choked, and getting thrown against a wall by a man twice my size.

“I can’t go home looking like this.” I said pulling away and motioning to the bloodstains on my black leather clothes. He looked me over, up and down before silently coming back to my face.

“You can probably borrow some of Erica’s clothes,” he paused, looking at me for a few seconds, making blood rush to my cheeks. “I have to say, though, you look good in that.” his smile was sly and playful. I couldn’t take my eyes off of his as he stared at me, something unfamiliar burning in his eyes.

I grinned back at him, a warm, glowing feeling flowing through my veins. He slowly leaned towards me, his eyes never leaving mine as his hand caressed my cheek as if I were made of glass. There was nothing in the world that could ruin the moment, except for the whole Lochlan family coming up the stairs. Their footsteps could be heard from the very first step and Jaxon growled under his breath, his eyes leaving mine and going to the staircase where Terrence emerged first. I pulled away and turned around, sitting cross legged with my back leaning against the couch. The disappointment of being interrupted surged through me, though all I could feel was Jaxon’s lips lingering on mine from his previous kiss.

Khione came up the stairs last, her eyes finding mine in an instant. She noticed the way I sat protectively at Jaxon’s feet, something the werewolves in their human forms did to show protectiveness and loyalty. Her lips twitched into a smile but even I could see that she didn’t trust the Lochlan’s when Jaxon shifted on the couch behind me and sat up. Jaxon and I didn’t touch but now that I finally knew why he had made me so anxious from the moment we met, we didn’t need to be touching to be close. Of course, I would’ve rather been touching him but for now, while we had an audience, I was okay with just being near him.

"So, how are you guys different?" I immediately asked the question that had been burning in my mind for a while. I finally identified the emotion that crawled steadily up my throat that instant… guilt. I glanced at Khione who stood in the back corner of the room, away from the opposing pack obviously uncomfortable.

"What do you mean different?" Jaxon asked above me and I slowly stood up, the soreness and possibly broken bones catching up to me quickly. I turned to face the whole group, my back to where Khione stood silently.

"Obviously," I said, "You guys were… turned into werewolves by alteration of DNA but Khione," I had to struggle not to say I, "was born a werewolf. She can shift different parts of her into the wolf without completely shifting. What about you guys?" I finished and saw them carefully avert their gazes to Khione's and then back to mine when they saw her icy stare.

Erica spoke up first, "Only our eyes change colors when we get angry or whatever." She flashed gold eyes just for show but I wasn't at all impressed. Being born a werewolf had its perks. Khione raised her eyebrows in a sarcastic, mocking way.

Kate said softly, "We can also shift whenever we want but the cold makes it almost impossible not to. It's an instinct."

I looked back at Jaxon and remembered when we had been walking through the woods and he had started to shift. I just hadn't known it yet. That was also when I established my status as the unofficial alpha of the Lochlan pack.

Erica was glaring at Khione when I turned back around, "Do you have something to say?" I could tell in the way Khione's blue eyes lit up that she was about to do some of her world famous trash talking about the Lochlan's less impressive wolves.

Her lips curled back in a tight, threatening smile. I knew I should've stopped things before they got worse but I honestly wanted to see what was going to happen between the two betas. Terrence's eyes darted between the two girls but lingered on Khione and I knew that if things escalated, his alpha instincts would intervene and I was afraid mine would too if I needed to protect my pack.

Khione stayed where she was in the corner, though. Her shoulders, stiff against the wall, showed that she was prepared but wasn't at all threatened by Erica who bristled next to Terrence.

"I was just thinking how it must bite to be you. All alone in the world against a pack like ours." Khione snarled but my insides froze when I realized she had said ours instead of mine.

Erica snarled back though she didn't look half as intimidating as Khione did with her fangs bared, "You are in our territory and without a pack so stand down."

"I understand this is your territory and I understand I don't…" she paused and glanced at me, "have a pack but I want you to understand that I'm not some worthless beta." The flash of gold in Erica's eyes told me she took that comment the wrong way. She took a step towards Khione but I intercepted her in an instant.

Erica's voice rose to a vicious, angry snarl, "At least I'm not a murderer!"

Everything went deadly silent. Erica's words rang in the air like church bells. *Murderer.* Khione and I simultaneously went stiff all over, our breaths freezing in our lungs. Something gripped my chest hard as I reached the table beside me to steady my shaky legs both from exhaustion and the hard truth. I was a murderer. My mom and dad were killers. I dragged in a long, broken breath as the world seemed to spin as truth became a horrible player in this stupid game. I couldn't focus on Khione's reaction while my world was turning upside down. All I could see behind my closed eyelids were the faces of the people I killed in the church that day, bloodied and angry. Lydia and Marcus's voices swirled inside my head, telling me who I was and that my destiny was inevitable. Someone's hand gripped mine but it was just a dull feeling even though I knew it was Jaxon's. My eyes snapped to where Erica stood her face a white sheet of horror as she realized what she had said to us linked back to what had happened earlier. Only she didn't know that what she said had been a problem my whole life.

My eyes blazed and my voice came out stronger than it felt, "Don't tell us we are murders when you don't know anything about the past." Khione didn't let Erica know that her words had affected her but I had known Khione long enough to see that they had buried their way into her mind. I paused and surveyed the looks on everyone's shocked faces, "I'm leaving. You crossed a line, Erica and I need some time to get used to all of this." At the last sentence, my eyes lingered on Jaxon's as emotions rolled head over heel inside of me.

Jaxon

What had just happened? Allie found out about us and I thought she had gotten past the initial shock of me being a freak but after Erica had said that to Khione, it was like someone stabbing an old wound over and over again. Something had happened back then when she was younger, something that she didn't want me to know but the way she acted whenever someone brought up the past, she immediately shut down. Being near her after two days of not knowing if we would make it felt like breathing in gulps of air after nearly drowning underwater.

Erica had locked herself in her room after looking like she had spit on a puppy when Allie and Khione left. Terrence and Kate were stowed away in the kitchen making dinner as if nothing had happened at all while I had shifted into my wolf form and roamed aimlessly around the forest in the middle of the night. Allie was most likely already asleep but every part of me ached to go to her house and clear things up.

My chocolate paws thudded quietly on the hard ground of winter as I walked in circles around the woods outside of my house. My ears picked up tiny sounds and for once I wondered what exactly the world was hiding from me. I had just found out that the wolves Terrence and I had been hunting were werewolves and even more powerful than us. Maybe we had gotten lucky by getting captured. The only problem was that had put Allie in danger, something I was very unwilling to do even if that meant risking my life. One day reality was going to catch up to us and it might not always be as forgiving.

Allie

The walls of the abandoned church seemed to grow smaller, caving in on me as I stood in the middle of the aisle with the wooden pews on either side of me. The sharp tang of fear and blood lingered in the air as my head whipped back and forth, wondering where I was. My fingers wrapped around the back of a pew but something warm and metallic soaked into my palm. I screamed, leaping backwards, and staring wildly at the blood on my palm. When I blinked again, there was nowhere that wasn't covered in the crimson red. Tears streamed down my cheeks as my breathing became puffs like a train. "Hello?" I called out but my voice echoed, slamming back into me. When I turned back around I was met by a familiar face.

"Mom?" I asked as I stared at the faraway look in my mother's eyes. She was dressed in gear as if she had come back from a successful hunting of werewolves.

"Run! You are all alone. You have ruined this family with your secret. Run, Allie, run," She cried her voice turning into an awful screeching sound.

I turned.

And I ran.

Sobs threatened to choke me as soon as my eyes flew open, coming back to reality. My window was open, blowing sharp gusts of wind into the room and showing signs that a storm was on its way. The clock said 1 o'clock and I knew there was no way I was going back to sleep. Wiping the tears from my eyes, I made my way down the creaky dark hallway towards the bathroom. Peering in the mirror, I was shocked to see a bruise wrapped around my neck from where the man had strangled me. I lifted my fingers to it, flinching when they grazed the tender skin. The bruises on my back had started to form last night but they had only gotten worse when I lifted up the back of my shirt. With puffy eyes and cheeks from crying, I pulled on a sweatshirt, jeans, and my paddock boots so that I could go see the horses to give me something to do instead of dream.

For a werewolf, Khione was a deep sleeper because even when I tripped over her mattress she didn't wake up, she only groaned and rolled over. That was how I knew she wasn't dead, I thought to myself with a little laugh. I stepped out onto the roof and used the tree to climb down instead of jumping. Every muscle in my tired body ached and groaned as I landed on the ground with a soft thud. I pushed my hair angrily from my face as the wind blew violently as if it had something to prove.

I made my way into the dark barn, the scents of the horses automatically calming my twisted nerves. How Khione slept after what had just happened was a complete mystery to me. I ran my hand along the wall to my right, searching for the light switch and right when my fingers landed on it, I heard another set of lungs taking in air. I wasn't alone. I froze, putting my hand up to cover my mouth and listen quietly to the other breaths. They didn't sound human, though. I had to fight hard not to let my breathing get out of control and complete panic control me. I prepared myself for a fight with this unknown animal, lowering my center of gravity so that I could take it down. I flicked on the lights.

I moved forward to attack but when I saw what it really was, I stopped and straightened up. The wolf standing before me stared at me with gold eyes, its muscles relaxed underneath its thick, brown fur. I watched it and automatically knew that I was standing face to face with Jaxon in his wolf form something I hadn't done since I almost ran over him with my truck. The air had turned frigid but it didn't bother me, the cold always comforted me when I didn't know what to do. Jaxon stared back at me as if he didn't quite know who I was but something about me was familiar. Ash stuck his head out of his stall, right across from where Jaxon was standing. Ash being Ash was more curious than afraid as he puffed out his nostrils and gave a small nicker that got Lincoln, a small black pony, to join in too. Jaxon's body tensed as he was surrounded on either side by two animals three times his size in height and weight. His lips curled back, exposing sharp fangs when he snarled at Ash who flung his head in the air and spun in his stall as if he were attacked. Jaxon's growls didn't quiet as Ash's cries grew stronger.

"Jaxon! Stop it!" I yelled at him so that I would be heard over his snarls. Sure enough, his ears and eyes turned to me, his gold eyes filling with comprehension at the sound of my voice. When I blinked again, a very confused Jaxon took the wolf's place.

"What am I doing here?" He asked with unfocused, dazed eyes as the wolf left his mind. His eyes then found mine and the confusion on his face grew even deeper.

"I don't know, you just showed up here as a wolf." I shrugged leaning against the wall when I was positive danger became impossible. Something… unfamiliar plagued my tone. It took me a few seconds to realize it was scorn but I wasn't trying to sound angry.

Jaxon noticed it too, his eyebrows rising at my tone, "Sometimes, I don't remember things when I come back into human form from a wolf." He said in a sad, small voice that made me want to wrap my arms around him but I stayed where I was, not sure how I felt about the day's events.

I didn't know what to say to that so, instead of answering, I busied myself by cleaning the bridle I had left out a couple of days ago. I turned my back on Jaxon, dunked a soapy sponge into the water bucket, and ran it over the tough leather. The only sound was the rhythmic chirping of the crickets and steady breathing of dozing horses. Jaxon stood behind me, his eyes a heavy weight on my back as I tried to concentrate on the bridle that dangled on the hook in front of me. It was nearly impossible.

"Allie," Jaxon said much closer behind me than I thought. His scent flowed into my nostrils, turning my legs to spaghetti. He continued, "What happened today, I'm so sorry. I wanted to tell you so badly but Terrence…" I spun around as anger flared in the pit of my stomach, my eyes flashing with fury.

I poked his chest with my finger, stepping forward as he stepped back, "You know you weren't going to tell me," I yelled in a half whispered voice when my hand curled around the fabric of his black t-shirt. "I don't care if your alpha told you that you couldn't tell me the truth! You can make your own choices! It's not an alpha's job to tell you what to do and how to do it. So man up and make your own freaking decisions, Jaxon. Let me know when that happens. Right now I just want to go back to sleep." I said my voice going from a yell to a barely audible whisper as I stared into his dark eyes that nearly matched the darkness of the outdoors. We were face to face, our noses nearly touching but I was too angry to enjoy the closeness of his body. "See you tomorrow," I whispered hoarsely and then turned to go.

I had nearly made it out the barn doors when a hand wrapped around my upper arm and spun me around. My hands came up to rest on Jaxon's chest for balance as his arm encircled my waist and his other fingers gently traced the bruise on my neck. I could barely feel it. I wanted to be angry so badly but the other part of me, the part of me that was in love with Jaxon, told me to get closer. Wait… I loved Jaxon.

His voice was a soft whisper in the wind, "You're right and I didn't want you to get hurt. It's my job to protect you and I failed but I want you to know that I will always be here for you whenever you need me," his voice was full of promise that it made every part of me ache and I couldn't stand it anymore.

Nerves racked my body as I stared at him in silence, trying to clear my mind of his scent so that I could actually speak in words. He didn't make a move as if he was waiting for permission but I had something to say first and I needed all his attention.

Tears filled my eyes as I said softly in a shaky voice the three words I had felt for so long, "I love you, Jaxon." His eyes widened and at first I thought he was going to bolt but his expression mirrored mine, full of love and promise.

"I love you too, Allie." He said and then he kissed me.

His arms tightened around me, pulling me closer to him and forcing my feet to climb on top of his shoes so that I was an inch taller than my usual height. His words vibrated through my body as I fisted his t-shirt in one shaky hand while the other curled around the hair at the back of his neck. The soreness from the day had completely vanished from my mind as Jaxon invaded every part of my brain. I opened my mouth, his lips no longer hot from the fever but cool and soft just like they were supposed to be.

I pulled away but kept my forehead leaning against his. My breath came in short gasps as I tried to catch it when I said, "I know I act like I don't need you," I sucked in a breath, "But I will always need you, Jaxon, that's a guarantee." I brushed my thumb lightly across his cheek, his eyes fluttering shut at my touch.

He brushed his lips across mine, not really a kiss but just as satisfying. "And I promise," he whispered, "That I will always be here." He pulled away so that he could look at me but I saw the fear and worry in his eyes when they found the bruise around my neck.

A smile played across my lips and I trailed my fingers down his cheek, "Hey, don't worry about me. It doesn't even hurt that bad." I faked and thought he believed it until his eyebrows rose and the worry didn't lessen.

"Your heartbeat fluttered." He said forcing me to roll my eyes and smile wider. I pressed my lips to his briefly before looking at him again.

"Okay so it does hurt." I shrugged moving slightly away from him but not because I was angry, it was because I couldn't think straight when I was too close to him. "But that doesn't mean you have to worry about me. I'm a big girl and I can take care of myself." His lips hardened but I laughed lightly, "Plus, it was kind of fun, you know? I felt like I was in the Hunger Games."

Jaxon chuckled quietly, shaking his head at me. "What are you going to tell Blake and Miles about running out at school?"

"How'd you know that?"

"Blake called me a couple of hours ago because you wouldn't answer your phone. I told her that you had just left an hour ago." He said with a shrug as I sat down on one of the tack trunks outside of Catcher's stall, a giant Belgian warm blood.

"I have no idea. I ran out of there crying. She probably thinks someone died or something." I sighed and ran my fingers through my wavy brown hair that was finally free of the sticky blood.

"Crying, huh? You were that worried about me?" He said his eyes challenging and glittering against the soft lights of the barn.

I narrowed my eyes at him and threw one of the horse brushes in his direction, "Shut up." I laughed when he dodged the brush with ease.

"I have to say, though, that ambush was pretty insane." He looked at me through wide eyes but underneath the worry I saw a little smidge of admiration.

"Thanks, it was my idea." I smiled proudly, "I've been known for insane plans. So, if you ever get into trouble, I'm your girl." He came to sit beside me and I leaned my head on his shoulder, his arm surrounding my shoulders as if he could shield me from the world. "That is a good question, though." I said thoughtfully about Jaxon's earlier question. I moved closer to him, the frigid winter wind cutting through my thin sweatshirt and jeans.

I said quietly, "I have no idea what I am going to tell them. I can't lose them due to a white lie. I mean, yeah, I have you guys but, I also need a human part in my life." Jaxon's fingers trailed aimlessly down my arm as if he didn't notice he was doing it. Suddenly aware of the exhaustion that ran bone deep, I fought hard to stay awake.

"I understand," Jaxon said in a soft voice, threatening to put me to sleep. We were lost in silence for a few moments. His hand froze in the circle it was drawing on my arm and I got the notion that he was thinking about something, hard. He took in a long breath, "What if we don't have to lie? Why not tell her the truth about me?"

he asked but every instinct screamed at me not to risk Jaxon's life just so I could keep my friends.

I pulled away so that I could look in his eyes. I said in a hard voice, "My mother has a whole team of werewolf hunters right on your tails and my friendships with Blake and Miles aren't worth risking you and your family's lives." The look in Jaxon's eyes told me he was grateful but oblivious to the hunters.

"I didn't even know she was still looking for us. They already killed my parents. What else do they want?" Jaxon asked with pain and remorse burning through his words.

I stood up, slowly my muscles objecting to the movement with a flare of pain. I made my way directly underneath the hay loft where I had thrown the lab notes a couple of days ago. Picking it up, I delicately smoothed out the creases and brought it back to Jaxon, sitting beside him as his eyes scanned the lines of notes. His frown deepened when he got to his name and I knew that he didn't like the analysis considering it practically called him an uncontrolled killer.

"Of course we were out of control," he snarled thrusting the paper back into my hands, "She took these notes right when we were injected." His hands, clenched into tight fists, shook slightly with rage.

Slowly, I unfolded his fists, lacing my fingers through his to keep them still. I wanted to tell him the bad, nasty facts but I also knew that wouldn't help the situation. Instead, I told him about something else.

"When I was eight years old," I said squeezing his fingers. He didn't look at me as I continued, "I ran away from home and found my way here. I had finally found a nice, happy family that loved me. Mom took me to the lab one day, saying that she was working on something big and couldn't leave me home alone. Dad had been overseas at the time and Dallas was in school. I was… unusually mature for being only eight years old. I understood most of everything she said that wasn't too scientific and I remembered hearing one word that made me want to sob. Werewolf. I didn't show any weakness, though. I just held onto her legs and watched people go by." I closed my eyes, reliving the blurry but significant memory. Jaxon still wouldn't look at me but the way his eyebrows were raised said that he knew the story well. I continued, "The scientists had been chatting loudly until an unfamiliar family walked into the white room. I hid behind mom's legs and peeked out. It was then that I saw a little boy about my age with dark eyes and hair. We stared each other with wide eyes. I knew what they were going to do to him but all I could do was stare. There was something about the little boy that captured my attention. I guessed he hadn't heard me but I told him quietly, I'll see you later." I finished and tears pricked my eyes, blurring my vision. I took my fingers from his to gently caress his face in my hand. He finally looked at me, eyes so full of love and compassion that it made my heart ache. I swallowed hard before I spoke again, "I saw him again, you know. Nine years later when he picked up my books for me in the hallway. And then not long after that, I fell in love with him," I paused and took in a shaky breath, "I fell in love with you."

Jaxon's lips parted and I smiled victoriously when he was rendered speechless. He leaned forward slowly as if he were afraid I wasn't real. Our lips met, innocent and familiar as all the doubts I had felt before melted away when Jaxon kissed me, hard. A surprised sound escaped my throat but I wound my fingers in his hair, kissing him until his eyes opened gold and I could no longer breathe.

Jaxon pulled away from me, his eyes wild and his chest heaving up and down. I wanted to pull his lips back to mine but I knew he needed time to gain control of the wolf before I was forced to defend myself against him.

He said softly, "I remembered you a couple of weeks ago. I only wish that I would've heard your voice back then. I remember hoping that you would be there when I got out but I never got to go back home." Jaxon's voice cracked with sadness and all I could do was stare at him with the same wide blue eyes that I had back then. He bent his head, pressing his lips to the crown of my hair. I rested my forehead against the crook of his neck, closing my eyes and breathing in his scent.

In the distance, a rich howl sounded through the night, breaking our moment. Jaxon stiffened beside me, his head swinging in the direction of the sound.

"Terrence," Jaxon growled, "We have to hunt to get our strength back up from yesterday. You should sleep." He trailed his fingers down the side of my neck, my eyes fluttering shut.

I didn't want to sleep. I didn't want to see Lydia's bloodstained teeth in my nightmares. There was no way I was going to sleep after those dreams haunted my mind every night. It didn't help that my head had begun to pound with a painful headache as I squeezed my eyes shut. All I wanted to do was sit here with Jaxon so that he could protect me from the nightmares that plagued every dream.

I lifted my head to look at him with pleading eyes, "Listen to me," I said in a serious voice, "You have to be careful out there. Those hunters are out there every night with guns and crossbows. They are skilled killers. And no offense, but from what Khione tells me, you are not very good at killing." He narrowed his eyes at me, making me unsure of my choice to say that to him but he needed to hear that.

"Well, sorry for not killing her on the spot…" His voice, dripping with sarcasm, cut through the space between us. I decided to drop the subject, even though I could've easily fought him hard on it.

“Just be careful,” I resigned right before Terrence’s impatient howl sounded in the woods again.

Jaxon kissed me gently, “Goodnight.”

“Love you,” I said the sweet, unfamiliar words.

“Love you too,” He smiled before his brown eyes bled out into gold.

His wave was sad as he fell to his knees and the wolf overtook him, the recognition fading from his eyes as if it were the darkness turning into light. I lifted my hand to wave goodbye but when I blinked, I stood in the aisle alone with just the sounds of the horses surrounding me.

Jaxon

Jaxon, go! Terrence’s yell vibrated through my whole body as the sounds of gunfire filled the night.

My teeth closed around the scruff of Kate’s neck, her body limp and heavy as I dragged her into the trees to hide from danger. A man screamed in pain and through the shadows of the night, I saw Terrence’s red eyes darting through the trees as another hunter fell. Kate’s whine sent a pinch of guilt through my stomach, the blood from her bullet wound flowing steadily now. Erica was surrounded by two men who pointed guns straight at her skull which I knew would kill her instantly.

Kate, I aimed the thought at her and her sad gold eyes looked up at me, *I have to go get Erica, I’ll be right back.*

Go… She thought back but I was already dashing through the trees, my paws thudding quietly on the forest floor as I charged the men.

I leapt onto one's back, sinking my teeth into his shoulder as he cried out in agony. All the control leaked from my body as I stood over the suffering hunter while Erica's snarls ripped through the night as she killed the other man. I stared into the man's frightened green eyes and the human part of me said to leave him alone but the wolf said to kill him now and get it over with.

Move! I'll do it! Erica howled the thought and before I knew it her grey body collided with mine as she tore the man's throat out without any hesitation at all. I was both impressed and horrified.

Kate's in the woods. The wound is bleeding badly. I told Erica when her ears whipped towards the sound of Kate's cries of pain.

Right before I was engulfed in the trees, I turned back to look at the mess we had made. Hunters lay scattered around the field far away from Sweet Home, Oregon. Mistakenly, Terrence had led us farther than we were supposed to go which had also been the place the hunters were searching for us. Things just got worse when we ran into them. Guilt was always present as we walked home, Kate dragging her leg behind her and trying to hold in her cries of pain. I wouldn't tell Allie about what happened that night.

<u>Allie</u>

My phone dinged around five o'clock, waking me up about two hours before I had to get up for school. I wasn't happy about that. What I was happy about was the text from Jaxon telling me that everything went fine last night and that he loved me. Slightly disappointed that he didn't call me, I texted him back saying I loved him too.

Khione, Dallas, and I made our way downstairs for breakfast but all the while I never took my eyes off my little brother. Something was wrong with him but I didn't know what. If we made eye contact, he would quickly look away as if he were afraid I was going to hurt him. There was also the fact that Oliver had pulled me aside and told me he was going to start training me for hunting due to the shortage of hunters because of what happened last night. What was Jaxon not telling me? Or was it just a coincidence that there were five less hunters than there had been the day before?

Oliver looked at me with his black eyes, "We are practicing after school. Meet me in that warehouse just down the road. Please come alone, I have to talk to you about something very important." The way he said it made me believe that there was something important I was missing. I nodded, speechless at his serious tone, and then left for school.

The question about what happened last night threatened to pass my lips every time I saw Jaxon in the hallways or in my classes. Something held me back from asking, though, and maybe it was the fact that Oliver wanted to tell me something important. But Jaxon wasn't stupid. He knew there was something wrong with me and I knew he knew it when he dragged me under the staircase between fifth and sixth period.

"What the…?" I asked him as I stumbled after him when he grabbed my arm, hard. "Ow," I said in a flat voice when he let go of me and I rubbed my wrist.

"Sorry," he said though he knew I wasn't really hurt, just annoyed. "Are you okay?"

"No,"

"Why? What happened?"

"You lied to me."

He froze, his mouth opening and closing as if deciding whether or not to say something, "What are you talking about?"

Sarcasm found its way into my words, "Oh, I don't know, maybe the fact that your pack was out hunting last night and now Oliver wants to train me because we have five less hunters than we did before." I found that I wasn't angry, just very annoyed that he lied to me.

He sighed, giving up, "Fine, okay we had some problems last night… but I didn't think it would be that big of a deal. I thought the hunters were the bad guys." His voice was angry, making me believe that someone had gotten hurt.

I gave an exasperated sigh, throwing my hands up, "Of course they are the bad guys. But they have everything to do with my family." My voice rose to a hushed yell, "So, control your wolves and don't let them kill anyone else. Or…" I drifted off.

"Or what?"

"Or I am going to get involved." I said giving him the coldest stare I could conjure up before shouldering my bag and sauntering out into the hallway. My threat about getting involved went much deeper than I thought he knew.

If I got involved, Khione would be on my side and she was a better fighter than the entire Lochlan pack put together. There was a difference between the way Khione and Jaxon fought when they were wolves. From what Khione described to me about her encounter with him and Terrence was that the two didn't know how to fight together in order to take down an enemy. While Khione fought Jaxon, Terrence prepared for his brother to send her his way but he never attacked. So, going against a group of hunters who are skilled at fighting together, Terrence's pack wouldn't survive if they were outnumbered by too many. Also, if Oliver was able to teach me how to fight like one of them, I could get involved, either on the side of the pack… or on the side of the hunters.

As angry as I was at Jaxon, it helped fuel a believable lie as I told Miles and Blake why I ran out yesterday. I told them something simple consisting of the fact that Oliver had gotten into a minor car crash but the medics that called me made it sound a lot worse than it actually was hence the fact that I was crying. I got away with it, making me realize the trust my friends had in me. I didn't deserve that.

After school crawled by slowly like a wounded snake, Khione and I were probably the first ones out of there. I told her she had to stay home while I went to train with Oliver because I needed to talk to him. Of course, Khione had objected for about five minutes but eventually she decided she would just go hunting until I got home.

"The hunters shouldn't be out today." She said to me as she fixed her lipstick in the mirror of my truck.

I was thinking about Jaxon, though, "Do me a favor," I said with a sly smile, "If you see the Lochlan pack out there, show them what a real fighter looks like and then tell me about it."

Khione's lips turned up, tips of white fangs barely showing, "You can count on it. I've been dying to teach Erica a lesson about born werewolves." I didn't object, just laughed at the deadly look in her eyes.

I quickly changed into the clothes that were still shoved in the back of my closet that I wore last full moon. The leather clung to the curves of my body comfortably and I found comfort in the feeling of being powerful. I made my way downstairs where mom had a display of weapons laid out on the table for me. We had made sure that Dallas wasn't going to be home because he didn't need to be brought into this cruel, complicated world.

I was on the road in ten minutes, loaded with two guns strapped on either side of my belt and a bow and arrow slung across my shoulder. I couldn't help but be excited to finally start training and be ten steps closer to defeating Lydia and Marcus. The trees zoomed by me, growing denser and denser as I drove into the part of the town with very little population. I was ready to show Oliver just what I was made of.

I pushed open the nasty metal door of the abandoned warehouse, which smelled like rotten eggs and dead rats. Not a good combination. The silence was so heavy that it was almost tangible and the wolf in me knew that was wrong. I pulled the gun out of my belt, keeping my finger on the trigger and the safety. I walked down a long corridor, the only sound were the pipes dripping water. The hallways lead into the main part of the warehouse, a giant room that could probably fit ten houses inside of it. Various crates and trash bins were scattered around the concrete room, giving someone the perfect place to hide. I clicked the safety. Training started now.

I rolled to the side when out of nowhere an arrow whizzed towards me. I came up on one knee behind a crate, blocking me from the view of the shooter. I hoped it was Oliver and that I hadn't just walked right into a death trap. I aimed the gun at where the arrow had come from but all of a sudden arrows flew at me from behind and I leapt on top the crate, front flipped off of it and took off at a dead sprint across the room. I stood in the center, dropping the gun and replacing it with my bow and arrow. Everything was silent, fear and anxiety rushing up my throat.

"Come on!" I yelled at whoever was shooting at me and then I was body slammed from the side.

I cried out as the other person and I skidded across the floor but I kicked him in the stomach, getting away from him quickly. Oliver stood above me, a bloody gash down the side of his face from one of my arrows that had cut him. I stood up slowly, assessing my competition and remembering something Lydia used to say to me. *Don't be on defense. Always be the first to attack.* I leapt up, spun in the air, and kicked Oliver square in the chest but he was powerful too and he grabbed my ankle and then twisted my body so that I landed on the floor on my hands in a push up position.

"Good strategy," Oliver said, thinking that I was defeated. Yeah, in his dreams.

In one swift movement, I flipped onto my back and swiped Oliver's legs out from under him, both of us landing on our backs breathing heavily. I stared at the ceiling of the warehouse where afternoon sun streamed in through small windows above me. Oliver helped me up, his hand enveloping mine completely as I was pulled up off the ground.

I dusted off my pants, laughing, "You're good." I nodded respectively to him and was rewarded with an actual smile, something that seemed…natural on Oliver's face.

Just then, as I looked at him, there was something strangely familiar about the shape and look of Oliver's dark eyes. I ran my fingers through my hair, uncomfortable under his scary familiar gaze as we stood in the dank warehouse.

"What did you need to talk to me about?" I asked breaking the silence that seemed to separate us with a piece of glass. I slung my bow over my shoulder and slipped my gun back into my belt.

"I know who you really are, Allie." Oliver said as every bone in my body turned to Jell-O. I aimed an arrow at his chest with shaky hands because I didn't really want to shoot him but he knew who I was.

He dropped his weapons, surprising me and I lowered the bow. "You're not going to kill me?" I asked in a voice barely above a whisper.

"I'm on your side, kiddo." He said smiling at me, "After all, the hunters are after my children."

"Excuse me?" My voice came out an octave higher than it was supposed to be.

"Terrence and Jaxon are my children." Oliver said as my eyes grew wide, taking in the shocking information about Jaxon's past.

"How? Their parents are dead. The FBI killed them, I thought." I said leaning back on one of the crates behind me, folding my arms across my chest.

"Here's what happened." Oliver said, "I was married to Annie Lochlan many years ago. I was never around and consumed with my work twenty four seven. She got pregnant with Terrence and I was around most of the time. Then, she was pregnant with Jaxon. She kicked me out a few months before he was born and for so many years, all I wanted to do was go back and see them. I just wanted to let my sons know that I care about them. But, I was afraid and then I saw Annie, her new husband, and my children changed into werewolves and I knew it was too late for me. The next thing I knew…" Oliver's voice cracked and a tear found its way into my eyes, threatening to spill over. The next thing he knew Annie and Dan were killed.

"Oliver," I said quietly, "There's still a chance for you to make things right between you and them." I was an expert on messing up relationships with people which also made me an expert on fixing them. Maybe Oliver and I weren't so different.

"How?"

"Here's the deal," I told him in a matter of fact voice, "If you help me keep the hunters off their trail, then I'll help you strengthen your relationship with Jaxon and Terrence." I unfolded my arms and held out my hand, raising my eyebrows in question.

"It's a deal," Oliver smiled and I could see Terrence and Jaxon in his face clearly now. I liked it. I shook Oliver's hand once and a taunting glint lit my eyes.

"Let's start training, then." I smiled and swung my fist at Oliver's face.

Jaxon

Erica's fur brushed against mine as we trotted through the woods, light snow dusting the ground as the day grew colder. Kate had stayed home due to her still injured leg from the night before and Terrence stayed ahead of us, sniffing for any signs of the hunters. All I could think about though, was how angry Allie had been at me when she found out about the hunters and the fact that I lied to her about it. I trotted with my eyes straight ahead and ears pricked forward, alert and aware of my surroundings so that we didn't create any casualties. Allie's face burned in my mind, scary calm but screaming with anger. I caused that because I completely abused her trust. Allie's trust was something very fragile.

Wait, Terrence thought, pausing in front of us and causing me to accidentally bump into him. He growled at me but his attention was focused on something else in front of me. I listened carefully, our breath freezing in our lungs.

There's another one close by, Erica thought as Terrence had. She and I stood in a circle facing out.

Sure enough, a white flash darted in and out of the trees and then disappeared. I snarled at the unknown wolf though, I had an idea who the pure white wolf was. A steady growl flowed from the complete opposite direction she had been running. How can a werewolf move that fast? The she wolf went silent and fear filled my chest because Allie's words were correct. We didn't know how to fight an experienced killer like Khione. Something body slammed me from the side and Khione and I skidded across the ground, her teeth sinking into my shoulder but before I could fight back, she had disappeared again.

Blood leaked out of the torn skin as I staggered back towards my pack who snarled in the general direction of Khione but I knew she was on the move. A howl sounded through frigid air as snow coated the ground in thick layers. Blue eyes stared at me from a distance but Khione's white body blended in with the cold environment around her. She licked her blood stained lips and disappeared again. I opened my mouth, exposing threatening fangs to no one in particular just as Erica flew across the clearing with Khione digging her claws and fangs into my sister. *We have to fight like a team.* I lunged for Khione, tackling her from the side and tumbling head over heels in the thick snow. I snarled viciously as saliva flew and teeth snapped the air. Good at dodging my blows, Khione made it impossible for me to bite her. She threw me off of her, swiping her claws across my chest and stomach. Terrence and Erica were about to attack but Khione was nowhere to be seen.

The three of us shifted, Erica and I bloodied but Terrence was just tired. Khione's claws had shredded my shirt and it lay in pieces scattered around the forest. I leaned back on my hands and carefully touched the four deep, claw marks that trailed blood down my body. I groaned, finding the other jaw marks from that pesky she wolf.

"Ugh," Erica half snarled half groaned as she rolled onto her knees, "That wolf is insane," Terrence helped the two of us up painfully and we made our way slowly home at a pace that a snail could most likely beat.

An hour passed and we were still only by the abandoned warehouse that was just outside of town. The claw marks were now searing pains through my whole body and it took all of my will power not to curl up on the snowy ground and go to sleep. Why had Khione attacked us if she knew we weren't the bad guys? What had Allie told her to do? A loud crash and yell disrupted the quiet evening, my body spinning in a complete circle to see where it had come from. The warehouse was all of the sudden ignited with sound.

"Come on!" Allie's scream vibrated through my whole body as another crash echoed through the air.

"Block me!" A man with a deep voice yelled at her from inside. She cried out in pain, grunting again in anger.

"What's Allie doing in there?" Erica yelled at me as my two pack mates sprinted behind me.

"I don't know but something is wrong!" I yelled back at her, holding back the cries of pain as I stretched my legs further and further until the claw marks threatened to destroy me.

I had to get to Allie.

Allie

I lay on my stomach with Oliver's knee on my back and my right arm pinned behind my head, my shoulder stinging with pain. I gritted my teeth tightly together, banging my fist on the ground and screaming in pain as I tried to think of a way out.

"Think fast!" Oliver yelled advice to me like he had been for the past hour or so.

Beat up, bruised, and out of breath, I gave it one last shot. I conjured up the strength of the wolf, reached up with my free arm, grabbed the collar of Oliver's shirt, and flipped him over me. He crashed into the broken boards of the crates and I smiled proudly at my work. I rolled onto my back, rocked back onto my hands, and then launched forward as I landed on my feet. Sweat dripped down my face, my hair hanging in my face like a curtain. When I pushed it back, I stood face to face with Jaxon, Terrence, and Erica who were cut up and bleeding.

"Allie?" Jaxon asked as he stared at me with wide eyes but I found myself unable to look away from his ripped up, bare chest.

I was still breathing heavily as I looked at him incredulously, "What… are you doing here? And what happened?" I asked him running my fingers through my wet hair. Oliver had roused from the pile of crates I had flipped him into earlier.

"Your friend Khione happened," Erica snarled, the blood from a cut on her shoulder trailing down her arm. "Then, after she nearly killed us, your boyfriend over here heard you screaming like your life was ending."

"Dad?" Terrence said coming out from behind Jaxon and Erica, looking at Oliver who stood just to the right of me.

I felt Oliver's breath freeze in his lungs when he heard Terrence call him the one thing that he had always wanted to hear. Emotions like anger and love warred on Terrence's face as he stared at his true father. I looked over to see tears welling up in his dark eyes and for once I saw where Terrence got his serious face. I couldn't decide if he wanted to go hug his long lost dad or punch him in the face.

"Dad?" Erica asked looking at Terrence in confusion as her and Jaxon tried to put together the puzzle pieces.

No one answered her though because all I could do was stare at Terrence as he tried to figure out his feelings about Oliver. Oliver took a few steps forward so that he was halfway between Terrence and me. As if he couldn't contain it anymore, Terrence stepped forward and wrapped his arms around Oliver's neck and hugged him with the biggest smile on his face. My hand came up to cover my mouth as I laughed and cried at the reunion, knowing that Oliver would do anything to keep the hunters at bay.

“I’m so sorry,” Oliver whispered when Terrence pulled away and looked at him, “I’m so sorry I wasn’t there for both of you.” Oliver looked at Jaxon but there was no way he knew what was going on.

Terrence turned to face his brother who looked even more panicked as the confusion piled up. Jaxon asked, “Can someone please tell me what’s going on?” I thought about the fight we had gotten into and how I had taken my anger out on Oliver when we fought but the way Jaxon was looking at a father he had never known, made all that fear go away because I missed my dad so much it hurt.

I crossed the room and made my way to Jaxon’s side, looking up at him with sad eyes as I laced my fingers through his. I leaned into him, meeting Terrence’s eyes with a pained expression but Jaxon held onto my hand as if he were going to faint. I looked to his bare chest where the claw marks were, realizing the blood flowed faster and his skin was no longer a deep tan. He made a small whimpering noise right before he fell to the ground with a thud.

Jaxon

Faces swirled behind my closed eyelids as my fuzzy brain tried to pull itself out of the confusion. Mom, dad, and Allie faded in and out of the darkness but I could never reach them. I tried to force my heavy eyes open but they didn’t want to. The static in the back of my head turned into clear, familiar voices.

“… And he won’t know how to handle it when he wakes up,” Terrence’s voice was close, “I barely knew how to handle it. It took all of my willpower not to punch you in the face, no offense.”

“I deserved a punch in the face,” A strange male voice, “But I appreciate your willpower.”

Laughing.

Then Allie's voice floated through the air but she sounded far away like she was standing across the room from me. "By the way, Khione," She said in a pointed voice, "I told you to teach them a lesson about fighting, not to actually hurt them." Anger electrocuted her words like lightning.

Khione snarled, "He attacked me. I was only defending myself. I played defense most of the time."

"You call body slamming us defense? What land do you come from?" Erica bit off each word bitterly as she threw them at the opposing beta.

"A land where warriors are born instead of pretty little princesses like you." Khione spat and the tension in the room grew so large I could almost hold it.

A searing pain shot through my chest, a small gasp escaping my lips and my eyelids flew open, revealing the world in harsh, annoying lights. Terrence and the strange man were at my side in an instant, kneeling on the ground beside the bed I was lying in. My eyes flitting around the room, I caught a glimpse of Allie leaning against the wall in a corner with her arms crossed and a smirk on her face. I couldn't decide if it was because of Khione's earlier comment or that I woke up. I stared at the dark haired man beside me.

"Who are you?" I asked him slowly, afraid to know the answer.

"My name is Oliver Bryn," He said, "And I'm your biological father."

"What?" Erica and Kate said the word before I could but it sounded just as shocked.

Biological father? What was he talking about? I knew who my father was and he was not the man standing in front of me. My real father was there for me. He walked me to school and taught me how to play football. He was always there. This man… this man was just another face that I passed by on the sidewalk. I sat up quickly in the bed the world doing a 360 flip. I squeezed my eyes shut, shaking my head back and forth as Allie came to sit cross legged beside me. She looked at me with a sad smile as if she knew all along who Oliver really was and felt bad for me.

I looked to Terrence, "It's true, Jaxon. He is our father, just you and me."

Oliver said, "When Annie was pregnant with you, I was busy with my job and was never around. Right before you were born, she kicked me out and I missed the birth of my second son. Instead, Dan was there as her best friend and helped raise you. They got married not long after that and then had Erica and Kate." The look on his face was pure regret and hatred for his actions but I couldn't bring myself to take pity on him, not when everyone had lied to me for so long.

"How come no one ever told me?" I demanded my fists clenching and unclenching in anger.

"Because even back then I was a hunter and Annie didn't want that life for her children so she thought it would be best for them not to know. We convinced Terrence never to say anything about me and to forget I ever existed." Oliver's hand came to rest on Terrence's shoulder lightly and I knew that my brother had missed him even though he was supposed to forget.

"I… I don't know what to think of this…" I was at a complete loss of words. Luckily, Allie came to my rescue.

"Maybe we should give everyone some time to process this… bomb that just exploded." She said shooing everyone out until we were alone and the others footsteps faded away down the stairs.

Allie told me to lie down due to the dizziness that was getting worse by the minute. The shirt that I wore clung uncomfortably to the sticky blood that was healing slowly. She leaned against the back wall and stretched out her legs beside me, running her fingers through my hair but I could tell she was thinking about something else. Her touch made it nearly impossible to stay awake.

"You know," Allie said softly, still combing her fingers gently through my hair, "Oliver just wants to make things right between the three of you. Plus, he can help me fight the hunters and protect your pack." I didn't want her to protect us if it could get her and Oliver killed. Even if I didn't exactly like Oliver… he was still my father.

"How am I even supposed to trust him?" I asked turning over to look at her but there was no expression in her blue eyes as I continued, "He just waltzed in here and dropped a bomb on us saying he was my dad." She smiled lightly but it was a sad smile as she reached out, trailing her thumb down my cheek.

"Dan Lochlan was your dad but Oliver is your father." She told me, forcing my eyes to meet hers, "Yeah, he screwed up back then but who cares. The past is the past and you are short on parents and Oliver is willing to lay down his life to protect his children. He was given a second chance and you were given a second dad. He will never replace Dan and he doesn't have to but give Oliver a chance." I didn't know what to say to that but could she be right?

"It sounds like you speak from experience." I said taking her hand in mine from where it rested on my cheek and lacing my fingers through hers. She looked away and out to the window where the sun shone brightly.

"I do," Allie said in a small, sad voice that made my heart ache. She whispered, "My real mom and dad… they tried to kill me multiple times." My eyes widened and fear corrupted the anger I felt towards Oliver. I didn't realize how hard Allie's life was until all the pieces came together.

"Allie…" I started but she shook her head, a single tear falling down her cheek. She swiped at it angrily, a bitter laugh escaping her lips.

"God, I am so sick of crying." She growled but I sat up and wrapped her in my arms as unwilling tears fell down her cheeks. "When I ran away and came here," She whispered, "I was given a second chance and a second father. But that chance was ripped away from me and he was last seen in Afghanistan trying to save another soldier." Her body shuddered against mine when I rested my chin on top of her head, her fingers curling around the fabric of my shirt. Even though the claw marks shot pain through my body, I didn't let go of her. How could someone do that to her? Someone like Allie deserved a better life than what she was given. In that moment, my goal for the rest of my life would be to give Allie the life that she deserved from the very beginning.

"I didn't know that," I whispered against her hair, "You trust Oliver?"

"With my life," She said and I trusted Allie's judgment because she hadn't been wrong yet.

"Then I'll give him a shot but what were you guys doing in the warehouse?" I asked her when the shuddering in her body had stopped and she pulled away from me.

Allie smiled, wiping the tears away, "He was teaching me how to fight."

"I thought you already knew how to do that."

“I know how to fight people.” She said raising her eyebrows with a smirk.

“Then what was he teaching you?” I thought I already knew the answers.

“He’s teaching me how to fight werewolves.” She said looking at me with a challenging gaze that screamed alpha. “Which reminds me; you should come because I need someone to help me practice. Oliver is hardly as strong as a werewolf and Khione is unpredictable.”

I considered the proposition and figured if I went it would be a way to bond with Oliver and protect Allie. “Sure, but I don’t want to hurt you.”

She laughed as if the idea was impossible, “Hurt me? I’d like to see you try.” She kissed me lightly before climbing off the bed. “You should get some rest. Khione nearly killed you.” She strode across the room, the sun outlining her figure as if she were from heaven.

“Are you going home?” I asked as my eyes became heavier and threatened to shut but I forced them open.

“No,” She said as she turned out the lights which didn’t really do much, “I’ll be downstairs until you wake up again.” Her voice dropped to a whisper and I nodded right before everything went black.

Allie

I made my way downstairs after shutting Jaxon’s door tightly behind me. I was met by laughter and chatting mainly coming from the Lochlan family and Oliver. Khione had gone home which I was slightly thankful for because I didn’t know if I could talk to her without yelling at her. I couldn’t believe that I had told Jaxon my biggest secret. Well, half of my biggest secret. Lydia and Marcus had tried to kill me when I would step out of line or say something that had the hint of challenge in the words. I had never been so glad to be living in Oregon.

Every part of my body was sore and small bruises started to form on my wrists from Oliver's tight grip and one spread across my cheekbone from where his fist had connected with it. I limped downstairs and flopped onto the barstool in between Oliver and Kate, who were laughing hysterically at something I missed. Erica was cooking something on the stove that made my stomach growl.

Terrence looked at me with a very uncharacteristic look on his face. He was smiling when he said, "Did you talk some sense into him?"

"Of course, that's my job, isn't it?" I smiled jokingly though it was pretty much true. "Erica, can I please take a shower and borrow some different clothes? I look like I just went through the sewer." I ran my fingers through my still sweaty hair, making me wonder how Jaxon had sat next to me.

Erica laughed, pointing up the stairs, "You can use my bathroom. It is up the stairs and to the right."

"Thanks," I nodded to her and pushed my sore muscles back up the stairs and closed myself in the bathroom.

When I was alone, I gripped the edges of the sink and stared at myself in the mirror. I pressed my forehead to the glass and let out a breath, thinking about what I had told Jaxon and how much I wanted a third chance. But everyone knew that three chances never happened. I stared at my reflection, curly brown hair, pale skin, and gold eyes.

"Oh crap," I whispered urgently when I saw the gold eyes glinting in the lights. I brought my fingers up to my cheek and traced the outline of my eyes, in amazement and fear. "What is happening?"

In the next instant, they melted back into their familiar light blue and I let out a breath of relief. I assumed it was because of the adrenaline still coursing through my veins from fighting with Oliver and the whole crisis with Jaxon and Khione. When I was positive my eyes had gone back to normal, I turned on the shower, stripped down, and let the hot water wash all the stress away.

A few minutes later, I was dressed in a too big sweatshirt that I was pretty sure wasn't Erica's but it was warm and smelled familiar. I pulled on the same jeans I had trained in because they had stayed in pretty good shape surprisingly. Twisting my hair into a braid, I made my way downstairs and joined in the conversation of old memories and good times.

Jaxon

My eyes fluttered open about two and a half hours later and I was met with laughter and voices from downstairs. I was surprised by how rarely I heard the whole family laughing. I pulled back the blankets, realizing it was now dark out and limped downstairs in a green t-shirt and jeans.

Everyone was crowded around the coffee table, sitting on the couches and the floor eating the ice cream that Erica had bought and drinking various drinks. The fire crackled in the fireplace, reminding me of a scene from one of those old time movies. I spotted Oliver first, who was sitting next to Terrence on the ground and I was shocked to see my stoic brother laughing and smiling. It spread joy through me to see him happy for once. Next, my eyes traveled to Allie who was curled up on the end of the couch wearing a large black sweatshirt that completely engulfed her tiny body. I looked closer, realizing she was curled up with my sweatshirt and the joy inside of me spread like a wildfire, knowing that when I got it back it would smell just like her, citrus and jasmine.

"Hey, you're awake." Allie looked up at me where I stood on the staircase, a bright smile lighting her features.

I grinned back at her as I sat beside her on the couch and she leaned her head on my chest, holding her bowl of ice cream in her hands. My arms came around her, wishing that I could shield her from all the werewolf drama. She was about to put a scoop into her mouth when I grabbed the spoon from her hand and plopped the blob of ice cream into my mouth instead.

"Hey!" Allie giggled grabbing at the spoon but I held it away from her, laughing the whole time. She reached across me but I pressed my lips to hers instead of handing her the spoon.

I felt her smile against my mouth as she kissed me, making me crazy. She pulled away laughing when Erica cleared her throat. Heat spread across Allie's cheeks as she looked down, embarrassed but I didn't miss the black and blue bruise that was forming on her cheekbone.

"What happened?" I asked her when everyone was quiet. I reached out and touched the bruise lightly. She flinched.

"What? The bruise?" She asked and I nodded, "Oh, it's nothing. It's just from training today." Allie brushed off my question and laced her fingers through mine, the sleeve of the sweatshirt she wore pulling back to expose dark purple bruises encircling her wrists. She saw the look on my face and quickly pulled the sleeves back down but it was too late. Anger already flooded my vision and mind, turning everything red.

My predatory gaze found Oliver's in an instant, "You did that?" My voice shook with anger but Allie's hand came down on my chest, purposely hitting my cuts to focus me on the pain instead of the anger.

Without being able to control it, a vicious snarl clawed its way out of my throat. Allie's eyes widened but she kept her steady gaze on mine, unwavering and very angry.

"Come here, now," She said wrapping her small hands around my wrist and pulling me off the couch and out the front door.

Icy air washed over me as Allie pulled me onto the porch and closed the front door behind us. I wrapped my arms around myself and shivered as I realized I was only wearing a short sleeve shirt. I looked out over the field that was now covered in fluffy white snowflakes, my favorite time of year to be a wolf. I growled and shook the idea out of my head, focusing on Allie who paced back and forth barefooted on the porch.

She threw her hands up, "I don't know how else to convince you. Jaxon, it is called training for a reason. Of course I am going to get bruised up but they are just bruises." She paced faster, the boards on the porch creaking underneath her angry footsteps. She said, "Next time, come to the training session on Saturday and I'll show you that I can take a hit." Allie finally stopped, folding her arms across her arms across her chest as she glared daggers at me.

The cold had cut its way deep into my bones and my voice shook as I said, "Look, I'm sorry," I ran my fingers through my hair, letting out a sigh, "I just…" I growled not knowing what to say. I couldn't focus on anything but the wolf as it tried to claw its way out. I stared at the dark sky, gritting my teeth and pinching the bridge of my nose as a wave of nausea washed over me.

"Here," Allie said pulling off the sweatshirt and shoving it at me, "We are not done having this talk and you are not about to get out of it by turning into a wolf."

I smirked and pulled the sweatshirt over my head, the wind shielded by the fabric that now smelled of Allie. The wolf crawled back into its hiding space. The only problem was, now that I could actually focus on Allie, she was only wearing a low cut black tank top that made her blue eyes stand out. I swallowed and focused on the fluffy snow lying peacefully on the ground.

"I don't understand why you can't trust him." Allie whispered so quietly that if I didn't have the hearing of a wolf, her words would've been lost in the wind.

"It's not that I don't trust him… it's just…" I didn't know what to say but Allie's expression softened.

"It's just that you don't want him to replace your real dad." She said looking down at her fingers.

How did she know me so well? I looked at her for a few moments in silence before I nodded slightly, giving into what I was really thinking. Allie sighed, running her fingers through her hair and I wondered how she wasn't freezing cold. Allie looked at me with a look I had never seen before; she looked like she couldn't decide whether to hug me or slap me.

"He's not going to replace him," Allie whispered, taking a step towards me, "Please, come to training with us Saturday morning."

"Yeah, I'll come," I said lacing my fingers through hers and bending down, "Thank you," I brushed my lips against hers. It wasn't really a kiss but the way her eyes lit up told me it was just as satisfying.

Allie's eyebrows knit together, "For what?" She asked sliding her hands up my chest lightly and lacing her fingers behind my neck.

"For helping me through all of this," I said my forehead resting lightly against hers. I cupped her cheek in my shivering hand, her skin hot underneath mine. Allie's eyes fluttered shut as she took in a deep breath.

She opened them and smiled slyly at me, "That's what I'm here for."

Allie

Jaxon's lips were inches away from mine when Terrence swung the door open, clearing his throat. Jaxon's eyes opened and he looked to his brother out of the corner of his eye, growling quietly before straightening. I looked at him silently for a few minutes before crossing my arms and turning towards Terrence.

"Yes?" Jaxon asked in an annoyed tone as he watched Terrence close the door behind him, shutting out the chatting.

"We're going hunting," He said and even though his voice was serious, the lightness was still there.

"Question," I said looking back and forth between the brothers, curiosity consuming me, "How come every time something happens, you have to go hunting?"

Terrence looked at me like I was crazy but said, "It's a metabolism thing. Whenever a lot of energy is exerted, we have to get it back by hunting."

"Interesting," I shrugged folding my arms across my chest, wondering why born werewolves didn't have to hunt like that.

"Let's wolf out," Erica appeared in the doorway with Kate and a sly smile on her tan face. I realized they had changed into short shorts and a tank top which made sense now that I knew the cold weather made them shift.

In the next instant, Erica and Kate had melted into their wolf forms. Erica's light grey fur looked like a duller version of my silvery coat and Kate's looked like the night sky. A smile lit Terrence's face as he pulled his shirt over his head, revealing carved muscles and tan skin. His eyes faded from dark brown to piercing red, the color of the alpha right before he leapt off of the porch and exploded into a midnight black wolf. He let out a giddy howl, automatically making me smile at the joyous sound. I turned my back on the house and watched as the wolves, barked and nipped at each other but they waited for the fourth member of their tight knit pack.

Jaxon pulled off the sweatshirt and shirt like Terrence had, taking in a deep breath as he stared at the pack. He shook his head, trying to hold back the wolf, and turned towards me, taking my face in his hands gently. I rested my fingers on his bare chest, right where his heart was beating wildly. He looked at me with gold eyes right before he kissed me as if it were the last moment of his life.

I accepted the warmth it spread through me and opened my mouth as he kissed me. I curled my fingers in his hair, a small growl of pleasure crawling out of his throat. All of the sudden, Jaxon shuddered once and backed away from me as quick as he could. Before I knew it, a chocolate brown wolf with gold eyes replaced Jaxon. The wolf and I looked at each other for a few moments before he took a step towards me, hesitant and unsure. Tears pricked my eyes as I bent down, holding out my hand for him to sniff. His cold nose touched my fingers lightly and a laugh escaped my lips. Jaxon pricked his ears up at the sound of my voice and all together, the recognition poured over him. He wagged his tail, back and forth slowly as he padded towards me, licking my nose without any hesitation. I laughed, Jaxon yipping and hopping around me as if he were laughing too. The next thing I knew, he threw his head over my shoulder and I wrapped my arms around his body, both of us hugging each other tightly. I ran my fingers through his fur for a few minutes before Terrence growled and Jaxon leapt off of the porch, disappearing into the trees before I could say goodbye.

A hand came down on my shoulder as tears streamed down my cheeks. I looked back to see a blurry Oliver, "You okay?"

I said the one thing I had wanted to say for a long time, "I miss it… I miss it so much it hurts." Sobs racked my body and I crumpled to the floorboards of the porch, cradling my face in my palms.

"Oh no," Oliver sighed sitting down beside me and wrapping me in his arms as I buried my face in his chest, "Crying girls is not my specialty."

He rocked me back and forth as I cried softly, "I always said that I didn't want to shift again because I was afraid of what I might do but every time I see them, I forget about all the bad stuff and I just remember the good. They all seem so happy, and I wonder to myself… why can't I be that happy too?"

Oliver sighed and petted my hair gently when he said, "You don't have to be a wolf to be happy, you know. I understand that's the only life you've ever known but here, you have a caring family and this family adores you too." His words sunk into me like the snow would melt over the summer. I wiped away the tears and pulled away from Oliver.

I nodded and looked at him with apologetic eyes, "I know that I haven't always been very welcoming to you. Only a few years ago I lost my second dad and I was pretty sure I didn't have any more chances left because no decent people deserve three chances but then you came and I thought to myself… what is mom doing? And I was so angry with her. But I just didn't realize it was a blessing in disguise. And mom cares about you so much… You guys would be a perfect couple." I said but an inkling of a thought crawled into my brain. I made a face, "Wait, if you and my mom get married then Jaxon and I would be brother and sister…"

Oliver looked confused and shocked, "Married? Where'd you get that idea? We aren't even dating." He laughed lightly when he saw my wide eyes and bewildered expression.

"But I heard you guys saying you weren't going to tell Dallas and me about you until we got used to you staying here. And then when we went out to lunch and the museum that one day. You guys acted like you were in love." I insisted turning so that I was facing him with raised eyebrows.

Oliver laughed quietly, "I didn't want you to find out that your mom had called my hunters and me in for backup because she was sure that wolves were coming. We did the whole dating thing as a cover up so that I had an excuse to stay here." He pulled me up to my feet and handed me my combat boots.

"Nice acting," I said pulling on the boots and my leather jacket, "I believed it, that's for sure."

Oliver and I drove home as he told me the details of the plan that he and my mom had cleverly made behind my back. He never lost my attention as he told me the story of how mom and he dated back in high school and how he was best friends with my dad. It amazed me how much I had not known about my parents' past but it also made me feel empty, like I never really knew them. The sky had turned black; the color of Terrence and Kate's fur and all I could think about as I stared out the window was that I wanted to be out there with them, running through the snow with silver fur glinting in the moonlight. I ran my fingers through my curly hair as Oliver pulled the car into the driveway.

"Don't say anything about you dating Jaxon or the whereabouts of the others. She doesn't know where they are and I have been leading her off their scents." Oliver said when mom turned on the porch light and looked out the door with a smile.

I nodded and pushed my sore legs out of the car and inside the warm house. I couldn't wait to get a good night's sleep in my own bed. I stepped into my bedroom and was met by Khione's steely stare where she was sitting cross legged on my bed. I knew she was angry with me for blaming her for the Lochlans' injuries and an angry Khione was something I wasn't in the mood to deal with when my head was pounding like a bowling ball. I massaged my temples with my cut up fingers.

"Hey," I said turning away from her and pulling off my shirt, changing into one of my dad's old t shirts that hung down to my knees. Khione made a *humph* noise from where she sat on the bed. I pulled on leggings and turned to look at her, "Look, I'm sorry about yelling at you at Jaxon's house but I was worried and stressed out."

"I accept your apology," She said in her thick Australian accent and then smiled slyly, "Besides, it's a once in a life time chance to hear you apologize to someone." She giggled and threw a pillow at me but I caught it before it hit me.

I was about to say something clever back to her when a sickening wave of nausea washed over me, causing my knees to shake and a nasty feeling crawling up my throat. I looked at Khione in horror, dropped the pillow and sprinted to the bathroom right before puking in the toilet. Acid burned my throat as I gripped both sides of the toilet and my stomach was emptied of all its contents.

"Allie?" Dallas and Khione burst into the bathroom behind me. Mom and Oliver's rooms were downstairs so most likely they couldn't hear us all the way up here. I gagged and coughed but Dal was by my side in seconds, his hand rubbing circles on my back.

"Can I have a tissue?" I asked in a grossed out voice, reaching out my hand when Khione placed one into my palm. I wiped it across my mouth, coughing again but the burning in my throat was painful. I stared at Khione in bewilderment but she was just as freaked.

Werewolves didn't get sick. I had never had any sort of disease in my entire life, even when I stopped shifting. Maybe that was it. Maybe since the wolf's magic was so low from not shifting, I was open to viruses. That was one of the problems with being human. When I was done barfing up all my food, I rolled onto the cold bathroom floor and lying on my back. The tile felt like ice on my feverish skin.

"Ugh," I gagged one more time and Dal pressed the back of his hand to my heated cheek. My brother's touch felt refreshing on my skin, "I'm fine." Dal helped me up, keeping one hand on my back because my legs still felt like Jell-O as I lay down in bed.

I didn't go back to sleep that night, plagued with false alarms of puking. Dallas ended up staying on a blanket on the floor after the third time that I almost threw up. Mom and Oliver had come up to but I told them I was fine even though it was a complete lie. I rested my fiery cheek on the window sill and let the winter wind wash over me until my eyes drifted shut for an hour or two before my alarm clock went off.

The good thing was, mom said that I didn't have to go to school but I did get up with Khione and Dallas, driving the two of them to school. I pulled into the parking lot, a few spots away from where the Lochlans were getting out of Jaxon's car. Dallas met up with Kate, lacing his fingers through hers instantly. Jaxon met my eyes with a confused look as he saw me start the car again to leave.

"You're not coming to school?" he asked when I rolled down my window and he leaned his elbows on it.

I shook my head, "No, I spent all last night puking. I'm going to the doctor right now." I said smiling when I saw his eyebrows pull together in worry, "The strange thing is that I feel fine right now just a little tired."

"Call me afterwards, okay?" he asked and I nodded with a bleak smile, "See you later." He patted the side of my truck with multiple thuds before kissing my forehead and running to catch up with his friends and family.

I shook my head, sighing as I pulled out of the parking lot and sped down towards Spencer's shop where hopefully I could find some answers about what was wrong with me. The pounding in my head had returned, forcing me to grit my teeth and grip the steering wheel tightly. I took out my cellphone, dialing Spencer's number with shaky hands.

"Hello?" he asked shuffling papers in the background but he seemed distracted.

"Spence, I need help. There is something wrong with me and I think we need to run some tests again." I groaned remembering the tubes and syringes that Spencer had hooked me up to when I first found him. He had done it to learn how my body worked since I was a born werewolf.

"Get down here, Allie." Spencer snapped and the call ended in an instant.

A couple of minutes later, I pulled into the parking lot of Spencer's shop none too gracefully because I felt another wave of nausea wash over me. I covered my mouth with my hand and dashed inside as fast as I could, shoving open the glass door where I saw Spencer and a black haired girl kissing behind the counter.

"Uhhh…" I muttered awkwardly, the nausea suddenly disappearing as the two whipped around to stare at me.

The girl next to Spencer was probably a head smaller than him and twice as thin. Her hair was short, a feathery pixie cut that made her look like a magical fairy. Her eyes were startlingly blue but they looked more like ice than water. Her skin was in between pale and a deep tan and I liked the way she looked standing next to Spencer. He cleared his throat awkwardly and raked his hand through his hair.

I licked my dry lips and plastered on a fake smile, "Well, this is awkward." The girl laughed quietly and came around the counter to stand in front of me.

"That it is," Pixie girl said in a high voice. She held out her hand and I took it, "My name is Eryn." Her smile was contagious when she shook my hand.

"I'm Allie Jennings," I told her with an equally warm smile, taking my hand back and crossing my arms over my chest.

Eryn looked back at Spencer with a laugh and a smile, "Spence, you didn't tell me you found a werewolf." Fear rocketed through me as my eyes widened and I backed away from the strange new girl.

"Who are you?" I hissed flattening my back to the door and staring daggers at Eryn who just held her hands up in surrender while Spencer came to stand beside her.

"Allie," he said quietly, "Eryn is like me. It's okay she was just leaving."

I looked at Eryn with narrowed eyes, "Trust needs to be earned, pixie girl." I snapped at her and pushed past them, walking across the shop towards the lair.

"Touché, wolf girl." I turned to see Eryn salute me before walking out the glass door and out into the parking lot.

Spencer closed the door to his lair when Eryn was officially gone and I once again felt safe. My legs swung back and forth from where I sat on the metal table and Spencer inserted a needle into my arm, sucking some blood out for testing. He did a series of different tests that I didn't understand at all while muttering scientific phrases about it.

"Okay," Spencer said rubbing his hands over his face, "I am going to run these tests but since everything about your body structure is… rather complex, it will probably take a while for me to figure all of this out." he handed me my leather jacket, "I'll call you when I get specific results."

I started to walk out but turned for a few seconds to say, "I think I like that Eryn girl." He smiled with a little laugh, waving before I shut the door.

Two days passed and I found that I had lost approximately one pound from puking for both those nights. I went to school on Friday though because I felt fine which made me feel even more uneasy about what happened. More bad news was that the Lochlans had killed some more hunters. Of course, Friday morning I had yelled at Jaxon about it but deep down I knew who the real enemy was and my wolf wanted to kill them too. I didn't tell anyone except Khione and Dallas about the barfing because I didn't need other people sympathizing for me.

Wriggling into my light jeans, I fastened the belt and to my surprise, I was one hole smaller than usual. I huffed out a breath, staring at myself in the mirror as I got ready for the bonfire everyone from school was going to tonight. It was a school sponsored event so, luckily, there wouldn't be any drunken teenagers staggering across the streets. On top, I wore a white lacy shirt with a tank top underneath it, tucked into my jeans. My hair came down in long, brown spirals and I did a quick spin, staring at my reflection with a smile.

"Are you sure you want to do this?" Khione asked from the doorway where she was wearing a pretty sweater dress and tall brown boots.

I looked at her through the mirror in confusion, "What do you mean?"

She ran her fingers through her straight blonde hair, "Allie, for the past two nights you have been up puking your guts out," she sighed in frustration, "And think about it, it's only been at night. What if it happens again?"

I folded my arms across my chest, "We will be in the woods, making it easier for me to just sneak off for a couple of minutes. I'll just bring a lot of gum. Plus, I don't even feel sick," I told her, smothering pink lipstick on my lips and smacking them together with a popping noise.

Khione held up her hands in surrender, "Okay, whatever." She sighed and made her way downstairs as I pulled on my tall leather boots.

An hour later, I parked my truck on the road beside the big field that Jaxon had taken me to right before he had left on that hunting trip. I smiled at the memory, looking up at the stars and remembering the gentleness of Jaxon's arms around me. Music blared from unseen speakers, all country music which was how we did it up here. The fire blazed, the flames reaching towards the stars with flaming fingers. People sat around the fire on logs but others danced in the field around them, laughing and chatting excitedly. Khione ran off, joining a group of kids who danced like they would never stop. Khione fit in perfectly. I sighed, glancing around the dark woods until my eyes landed on Jaxon and Erica. Kate and Dallas had skipped the bonfire and went to a movie instead.

Jaxon met me halfway, grabbed my hand, and spun me around in a circle until my back was pressed against his chest. His arms encircled my waist and I breathed in his scent, realizing in shock that I could actually smell the scent of his wolf underneath his skin. I could never smell it before. It drove me crazy. I giggled giddily, lifting my face to his and he pressed his lips to mine. I craned my head back; spreading my lips and tasting everything that made my world go round. I could feel the heat of his body through my shirt as he turned me in his arms so that I was facing him. When Erica whistled behind Jaxon, I pulled away, blushing uncontrollably with a little laugh. His eyes opened blazing gold, his skin about ten times hotter than it was a few seconds ago. I glanced behind me before shoving him into the trees before anyone saw his glowing eyes. He snarled in frustration, scrubbing his hands over his face right before smashing his fist into a tree trunk. It creaked and groaned but only wobbled a little bit, luckily. It would've been kind of hard to explain a fallen down tree. When Jaxon looked back at me and Erica, his eyes blended in with the darkness once again and he was in control. I had to say, though, I kind of got a feeling of victory inside of me when I saw what I could do to Jaxon's steely self-control.

Erica laughed from where she stood beside me, "Well, that was very fun. You, my friend," She pointed to me, "are really good at testing his self-control."

I did an exaggerated bow, smiling at the siblings, "Thanks, it's a great talent."

Jaxon rolled his eyes with a smirk as he threw his arm around my shoulders and the three of us walked back into the field where everyone seemed to get louder and now every kid had joined in the dancing. I noticed how they cast furtive glances over their shoulders at the teachers that stood around the field, supervising us carefully. Jaxon, Erica, and I found a vacant log and the three of us sat down, watching the flames lick the sky. I sighed contently, my body feeling relaxed for the first time in months and I loved it.

Tucked warmly in the blankets in my room, Friday night rolled around and I dreaded it more than anything in the world. I wanted to pause that moment by the fire forever but I was realistic enough to know that would never happen. So, I huddled closer into my sheets and either waited for dreams or sickness to overtake me.

To love is to destroy.

To love is to destroy.

The words bounced off the walls, filling my ears like a thousand wailing people. I was standing in the warehouse, the moon shining light into the cracked windows. The wailing grew louder, forcing me to cover my ears tightly and to grit my teeth so hard that I thought they would shatter.

To love is to destroy.

To love is to destroy.

A scream clawed its way out of my throat as the chanting grew louder, my head pounding and panic surging through me. Tears fell down my cheeks like a waterfall during a storm and all I could do was crumple to the ground, cringing on the concrete.

"Stop! Please!" I cried out with a sore throat from the screams earlier.

Silence. Finally.

Two dark figures stood in the doorway as one said in a familiar female voice that made my skin crawl, "Don't you remember? Run, run as fast and as far away as you can. Never look back, Allison because we will be right behind you every step of the way." Lydia laughed as if she were a witch about to put a spell on a little girl.

She and Marcus stepped out of the shadows, their teeth and clothes stained crimson. Marcus laughed, "We are coming, whether you know it or not, we will be there when you least expect it."

Two wolves in human form brought someone out of the shadows. The chained figure struggled and writhed but the wolves just laughed and tightened their grip. When they stepped into the pool of moonlight next to Lydia, a scream of terror rushed out of me. Jaxon stood before me, bruised, bleeding, and barely able to stand. I sobbed but knew if I went any closer they would kill him right away.

"No, let him go," I pleaded, standing up slowly on shaking legs, "He has nothing to do with this." A smile spread across both my parents' faces as they stared at me like prey.

"Oh but darling," Lydia said in her creepy, silky voice, "he has everything to do with this."

To love is to destroy.

The cries started up again, the pain in my head almost threatening to burst my skull. I stared at Jaxon with wide eyes but I knew if I ran forward, Lydia wouldn't hesitate to kill him.

"Mom," I sobbed and she paused, something dawning on her face but she regained her composure, "please stop this."

She moved in front of Jaxon, obscuring him from my view but Lydia stared at me with a vicious look in her eyes. She said in an eerily calm voice, "Can't you see? I can't stop. I am not going to lose my power to an incompetent girl." I didn't have time to think about that statement because she turned her back to me and brought her claws back in the air.

I screamed until my throat felt like it was bleeding when she brought her claws down with a whoosh and slashed them across Jaxon's throat.

"Allie!" Someone shouted at me through the haze. I realized I was still screaming, my throat feeling like it was bleeding.

I rocketed out of my room, burst through the bathroom door, and retched all my food into the toilet. Tears streamed down my sweaty face as I leaned back against the wall. Images swirled before my eyes, Jaxon falling limp in a pool of blood, the wailing voices, and lastly, Lydia and Marcus's bloodstained smiles. Khione and Dallas came into the bathroom, their faces identical masks of horror. But I was already pushing myself up off the floor.

"Your mom and Oliver aren't home." Khione said in a calm voice that betrayed the look on her face.

"I figured," I said in a small hoarse voice. I wiped the tears from my face as I flung open my closet door, grabbing the clothes I had trained in earlier that week with Oliver.

Before I put them on Khione said, "Where are you going?"

"Out," I stated in a detached voice that didn't sound like mine, "I need… I need to clear my head."

Dallas left so that I could change.

"Allie," Khione said softly, "You haven't slept in a while. You should go back to bed."

I spun around to look at her, "I can't go back to sleep," I pulled the black tank top over my head and wriggled into my jeans and lace up black boots. My black hoodie made me feel like no one, not even Lydia, could get to me.

As soon as my feet hit the ground after jumping out my window, I took off at a dead sprint into the woods across the street where I could disappear. Anxiety gripped cold fingers around the knot in my stomach as I scampered through the woods like a bunny running from a wolf. I was running from my parents. I hurdled over a fallen tree with ease and barely made a sound when my feet landed back on the ground. As I moved my legs faster, I felt as if I was running on air.

This has everything to do with him.

I snarled at no one in particular.

Run, run as fast and as far away as you can.

I catapulted myself over a ditch that I wouldn't have been able to make if I was human.

Never look back, Allison.

I didn't look over my shoulder as I dodged in and out of the dark trees.

To love is to destroy.

My foot caught on a rock and I stumbled, toppling head first down a steep hill that I hadn't seen before. I cried out and groaned all the way down until I came to a slow stop at the very edge of a cliff that dropped off sharply. I peered over the edge, coming face to face with a large lake that I had never seen before. My reflection wavered in the water but something strange caught my attention. I leaned closer to the lake, my eyes narrowing in the darkness. When I got close enough that I could see clearly, I was appalled to see red eyes instead of blue ones. I shrieked in horror, scrambling away from my reflection landing on my hands. My chest heaved up and down, unable to take enough air into my lungs. Red eyes? Only alphas had red eyes. To become an alpha, a beta would have to challenge and kill one. Unless…

Can't you see? I can't stop. I am not going to lose my power to an incompetent girl.

"That's what she meant." I whispered to myself in utter amazement, breaking the tranquility of the woods.

I am an alpha.

I crawled slowly back to the edge of the cliff, peering down into the water where I could see the blurry reflection of myself. But the red eyes weren't there anymore; instead they were my regular bright blue ones. I closed my eyes, taking in a deep breath and pinching the bridge of my nose. I knew my adrenaline was pumping a hundred miles an hour from the dream and running halfway across town in under ten minutes. I lay on my back, the grass soft underneath my clothes as I stared up at the stars. I imagined them turning into a whole pack of wolves, their bodies made of twinkling stars as they galloped across the sky. I lifted my fingers towards the sky, pretending I could reach the wolves and stroke their fur. A tear snuck its way out of the corner of my eye and I let it trail down my cheek onto the cold ground. I groaned in anger, pounding my fist on the ground.

"What am I supposed to do?" I whispered, my voice lost in the wind.

You can't live a lie, follow your heart.

Dad's voice echoed through my mind as a gust of wind washed over me, swirling my hair all around me. I sat straight up, my fingers curling into the dirt below me. A smile crept across my lips as I pulled my knees up to my chest, silent tears falling down my cheeks. I had been so caught up in the fear that I forgot to listen to what my dad had always told me. I didn't want to live a lie but it was the only way to protect the people that I cared about. I sighed in frustration, dragging my fingers through my hair roughly, not caring about the tiny pinches of pain. I crawled back to the edge of the lake, turning over and lying on my back again so I could watch the wolves run across the sky.

Jaxon

Utterly alone was not the way I wanted to be stuck in this type of situation. I was pretty sure I had lost the hunters a while back but I kept darting through the dank woods in case they were hiding. Lungs burning from the cold, I pushed my legs harder, leaping over a fallen tree and turning sharply to the left. My gold eyes shined brilliantly in the darkness, my brown fur turning me practically invisible.

The scent of citrus and jasmine flowed into my nostrils when I hit the edges of the woods in an unfamiliar place. My muscles froze in confusion as my wolf registered what the scent meant. Allie was here somewhere. Ears pricked forward, I stepped into the clearing to see a figure lying at the edge of a lake but as I stepped closer the figure took shape and became Allie. My tail wagged enthusiastically back and forth. She hummed a song that I didn't recognize but her voice was sweet and rich like honey. My gold eyes narrowed to see her dragging her fingernails up and down her arm, the slight smell of her blood filling my head. I snarled at the fact that she was hurting herself and as soon as she heard it, she froze and turned around slowly in apprehension.

When she saw it was me, her eyebrows lowered and she turned back around, obviously not in the mood to talk. Well, she was in luck then because it was too cold for me to shift back into human form. I trotted up to her, lying beside her so that my head was even with hers. I rested my chin on my paws and watched her curiously, wishing I was human but knowing she wasn't going to talk to me. I whined.

"Is it too cold to shift back?" Allie asked me in a soft, detached voice that I didn't recognize at all. I looked up at her, bobbing my head slightly in a nod.

Allie watched me quietly for a few minutes before reaching her hand out and combing her fingers through the fur on the back of my neck. My eyes fluttered shut and accidentally a groan of pleasure slipped out of my throat. She laughed lightly but her face became stoic in a matter of seconds and she turned her eyes back to the stars as if watching something. I rolled onto my side so that I could watch them too but I didn't know what the significance was for Allie.

She sighed again, wiping something from her face and moving her head so that it rested on my rib cage lightly. Still, Allie combed her fingers through my fur, lulling both of us into a deep, careless sleep.

The sky turned gold, the orange sun hanging low in the distance where the lake dropped off. The cold air had blown away, warmer air taking its place. My eyes fluttered open, my arm wrapped around someone's waist. Arms? When my eyes opened all the way and I took in my human body clothed in a grey tank top and black basketball shorts, I realized I must've shifted in the middle of the night. I looked down to see Allie resting her head on my torso, her breathing steady. I smiled, tucking a piece of her hair behind her ear gently without waking her and watching as she slept peacefully. The dark circles under her eyes told me that maybe I had missed something important, like the fact that she hadn't been sleeping. Guilt found its way into the pit of my stomach as I gazed at her sleeping form.

In the next second, her eyes darted back and forth underneath her eyelids impossibly fast. Allie's mouth opened, making tiny little gasping noises, her fingers curling into the dirt of the ground. Tears streamed from her still closed eyes. In an instant, her blue eyes flew open and she shrieked in fear, scrambling away from me in the haze of the nightmare. I sat up and watched as Allie scrubbed her hands over her face and shook her head, clearing it from whatever dream she had had.

"Allie?" I asked hesitantly and her eyes met mine, wide and scared, like a child's.

A smile spread across her face and Allie laughed in relief right before she moved towards me, wrapping her arms around my neck as if I had just come back from the dead. I returned her hug but deep down I knew something was wrong in the way she clung to me tightly.

"Hey," I said gently against her hair, "Are you okay?"

Allie pulled away hesitantly, looking to the ground. The black clothes that she wore made her sad blue eyes stand out even more. She turned away from me, moving to the edge of the lake and dangling her feet over the cliff. Allie flipped her hood over her head, obscuring her from my view until I moved to sit beside her.

"I haven't slept in about a week and I think it's starting to catch up to me." Allie said as she stared at the rising sun in the distance.

"Why not?" I asked but I saw the way she ground her teeth together in frustration and looked away. I touched her cheek softly and said, "Allie, you have to tell me what's going on."

She groaned again in frustration, picking up a rock and chucking it into the water with a *plop*. All of the sudden, she stood up, something fierce and angry burning in her eyes as she looked out over the lake. Allie turned away for a few seconds and I stood up, afraid she was going to bolt into the woods. But instead, she spun around, a loud shriek of anger bursting from her lungs.

"I can't do this anymore!" Allie sobbed but all I could do was watch in speechless horror as she finally broke, "I think… I think I need a break from… from everything."

"Allie, wait," I moved towards her but she stepped back.

“Stop,” her voice shook as she talked, “Please, I just need some time, Jaxon.” Allie backed away to the edge of the woods but paused before the trees engulfed her.

I didn’t answer her but when I blinked, she no longer stood crying in front of me. What had just happened? Did Allie just… break up with me or put us on pause? I snarled at no one in particular, raking my fingers through my hair in confused frustration. If Allie wanted to give up on us then I was going to go to training and show her just how much we needed each other. There was something she wasn’t telling me and if she didn’t want to, fine, but somehow I was going to find out. I sat back down at the edge of the lake, confused about what had just happened to a girl who I thought was even stronger than me.

In two hours, I was on the road, driving towards the warehouse that we were going to train in. I dreaded facing Allie after what had just happened but I also needed to make sure that she was okay and didn’t do anything to hurt herself. The agonizing drive would only take me about an hour but the pace I was driving would take me a little while longer. Snow and ice bleached the ground, turning it a glowing white and out of my rearview mirror I was pretty sure I saw pure white wolf with blue eyes running in the road behind me. Khione was coming. I ran my fingers through my hair and glanced out my left window, catching a glimpse of a very tired looking Allie trudging through the snow wearing mostly leather. I forced myself to keep the wolf down at the sight of her as I slowed to a crawl and rolled down my window. She didn’t look at me but I knew she knew I was there.

“Do you want a ride? It’s cold.” I asked thinking even if we were broken up or whatever I may as well try and win her back.

“No, I’m fine. I can walk. It’s good exercise.” Allie said pulling her jacket closer and hunching her shoulders against the wind.

I sighed and stopped the car, reaching across the seat and opening the passenger door.

"Allie, get in the car. I am going to drive you there." I snapped at her. At first I thought she would be offended by my tone but when she stopped and a smirk played across her lips, I knew it was the only way to get through to her.

We drove in silence for a few minutes, the radio playing a song that Allie knew in the background. She sang with it quietly, keeping most of her body turned towards the window watching Khione running alongside us. The silence cut deeper and deeper into me as a thousand questions burned through my mind about last night and this morning. Allie didn't seem to mind it though which kept me from saying anything. Alas, I couldn't take it anymore.

"Allie?" I asked feeling the silence shatter into a million pieces. She paused before turning around to stare at her hands in her lap. "Can we talk about what happened this morning?" She sighed as soon as the question left my lips.

"Look I'm so sorry about what I said. I… didn't really mean it." Allie said hesitantly but right before I could sigh in relief, she muttered, "At least I don't think I did."

"I just don't get why you can't tell me what's going on." I said and before I could stop myself, reached my hand out to her, tucking a piece of her hair behind her ear.

Allie squeezed her eyes shut, two different emotions warring on her face as she leaned into my fingers. I pulled the car to a stop at the side of the road but both of us waited before getting out, reluctant to ruin the moment that was forming. She looked at me through half lidded blue eyes that seemed to be filled with imaginary storm clouds.

Allie took in a deep breath, "I… it's really complicated and I don't want to talk about it right now. I'm so sorry; can you just trust me about this?" She asked me quietly and even though I wasn't happy with that answer, I nodded my head, smoothing my thumb over her cheek before hopping out of the car.

Khione's white form had already darted into the open door of the warehouse. I opened the passenger side door for Allie who stepped out a little too quickly for the icy roads. Squealing, her foot slipped out from underneath her but in an instant, my arms were locked tightly around her, and Allie's face was only inches from mine. Her eyes searched mine for a few seconds of empty silence right before she grabbed both sides of my face and pressed her lips to mine. I made a surprised noise in the back of my throat but pressed my hands in between her shoulder blades so that we were practically one person. Allie pulled away slowly, breathing heavily, her forehead resting against mine.

"We should go; Oliver is probably waiting to ambush us." Allie laughed lightly pulling away from me and folding her arms across her chest as she jogged slowly up the hill to where the warehouse stood isolated.

"Ambush us?" I asked running after her and then falling into step beside her. Allied rubbed her hands together and folded her arms across her chest to block the winter wind from cutting into our skin.

Allie smiled slyly as if there were some big inside joke that I wasn't a part of. She laughed, "What? Did you think this was going to be a walk in the park?" There was something challenging in her voice when she said those words, making me wonder if doing this was the right choice.

Allie must've seen the look on my face because she threw her head back and laughed out loud. I had never seen that side of her, the carefree side of her. Usually, all her emotions were rolled up into a tiny ball, unable to untangle themselves and come out. She barely let anyone see past her stoic side. It always seemed like even when Allie was fully engaged in conversation, she was in a secret world deep in the depths of her mind. I didn't understand why battle was something she liked when it made me want to puke. What had she gone through in the past? Every now and then Allie would give me pieces of her past but I always knew it was never the whole truth.

"When I first walked into that building on our first day of training, Oliver shot at me with arrows and guns in some hidden place up in the rafters. He probably nearly killed me," her smile spread from ear to ear when she said, "It was great." That stunned me.

"How was being shot at great?" I asked her as we came closer and closer to the warehouse, a sense of dread growing in the pit of my stomach.

"You don't like adrenaline very much, do you?" Allie asked her voice tinged with a tiny shred of disappointment that I pretended not to hear.

"I like adrenaline when I'm running through the woods as a wolf. To be honest, I am not looking forward to getting shot." I raised my eyebrows at her but she just smiled and laced her fingers through mine but I didn't miss the slight tightening of her jaw as if the words had stung. I narrowed my eyes in suspicion but she brushed the comment off like dust on a counter.

"Oliver said we aren't supposed to use weapons just in case one of you gets hurt." Allie moved in front of me as she talked, taking her hand out of mine so that we could pry open the heavy metal door.

"We aren't fragile cats, you know," I told her right before I dropped down into my wolf form, looking up at her through my gold eyes and wagging my tail.

The door shut with a loud clang behind us.

Allie

Jaxon's nails clicking on the concrete ground were the only sounds that echoed through the long corridor. I wasn't sure what to expect so I kept my eyes glued in front of me as we entered into the giant room. Jaxon slowed to a stop, his muscles tensing in apprehension and he did the worst thing that he could've done. He looked back at me.

Khione's powerful wolf slammed into him as she leapt from some unknown hiding spot. Her snarl overpowered Jaxon's yelp when the two wolves went skidding across the floor, slamming into a dumpster, the sound ringing through the air. Oliver appeared out from behind a crate, moving to stand beside me as we watched the two untangle themselves from the trash. I giggled when Khione snapped at Jaxon for getting too close to her when he tripped on a plastic bag that had gotten caught around his foot. Khione hopped lightly on top of a large crate, shifting into human form and sitting on the edge so that her feet dangled.

"That was too easy." She said in her thick Australian accent as she pretended to look bored and pick at the claws that were still extended.

Jaxon, still in wolf form growled at her, shifting back into human form… still growling. "That was not fair. I wasn't ready." He dusted off the tight black shirt he was wearing, the same one he had been wearing when we first met.

I crossed my arms, smirking at him, "Put your ego aside and listen." I told him as I walked out into the center of the room, "There is going to be a time when… you might have to kill… a human." I saw his eyes widened, "Not an innocent one but you need to know how to defend yourself. I am going to teach you how to do that. Shift and attack me."

“I am not going to attack you. What if I hurt you?” Jaxon asked but it only made my arrogant smile wider. Khione was the one who said something instead.

“Honey, trust me,” She said from atop the crate, “You are nowhere near as skilled as her. You’d be lucky if you even got in a nibble.”

I looked back at Jaxon with the same presumptuous smile as I did before. Uncertainty kept Jaxon from shifting into his wolf form. He watched me with fearful eyes but something in the way I held my ground told him there was nothing to be afraid of. His eyes melted from brown to liquid gold right before he dropped to the ground on all fours, transforming into the dark brown wolf I had come to love. There was a second when I wasn’t sure if Jaxon was going to go through with it but when I wiggled my fingers at him tauntingly, his lips curled back in almost a smile. Then, he lowered his head and charged straight at me.

I stood there watching him, waiting for the exact moment to leap over and away from him so that he wouldn’t have enough time to think. When he was a foot away from me, I sprinted full speed straight at him. I saw his gold eyes widen in shock but he didn’t stop. At the last second before we collided, I changed my plan and instead of leaping over him, I body slammed him right in the chest. Jaxon yelped in surprise as we skidded across the floor, a sharp pain stinging my stomach as he tried to get away from me. I unhitched my arms from around him and he scrambled away from my adrenaline filled body. I lay on the concrete ground on my back with a strange sensation flowing through my body and a wide, alien smile on my face. I stood up slowly, something warm trailing across my stomach. I winced when I looked down, seeing that my black tank top had three claw marks slashed through it. Jaxon was at my side in minutes, his chest heaving up and down, the horror on his face making the claw marks hurt worse.

"Allie," He said in a pained voice that I had never heard before. Gingerly, he helped me shrug off my jacket and I lifted the bottom of my shirt up, revealing long, thick claws marks that started just below my bra and disappeared into my belt.

Warm, crimson blood oozed from the marks but he hadn't gotten me very deep so I wouldn't have to get stitches. For some reason, when I looked at the claw marks, I felt no pain or fear for the wolves. Instead, I felt like I was me again like when Khione, Monica, Rachel and I would come home barely able to stand. It was the most fun we ever had, taking risks. I didn't realize how much I had missed that part of my life until I stood there staring at the marks.

"Well," Khione said hopping off the crate with raised eyebrows and a smile that matched mine. She clapped Jaxon on the shoulder and he jumped but never took his sad eyes off of me, "I guess you deserve more credit than I gave you, kid."

Jaxon growled quietly as Khione sauntered over to sit by Oliver. Jaxon whispered, "I… I didn't mean it… I didn't think you were going to do that and it surprised me and I tried to get away but my claws were out and you were too close to me and…" he stopped babbling when I laughed lightly. He gave me a confused look, cocking his head to the side.

"Jaxon," I said pulling my shirt back down, "I've had way worse injuries than some claw marks, trust me." I bent down to grab my jacket, desperately trying not to wince when a shooting pain wiped over me.

Oliver's voice floated through the air, "Allie, sit over here and coach them on the sidelines before you do anything else stupid." He rolled his eyes mockingly at me but I limped over to him and sat down, leaning back on my hands.

"Oliver, I think we all know that making me sit down isn't going to prevent me from doing anything stupid." I promised all of them with a wink before shoving Khione off the crate and into the center of the floor.

"That's not good enough!" I yelled at the top of my lungs, my voice bouncing off the walls like a roar.

The smell of wet dogs filled my nostrils as I watched Khione back away from where she had Jaxon pinned on his back on the ground. Both wolves panted strongly, their lungs heaving in and out as if they had run a marathon. Every time Jaxon went for Khione, she pinned him down in less than ten seconds. Khione looked to me with irritation in her blue eyes, flattening her white ears tightly against her head. Jaxon whined tiredly, his legs shaking slightly from pure exhaustion.

I stood up in frustration, combing my fingers through my hair, "Listen to me, Jaxon, you are not using your strength at all. I know you have it but you are treating Khione like she is a little girl." I told him although he looked like he was about to attack me. His lip curled back, exposing sharp fangs but I just narrowed my eyes at him.

"Put those teeth into Khione," I pointed my finger angrily at him, smiling when Khione's white wolf snarled challengingly at Jaxon.

I leaned back against the crates I had been sitting on. Oliver had left out of boredom which I was kind of glad for, it gave us more focus. I watched in frustration as Khione flipped Jaxon over, raking her claws across his cheek in annoyance most likely. Jaxon's gold eyes blazed like a wildfire, something powerful awakening in him. For a split second, the two wolves stared at each other, scorching anger pulsing through their veins. But as if he were a volcano, Jaxon's strength erupted and in the next moment, Khione was flying across the room and lying in a pile trash. Jaxon leapt up, throwing his head back and howling a joyous song that warmed me like the sunshine during the first few moments of spring. He shifted into human form with a very wide, proud smile on his face, the claw marks standing out like white flags.

"Yes!" I laughed running over to him and throwing my arms around his neck. I pulled away, "That's what I'm talking about."

Khione climbed out of the dumpster in human form, "Well," She dusted off the trash that clung to her, "I have to hand it to you that was pretty impressive." She combed her fingers through her hair as she walked by us, then tauntingly she said, "But, born werewolves are still ten times better," Deliberately, Khione patted the raw claw marks on Jaxon's cheek.

A whine escaped from his throat as I glared at Khione who just smiled and walked away. I turned back to Jaxon and gently, touched the tips of my fingers to the oozing red cuts. He squeezed his eyes shut and flinched and I pressed my lips together in concern.

"Hey Al," Khione called from where she sat, combing her fingers through her hair, "Spencer called."

I moved away from Jaxon, a split second of terror gripping my heart for a second. I glanced at Jaxon who was staring at the phone in Khione's hand as if it were a spindly cockroach. I swallowed, wiggling my fingers in her direction. Khione raised her eyebrows before tossing it to me and I snatched it out of the air with ease. I moved away from everyone so that I could read the many text messages he had sent me without any prying eyes.

Tonight's a full moon- didn't think you knew that.

Allie?

Allison.

Allison Brielle Jennings answer the freaking phone.

Shoot, the moon. I locked my phone and slid it back into my back pocket, wincing at the pain the claw marks made. I sighed, running my fingers through my hair before turning to Khione with a hard look on my face.

"Who's Spencer?" Jaxon asked when he saw the uncertain look passing between both of us. I took in a deep breath before turning to look at him with my lips pressed tightly together.

"Um, he's a friend." I kissed Jaxon lightly on his uninjured cheek, "I have to go, see you tomorrow?" I said but didn't wait for an answer from him because neither Khione nor I were ready for tonight.

Khione stayed human as we walked home together, silent and uncomfortable. I knew she was going to hunt tonight but trepidation crept through my veins as I wondered how well her control was when under the influence of the moon. Mine stunk. I shoved my hands deeper in my pockets, shivering because the rips in my tank top didn't keep the wind out. The snow blanketed the ground, covering every surface placidly. I couldn't decide whether I liked the snow because of the beauty or if it was because of the old memories of running through the snow as a silver wolf.

"Are you going out tonight?" I asked her slowly, keeping my eyes straight ahead of me.

"I have to," Khione said in a detached voice, "You don't want me inside when the moon comes out I'll kill someone." Her Australian accent made the anger and sadness stand out sharply.

"I'm coming too." I told her, gently tracing the cuts that were already starting to turn into scars.

Khione whirled in front of me, "Whoa, no you are not."

I narrowed my eyes at her and crossed my arms across my chest, "Oh, yes I am."

“I’ll kill you!” Khione exclaimed throwing her hands up in the air, “You cannot go out there with me.”

I hesitated for a few moments, “Fine, I’ll stay home.” I lied, keeping my heart beat steady.

Khione blew out a breath, “Good.”

The sky darkened.

Khione disappeared into the woods in a white flash after walking home with me. I sat down on the couch for a few minutes, staring at the blank wall as thoughts rolled through my mind like a tidal wave. With my head in my hands, I thought about what the darkness was going to bring.

“Hey,” Dallas said from behind me, making me jump slightly, “Are you okay?”

I looked back at him with wary eyes, tired from many days of stressing and fearing. Dal came around and sat on the couch beside me. I zipped up my jacket so that he wouldn’t see the scars and start asking questions about what I had spent my day and night doing. Seeing the stress on my face, Dallas took my hand in his and gave it a tiny squeeze. I gave him a tiny smile, wondering how my brother’s touch could make everything seem ten times better.

“There’s just a lot of stress,” I sighed leaning my head against his chest, both of us lying down, Dal’s head resting on the arm rest of the couch.

I rested my head on my brother’s chest, lying pinned beside him and the back of the couch. I closed my eyes, breathing in his scent and wishing I could stay there forever. I always watched other siblings fighting and screaming at each other and I thought, how could anybody hate their sibling? Dallas was the only thing that ever kept me from running away back then. He stroked my hair as if I was a child and sometimes I wondered how he was younger than me.

"I'm worried about you," He whispered, his breathing slow and hypnotizing.

"Don't be," I told him in a groggy voice, not wanting the exhaustion to overtake me.

Dal was silent for a few minutes, his breathing evening out until I knew he was asleep. I looked up at him, smiling at his relaxed features before I shut my eyes and let sleep take over.

Luckily, I woke an hour later, Dallas still sleeping peacefully beside me. I glanced at the clock on the mantel, realizing it was already midnight. Without waking Dal up, I climbed off the couch and dashed upstairs. I found the tiny hole in the wood floors and lifted up, revealing shiny black weapons. Slowly, I went with just a gun before leaping off my roof and sprinting into the woods where I was about to meet my greatest challenge.

The woods were quiet. Maybe a little too quiet for my taste but I kept walking on tired legs, stepping over fallen logs that were covered in snow. I looked up, watching the moonlight shining through the covers of the trees as something crawled right underneath the surface of my skin. The wolf felt… stronger than usual and I became uneasy because I actually liked it. I held onto the human part though as I walked through the trees, half expecting to see a white wolf dash from the woods.

But, instead of a vicious white wolf, I was met by a vaguely familiar light grey one with streaks of brown. I knew that wolf so I didn't go straight for my gun. I looked into the wolf's brown eyes and tried to picture him in his human form.

Aiden Walker.

I could picture then, pale skin, and blonde hair that flopped into his dark eyes. We were close friends as he was best friends with Monica and most likely going to become her mate. What was he doing here away from her?

"Aiden?" I asked his ears pricking forward at the sound of my voice.

But, when he didn't shift back, fear climbed into my throat right before he lunged at me. Aiden collided with me, mouth wide, claws out and we went tumbling down a hill. His claws and teeth sunk into my skin with searing pain and as soon as we came to a stop, his teeth pressed lightly against my throat. I swallowed, lying on my back pinned under Aiden's paws. I didn't feel any fear.

I whispered quietly, "I may not be able to shift but I am still a werewolf."

My canines lengthened into fangs, my fingernails into claws and I knew my eyes weren't gold. I slashed my claws across Aiden's rib cage and he yelped, dashing away from me in surprise. I staggered up, Aiden's blood covering my hands like thick, sticky syrup. I lowered my body, ready to fight for whatever it took. I opened my mouth, baring sharp fangs as a snarl exploded out of my chest. Aiden growled back and stalked in a circle around me, both of us waiting for the other to make a move. Aiden came at me like a bullet out of a gun. His claws sunk into my shoulders, forcing me to roar in pain. I flipped Aiden over, hovering over him as I tried to force his submission. He locked his teeth around my arm and with the strength of a werewolf, he launched me over his head and straight into the trunk of a tree. I hit the ground with a groan, my shoulder aching after a sickening crack.

Aiden stalked towards me, taller and much more intimidating. I watched him from where I lay on the dirt, barely able to hold onto consciousness. He towered above me and I know Lydia had sent him to kill me. I wasn't going to give her the satisfaction of killing me that easily. Aiden's mouth opened and before I knew it, anger surged through me and I had my claws sunk into the sides of his neck while my friend tried to jump away from me but the savagery I felt was unlike no other. Aiden cried out and howled but something gave me the strength to hold onto the struggling wolf whose fur was now stained crimson instead of grey and brown. His teeth snapped the air and I dodged his blows right before pulling him down to me with the quickness of a cobra and then sunk my fangs into his throat. He gave one last rich howl before Aiden's body went limp in my arms, falling to the ground where I still sat. My pack mate's blood flowed from my mouth, dripping down my chin and onto my clothes and then onto Aiden's still form on the ground.

My breathing puffed out hotly against the cold air, tears exploding out of my eyes. I screamed at what I had done, wanting to back up but the bark of the tree dug into my shoulders. I rubbed at the fresh blood on my chin with my hands but the crimson only spread more due to his blood on my fingers. How could this have happened? I sobbed tragically staggering to my feet, wavering slightly as I fought for air in my closed lungs. I bent down, wrapped Aiden's stiff body in my arms, and carried him all the way to the edge of the lake where the stars reminded me of the wolves.

I lay him down at the edge of the cliff, sitting down beside him, sobbing and running my fingers through Aiden's blood soaked fur. Stiffly, I realized I was no longer stroking fur; my hand was trailing down skin instead. I sucked in a breath of shock when I looked down to see Aiden, in human form, looking up at me through lidded eyes.

His chest moved up and down.

"Aiden?" I choked back a sob, taking his face in my hands and looking at him for the first time in so long. His body was covered in dirt and he must've taken his shirt off before he left to make the change easier.

He winced but whispered, "Hey, kid," Aiden smiled painfully, reaching up to touch my cheek. I covered his hand with mine, squeezing his fingers gently. His thumb wiped the tears away that fell down my cheek.

I tried not to look at the blood at the base of his throat, just shy of his windpipe.

"I'm so sorry," I whispered my voice cracking as I looked into his struggling brown eyes, fighting hard to hold onto life.

"I think Lydia knew I…" He coughed, "Wasn't going to make it back from this trip." His features turned into a sad smile, "She threatened Monica, and I had to go. But, I don't want this life so hopefully, I'll find another life where I can be happy." His breathing shuddered and his eyes fluttered.

"No, no, no," I sobbed lacing my fingers through Aiden's and squeezing hard, "Aiden, no! Don't leave me!" I cried leaning my forehead on his bloody chest.

"You'll be a good alpha," He sighed and the tears came faster.

"Say hi to dad for me," I whispered as Aiden took his last breath and died in my arms.

Jaxon

It was when Erica and I heard the scream that fear rocketed through me. We exchanged looks of uncertainty before shooting through the woods in panic towards the unmistakable sound of Allie sobbing uncontrollably. The smells and sights rushed into my mind like a whirlpool.

We skidded to a halt when the lake came into view and my eyes landed on someone in black lying across a dark shape. Erica shifted first and I followed, both of us walking cautiously to where I realized it was Allie who clung tightly to a grey wolf, his fur smeared with blood. Her back was to me as she lay alongside the dead wolf as if he were just sleeping. Sobs tore through the air like claws and Allie's body shook violently as she curled her body in tighter.

"Allie?" I asked surprised when she didn't turn around in fear like usual if someone scared her. She went completely still though but never looked back at me.

"Please," She sobbed, "Leave me alone." Allie's voice sounded broken as if someone took a sledgehammer to it, shattering it into a million tiny pieces.

I looked at Erica before bending down behind Allie and resting my hand on her shoulder, she flinched.

"I killed him," She whispered in a voice I could barely hear. Slowly, she sat up and I nearly yelped in surprise when I saw her mouth and hands stained in dried blood. Allie held the wolf's head in her lap, stroking his muzzle like he was made of paper. "I killed him." She said again before breaking down like water pushing through a dam after years of being held back.

I didn't know what to say. The wolf's smell wasn't human. I didn't understand why she was so upset when all she did was protect herself from ending up like the grey wolf. I glanced back at Erica who looked just as horrified and confused as I was. But, her eyes remained on Allie protectively. Her gaze was different than when she had killed those men in the church. This expression that she wore held a life time of pain, despair, and regret. It nearly killed me inside.

"Allie," I said gently but she raised her head as if I had fired a shotgun, "It's okay. It was just self-defense." I reached out to touch her cheek but she pulled away with fearful guarded eyes, making me retract my hand.

"It doesn't matter that it was self-defense," she whispered so quietly I even had to strain to catch her words, "Aiden was a good person and he didn't deserve to die like this. I did." Allie's eyelashes cast shadows across her cheeks as she looked down at the wolf in her arms.

"Wait," Erica asked bending down beside me with scrunched eyebrows, "This is a werewolf?"

Allie tucked a piece of bloody hair behind her ear and glared at Erica, "Yes, and I have known him since I was a little girl and he always protected me from everything and read stories to me and…" Her voice trailed off because she had begun sobbing again and the words were lost in her tears.

I couldn't sit here and watch Allie break down any longer but I knew she wasn't going to come with me. So, I reached my hand out towards Aiden slowly, cocking my head to the side in question, asking Allie if I was allowed to touch her friend. She pressed her lips together and nodded carefully, watching me with hawk eyes as I rested my head on the wolf's neck. I combed my fingers softly through his fur, not caring that his blood was getting on my hands too.

Allie watched me as I said to Aiden's still form, "I didn't know you at all but we had something in common. Both of us want to protect Allie from everything. You were noble and sacrificing and I admire you for that. But, now that you have passed, I will take care of Allie and I promise you will never have to worry about her ever again. She loved you," I paused looking up to see Allie's lips parted in astonishment and fresh tears welling up in her eyes, "So, thank you for taking care of her all those years before we met." I gave Aiden's fur one last stroke before I stood up, looking anywhere but Allie because the gratitude in her eyes was so powerful it hurt.

Erica and I started to turn away when Allie called out, "Wait," I looked back to see her staggering to her feet with Aiden in her arms. "Will you help me bury him?" Her fingers curled into his fur but I noticed the way her knees and arms shook as if she was about to collapse any minute.

I looked closer at her, my eyes straining through the dark of the night to see what had happened to her. Allie's shirt was no longer whole, it hung off of her in different places and underneath the fabric were grotesque claw marks, ten times worse than the ones I had given her before. Bite marks riddled her body like ants at a picnic, blood flowing down her limbs. Her skin, unnaturally pale, shone like the moon that loomed behind her.

"Of course," Erica said and started walking towards her to help her carry Aiden right as Allie crumpled to the ground unconscious.

Allie

Aiden, I miss you.

"Is she going to be okay?" a deep voice asked making my head throb even more than it already did.

Open your eyes.

"I think so," A girl said.

Why can't you open your eyes?

Something creaked beside me and I could feel blankets underneath me, warm and comforting. A door opened.

Talk, move, scream do something.

"Dallas is here."

Dallas? My brother? I want to see him.

"He didn't tell his mom, did he?" a younger girl asked from far away.

"No, Mary and Oliver aren't home," The person closest to me said.

A new voice came into my head.

TO LOVE IS TO DESTROY.

A whoosh of air burst into my lungs as the sound vibrated through my skull and I shot straight up in the bed I was lying in, my eyes flying wide open and taking in the harsh lights. My head whipped back and forth trying to regain my sanity as I tried to piece together where I was and what had happened. Fingers curling into the blankets, I realized how much every part of my body ached and I felt like I had just spun around in the dryer for an hour. I rubbed the sleep out of my eyes and looked around the room in confusion. Erica and Kate were in the corner of the room like I had been when Jaxon was unconscious. Terrence stood by the door with Dallas beside him who looked more horrified than ever. Jaxon was the person who had sat down beside me on the bed. I remembered the words he had said to Aiden earlier and felt a new wave of tears wash over me. *No, I am not going to cry in front of my little brother.* I blinked away tears and ran my fingers through my hair, heat flaring across my cheeks because I knew everyone was watching me closely.

Jaxon cleared his throat and said quietly, "Why don't we give Allie and Dallas some time alone, this is all kind of crazy."

"We'll be outside burying Aiden," Erica said with a sad smile.

I swallowed carefully and smiled at Jaxon who leaned forward and pressed his lips to my forehead before disappearing with the rest of the Lochlans through the door, closing it tightly behind him. Dallas came to sit beside me, holding my hand in his and something tugged at my gut. The truth. I wanted to tell him so badly who I really was that it almost hurt. Dal and Jaxon were the two people I couldn't live without but I knew for sure I couldn't tell Jaxon, not without messing everything we had up.

"What happened?" My brother asked in a small scared voice and finally I let the truth flow from my mouth. I couldn't handle it anymore.

"Dal," I said, "Do you remember when you asked me what in my past was so terrible?" I asked when I heard the front door of the house shut. Dal's eyes widened but he nodded mutely. "Well, I think it's time for you to know. You have to know that what I am about to tell you has to stay completely secret. No one, not even mom or Jaxon, can know this." He nodded again and I told him my story.

"I was born in London, Ohio but we didn't have to leave because of financial issues. My mom, dad, friends, and I had to leave because… because we killed too many people," I said not looking at Dal's face, "I'm not human, Dallas. I'm a born werewolf, an alpha in fact. I came here because I didn't want to kill people and now my mom and dad are trying to find me. The only problem is, once they find me… they will kill me for betraying them.

"I found this warlock named Spencer," I said, "You've met him. He gave me some potion that keeps the wolf away and won't allow me to shift anymore and I haven't shifted in nine years. But, they are getting closer and I'm afraid the only chance I have is to become what I have always feared the most… myself."

Dal's hand was no longer in mine. His eyes grew to the size of baseballs, his face a pale sheet of horror. He looked at me like I was some new stranger who captured his attention in a bad way.

“I don’t believe you,” He whispered in a cracked voice that sounded so broken I nearly regretted telling him the truth. He backed away from me, standing up and staring at me in fear.

I sighed in exasperation, moving off the bed in incredible pain. I hobbled over to the window, peeking out the curtains and seeing an empty field. They must’ve gone deep into the woods to bury Aiden so luckily, their powerful hearing wouldn’t listen in on our conversation. I stood in front of my brother, uncertainty and relief running through my veins but I held my ground firmly.

“If you don’t believe me,” I whispered softly, “Then, I need to show you.” A tear fell down my bloody cheek as I prepared to make the change… well half the shift.

I squeezed my eyes shut and let the powerful feeling rush through my veins. I felt the piercing pain in my gums and fingertips right before fangs lengthened my canines and claws grew from my fingers. When my eyes snapped open, they burned red and I watched as Dallas sucked in a breath and fell back against the door. I slid my tongue across my fangs, feeling them out with a smile.

“Dallas,” I said quietly, my muscles aching ten times more from the energy the change took, “Please, don’t tell anyone. I’m still me.”

He was silent for a few moments, watching me with horror in his eyes and my heart hurt at the sight of that. I swallowed hard, looking down at my torn up wrist from Aiden’s teeth. My claws and fangs retracted but I willed my eyes to stay red as I moved closer to him. He didn’t back up when I stopped a foot away from him, looking at him with my lips pressed together.

He opened his mouth, closed it, and then opened it again, “I… don’t really know what to say to that. In fact, I am secretly freaking out inside and I don’t really know how to handle this but… I am glad you told me the truth." Dal said with a bleak smile on his face but I knew he was still afraid and mad at me for hiding the truth.

"Dal," I reached out to him but he backed out into the hallway with a scared look in his eyes.

"Don't," he whispered a tear falling down his cheek, "I still need some time." And just like that he had disappeared outside. I watched him run across the street and towards our house.

Hobbling into the bathroom, I gripped the edges of the sink to keep from collapsing again and stared at my reflection in the mirror. My eyes had turned to their usual blue and the blood covering my body made them stand out more. I hated it. I ground my teeth together and screamed so loud my throat hurt, my arm swinging back and I slammed my fist into the glass. The mirror shattered and rained down onto the floor, cutting painfully into the flesh on my knuckles. White hot anger surged through me as I ripped off my bloody jacket, throwing it onto the floor.

I stared at the claw marks that tore up my arms. They weren't too deep so they would heal quickly but for some reason, I liked the way they looked against my skin. It reminded me of the old days and I had something to hold onto even if it was a little painful. I glanced down my cut up body and had an overwhelming feeling of defeat. I wanted to curl up into a ball, go to sleep, and never wake up to face the hard world. I did just that. I leaned my back against the wall and slid down to the floor riddled with shards of glass that poked in uncomfortable places but I didn't care at all. I folded my arms underneath my head and used them as a pillow. I shut my eyes tightly, a single tear dripping off my eyelashes, before sleep took me over and I was pulled under.

Someone's fingers brushed against my temple and down to my chin, "Allie?" Jaxon asked quietly my eyes fluttering open to see a blurry version of him looking down at me from where I still lay on the floor.

I groaned, pushing myself up with my hands and wincing when some of the shards poked into my palms. I sat back, leaning my head on the wall and feeling like I jumped off a cliff. Jaxon's room had turned bright from the sunlight that streamed in through the window.

I rubbed my eyes, "What time is it?" I asked but paused in confusion, "Actually, the better question is what day is it?" I laughed lightly, plucking a tiny piece of glass out of my arm.

Jaxon grinned, touching my face gently, "Its morning. We thought you were asleep on the bed, not the floor." He glanced down at the glass shards and pressed his lips together.

"Thank you," I whispered with a smile, "For saying those things about Aiden. I really appreciated that." I told him gratefully, a feeling of sunshine filling me like it filled the room.

Jaxon held out his hand and I took it so that he could help pull me off of the tile floor, "Both of you deserved it," He said and grabbed a damp wash cloth, dabbing at the blood still on my face.

"Sorry about your mirror," I said guiltily and holding up my scarred knuckles so that he could see. Jaxon raised his eyebrows in surprise but just laughed quietly, taking my hand in his before grabbing a bandage out of the cabinet. He wrapped the soft cloth around the scabs as if I was made of glass but, I didn't miss the slight narrowing of his eyes when he glanced at the shattered mirror one last time.

February rolled by, fading into March. Dallas was beginning to come around on the idea that Khione and I weren't human. Oliver's house had finished being built and he packed his bags, leaving us for a house twice as big and was on even more land than ours. Despite my sadness for him leaving, at least this would give me a new hideout place when life became too overwhelming. Without realizing it, I began to distance myself from everyone as if anticipating things were about to explode. Of course, it didn't help that the sickness that had plagued my nights now made appearances during the day. Spencer was holed up in his lair conducting test after test to try and crack the code. Khione spent most days and nights running through the woods as a wolf, making me feel like a caged animal. Jaxon and I hadn't seen each other outside of school lately. He didn't text or call and I began to wait for him to break up with me. After the whole Aiden thing, I thought that maybe he was starting to get suspicious about who I really was.

I was sitting on the couch cross legged with a carton of Chinese Lo-Mein balanced on my lap and watching a movie when mom came up from the basement, holding a little square box. I glanced back at her for a second but then turned back to my movie. Dallas and Khione were at school, leaving me to try and gain back the weight I had lost.

An annoying beeping sound pounded against my eardrums and I looked back in irritation to see my mom staring at the black walkie talkie thing in puzzlement. It was lighting up like crazy.

"Stupid thing," Mom said to the receiver, "It's been acting up all day." She tossed it onto the counter, silencing it immediately.

"What does it do?" I asked when I swallowed some noodles.

"It detects werewolves," she said and a ball of noodles nearly got lodged in the back of my throat. I coughed crazily for a few seconds before regaining my composure and she added, "It thinks there's one in the house right now." Mom laughed like it was an absurd idea while I was choking on my lunch and trying not to die.

"Ha, stupid thing." I said quietly before standing up and wrapping the blanket around my shoulders to keep the chills of the fever off of my skin.

"Where are you going?" Mom asked coming over to me and crossing her arms across her chest in defiance.

"Outside for a few minutes," I told her with my lips pressed together tightly.

"Honey," Mom whispered, "It's chilly out there," She pressed the back of her hand to my forehead, "And you're burning up."

"It's warm out, okay? And I just want to go see Ash, that's all." I said shrugging in annoyance and pushing past her.

"Allie," Mom said forcing me to pause in the doorway and turn around, "I am sick of your attitude." Her voice was scary calm but I didn't feel a twinge of guilt.

I looked at her for a few seconds before walking right out the front door.

In an hour, I decided to take a trip over to Oliver's new house to check it out and help him unpack. Clothed in jeans and a short sleeve shirt due to the now warmish air, I hopped out of my truck and knocked on the front door. Multiple voices came from inside and my eyebrows pulled together in confusion as Oliver opened the door with a huge smile on his face.

"I didn't think you'd be this happy to see me," I said pressing my lips together but Oliver laughed and moved aside to let me in.

"I have company," He said as we walked down the hallway.

I took a deep breath, smelling the air, "Jaxon and Terrence are here, aren't they?" I pressed my lips together with a slight nod.

We walked into the large living room and as I predicted, there was Terrence drinking a beer and leaning against the counter. I gave him a tiny smile before my eyes found Jaxon's where he was lounging on the couch, lying flat. The perfect strip of skin showed between the waistband of his jeans and hem of his t shirt. I averted my gaze as my heart contracted at the sight of him after not hearing a peep in a couple of days. He didn't look at me when I walked in like Terrence did, instead, he took out his phone and started playing on it.

I ground my teeth together and grabbed the phone from his hands, "Well, I'm glad to see this is working. I started to think it fell in the toilet or something." I threw it back onto his chest with a thump and Jaxon sat up slowly, coming around to stand beside me.

He kept his distance though, even when I could see in his eyes that he wanted to be near me, "Sorry, I've had a lot going on." Jaxon said tucking his phone back into his pocket.

I shook my head in annoyance and sighed in frustration, "Okay, whatever." I turned to Oliver, "Why are they here?"

Terrence answered instead, "We are thinking about moving in."

My jaw dropped in shock, "What? Why? What's wrong with your house?" I asked looking back and forth between the three of them.

Jaxon said in a satisfied voice, "It's getting expensive and we can't afford it much longer. So, since Oliver is our dad, we are thinking about moving in sometime in the future." He rested his elbow on my shoulder, sending electric waves through my whole body.

I narrowed my eyes at him and moved away from him so that he tripped, almost falling to the floor. Terrence snickered as I said, "Don't play the dad card with me. You guys can't live here. My mom will be here all the time trying to find you and the rest of your family." I told them with raised eyebrows to make my point stronger.

Oliver said from in the kitchen, "That's why we are going to wait for all of this to blow over before they actually move in." He poked his head out the doorway and smiled at me but I just sneered at him.

Pent up anger exploded out of me, "What if this never ends?!?" I paced around the room, spinning around to face everyone, "What if she never stops and just keeps hunting us and then Lydia and Marcus are going to try and kill me." My blood pumped in my ears as I willed my eyes not to change colors with the stress.

"Lydia and Marcus?" Terrence asked and heat rushed to my cheeks in fear when I realized what I had said. I swallowed hard, running my fingers through my hair. "Allie, what do you know?"

I lowered my eyebrows, "Nothing, I know nothing." I held up my hands in surrender but I knew my heart was racing insanely. My eyes met Jaxon's whose brown ones had flashed to a bright yellow.

He snarled, moving towards me, "What aren't you telling us?" When I hesitated, he moved blindingly fast and the next thing I knew he had my back pinned against the wall, his hands on either side of me.

Panic rose in my chest until it almost choked me as I closed my eyes and turned my face away from the heat rolling off his body. My breathing quickened as I was reminded of the countless times Lydia or Marcus had done this to me. I never thought Jaxon would do this to me and the betrayal I felt on the inside threatened to form tears in my eyes. I didn't want to cry but as he stared at me as if I were prey, my heart slowly broke. It took all of my willpower not to cry out in fear and bolt out of the door. Instead, I met his eyes like the alpha I was and placed my hand on his chest.

"Get away from me," I said in a scary calm voice as I glared at him in his gold eyes.

Jaxon didn't back away but he looked back at Terrence and Oliver and said, "Can you give us a minute?" the two dispersed after a few seconds of hesitation.

Jaxon turned his eyes back to mine, his gaze intimidating and strong until I felt like a caterpillar. My hand turned into a fist on his chest as I tried to keep the wolf down. His face was close enough that if I moved forward an inch, I could've kissed him. I thought about doing it but the way his arms shook angrily beside my head made me think maybe that wasn't such a good idea.

"What aren't you telling us?" Jaxon asked in a slightly calmer voice, though his eyes and breathing told me he was furious on the inside.

"I've told you everything." I whispered, "Yes, I have friends who are werewolves and I know things about them. The alphas are after me but that's all I know." I pushed my fist against his chest and he stepped back but I stayed flat against the wall.

Jaxon groaned and ran his fingers through his hair. He said quietly, "I love you, Allie." He said with unnatural pain in his voice, "But, do you want to know what the worst feeling in the world is?" I didn't answer him, "Not being able to trust the person you love and that's what I'm feeling right now."

I didn't know what to say but my heart stopped, "Why can't you trust me? I'm not lying to you." I ironically lied to him as convincingly as I could.

"That's funny because your heart is racing like crazy." He said with a bleak smile on his face that made my body ache with regret, "There is something about your past that you don't want anyone to know and frankly, it makes me think that you aren't who you say you are." The look in Jaxon's eyes made me flatten my back harder against the wall as if I could blend in with the cream paint.

Tears welled up in my eyes and spilled over, falling down my cheeks and clogging my throat, "Are you going to break up with me?" my voice didn't sound like my own at all. I felt like a child, looking up at Jaxon through wide, bloodshot blue eyes.

He looked at me for a few moments, his eyes full of pain and betrayal. He stood a couple of feet away from me but it felt like he was on the other side of the world and there were thousands of volcanoes in between us, waiting to erupt. Jaxon's face blurred in front of me and I knew this was the end. I knew my secret had caught up to me and there was no going back. I had a feeling it was time to move on and there was nothing left to do. I couldn't change what was happening any more that I could change who Lydia was to me.

"Yeah, I am," He said but before he could say anything else, I grabbed my jacket, bolted out the front door, and slammed it loudly behind me.

I sat in the corner booth alone, staring out the window of the café with anger and resentment coursing through my veins. I didn't bother to wipe the mascara out from underneath my teary eyes but I didn't care. I couldn't put what I was feeling into actual words. I stared out at the bleary skies that reflected my mood and tried to put together what had just happened. New tears welled up in my eyes and I covered them with my hand as I sniffled like a total kid. How was I supposed to get through this without Jaxon or any of the Lochlans? I couldn't be near them without breaking down. I knew Jaxon was never going to forgive me for not telling him the truth but I couldn't tell him.

"Allie?" Someone asked making me jump. I blinked the tears away and looked up to see Erica standing at my table. My heart thumped painfully. I wanted to punch her in the face.

"Um, can I just be alone for now?" I asked not looking at her, "I'm having a crappy day." I took an angry sip of my coffee and stared back out the window as if I was trying to burn a hole through the glass.

"What happened? You look like a mess." Erica said her brain having no filter what so ever. I rolled my eyes when she sat across from me.

"Tell your brother that he's a freaking jerk with trust issues." I snapped at her, grabbing my coffee and marching toward the front door when it opened in front of me and Jaxon walked through.

I stopped a few steps away from him, boiling with anger.

I turned back to Erica.

"Oh, look here he is now," I said caustically and when she smiled bleakly, I turned back around and dumped my coffee onto his head.

Jaxon sucked in a deep breath, his mouth dropping open in surprise as the brown liquid trailed down his face and neck, probably burning his skin. I put the cup in his hand and smirked, patting his chest hard and then walking past him and out the front door.

I groaned as loud as I could when I was across the street from the café and far away from Jaxon. What was I supposed to do now? I had nothing. I built up a mental wall to keep the floods of emotions from washing over me. I wasn't going to cry over a stupid boy. Jaxon meant nothing to me anymore.

He meant everything to me.

I was just lying to myself if I said I didn't care about Jaxon anymore. I loved him with everything I was and I knew all his secrets. I flashed back to the night of the first full moon when I was in Jaxon's house and he was telling me about his parents. I had told myself that I wasn't going to let him hold me because I didn't want to get close to anything. I wanted to prevent what had happened a couple of hours ago. I wanted to keep my already fragile heart from breaking all over again. A tear fell down my cheek as I started my truck, pulling out of the parking lot and speeding down the street. I grabbed sunglasses from my glove compartment, pulled a Yankees cap down on my head, rolled the windows down, and blasted music that disrupted the peace of the neighborhood.

The wind blew through my hair and I tapped my hand on the side of the truck to the beat of the music. It took all of my willpower to keep my heart from breaking as I drove to a place where I would fit in just a little bit, even if it was a tad risky. I cranked the radio up louder and smiled when The Midnight Hunter's Bar came into view. I couldn't help but feel giddy when the awful yet somehow pleasant smell filled my nostrils and I was reminded of the days when I would go there just to feel at home again.

I pushed open the glass doors and was rewarded with the loud sounds, smells, and sights of werewolves. Most people would probably think I was crazy for entering into the territory I had wanted to forget for so long but after the break up with Jaxon, I needed some time with my kind. The Midnight Hunter's Bar was run and owned by werewolves providing a peaceful, well sometimes peaceful, place for wolves in their human form to hang out. The perk of being one of them was that I could get in even when I was only fifteen. Of course, I wasn't allowed to drink but I still had some old friends here that I loved to talk and play pool with. I pulled my hat down and marched inside as if I had never stopped being a werewolf. I only went there once or twice when I was fifteen because things got crazy sometimes, especially when a human would accidentally come in and we would have to act normal.

"Well, I'll be darned," A voice said from my right very loudly, "Allie Jennings has come back from the dead looking better than ever."

I knew that voice. My face broke out in a bright smile and I turned to see Cole Jordan. He looked exactly the same as when he was fifteen, the last time I saw him, with midnight black hair, light skin, and freakishly blue eyes. His white teeth shone brightly as he pushed back his chair and sauntered over to me like the bad boy he was.

"Cole Jordan," I said smiling, "It's been a long time." I reached up on my tip toes and wrapped my arms around his neck when he hugged me tightly with all the strength of a born werewolf.

"Indeed," he laughed snatching the hat from my head and securing it on his own. I glared at him jokingly. His eyes flashed gold, trying to provoke me into getting it back from him. He didn't need to know that I was an alpha.

Instead, I rolled my eyes giving up and followed him to the counter where a waitress was serving drinks to wolves disguised as humans. Secretly, I wished a fight would break out between two betas or something, alphas didn't come here, and they would have to get dragged away, salivating and snarling. I swiveled in my chair so that I was facing Cole, who was watching and smirking at me. I narrowed my eyes at him and took a swipe for my hat but he jerked away quickly. Instead, he caught my hand in his, electricity running through my veins as I looked up into his eyes. I flashed back to a night two years ago in this same spot.

Our faces were inches from each other's and all I could see and smell was Cole Jordan with his fierce blue eyes and cocky grin. I was convinced that I was in love with him and maybe I was but it wasn't serious when I was fifteen. Cole's hand came up slowly to caress my cheek and my lips parted at his touch, my eyes fluttering shut. I couldn't take it anymore, I wanted him so badly. My heart hurt too bad to be alone and I was ready to do something stupid and reckless.

He crushed my lips to his the next moment and I let him move my mouth with his. He was fierce in a gentle way that made me feel like I wasn't some little girl. But then, as I was kissing him, all the cruel memories of wolves burst into my mind in a millions colors and I knew this was wrong. I jerked away from him, panic flushing my cheeks.

"Are you okay? I'm sorry if that was too fast." Cole said with wide eyes that made me want to kiss him again.

"No, it's just... I have to go." I told him in a shaky voice before bolting out the door and down the street. It was the last time I had seen him.

The way Cole was looking at me at that moment made me believe he was remembering that day too. I took in a deep breath, pulling my hand out of his and turning to face the counter in an awkward silence. Jaxon's eyes still lingered in front of my face and even though a part of me wanted to kiss Cole again, the other part said it would just make things messy. Cole handed me my hat back and I smiled slowly at him, tucking it back onto my head.

"Look," I said turning to face him in the chair, "You are one of the few werewolves I can trust and I have missed you a lot but things... have happened that have kind of messed me up a little and to add to more of that, my boyfriend just broke up with me." I told him twisting the ring on my finger anxiously but I couldn't help feeling like I should get back at Jaxon. I couldn't use Cole just to make someone jealous. That would go against everything I stood for.

But, I thought to myself, *I could keep him around as someone who was a very good friend.*

"Oh," Cole said looking down in disappointment, "I'm sorry, I didn't know that." He was about to get up from the chair when I grabbed his wrist, stopping him before he could leave.

"I need a friend, though," I said honestly, "And we are the same in so many ways."

He smiled widely, "Give me your number, kid."

I handed him my phone.

<u>Jaxon</u>

The world seemed upside down in so many ways. All I could see was a thick cloud of fog that wanted to cut me off from the world, from Allie. But, the feeling that she was lying to me about something important made my stomach knot up tightly. Then, the look on her face when I broke it off made me want to puke as she ran out. The worst thing was that I knew how fragile Allie's heart was and all I did was crush it under my boot.

I groaned in anger, regret, and uncertainty as I walked down the sidewalk, no destination in mind. I shoved my hands farther into the pockets of my jeans, wishing I could just curl up into a ball and go to sleep, never waking up. I turned a corner, entering into a dark alley that was lit dimly by the lamps. It smelled of garbage and other things I didn't really want to know about but I figured I deserved whatever came at me including a very pissed off Khione.

She rammed into me like a bulldozer, slamming my back into a brick wall so hard it cracked a tiny bit underneath me. I let out a cry as my head too cracked against the wall, the world spinning even more. Khione snarled, pressing her arm to my throat and staring at me with her intense gold eyes and thick fangs. Khione's other hand wrapped around my wrist, her claws digging into my skin and drawing blood painfully. I gritted my teeth tightly together, trying not to let her smell my fear. It didn't really work.

She snarled and said in her Australian accent that scared me, "I hope you feel like absolute crap after what you did to my best friend." I could feel her cool breath on my cheek when I turned my head to the side. "She trusted you with her life and trust is the last thing Allie gives to people. You took that rare thing and you tore it apart into a million unfixable pieces. You deserved a lot worse than a cup of coffee to the face and by the way, I've known Allie for her entire life and she is very capable of making your life miserable." She jammed her arm one more time against my throat before disappearing into the shadows and leaving me mortified and trying to catch my breath.

I knew every single thing that Khione had said to me was true and it made me feel the size of a worm. I fought back the urge to punch the wall even though I deserved far worse pain than the claw marks burning my wrists. I cursed myself before dropping to my hands and knees and shifting into my brown wolf to find at least a tiny shred of comfort.

Allie

"Why didn't you tell us?" Blake exclaimed when she and Miles bombarded me at my locker right before lunch.

"Tell you what?" I sighed exasperated slamming my locker shut a little too powerfully.

"You didn't tell us that Jaxon broke up with you." Miles said with raised eyebrows and sympathy written all over his face.

“Oh, yeah sorry,” was all I could think of to say as I gripped my books to my chest and started walking down the hallway with my two friends trailing noisily behind me.

“Um, excuse me?” Blake asked in a high pitched, insulted voice, “What happened? You guys are soul mates.” She and Miles sped up so that they could match my quick pace.

“I really don’t want to talk about it, okay?” I accidentally snapped at them and Blake raised her eyebrows in surprise but stayed quiet as we sat down at one of the empty tables across from Erica.

“Hey guys,” Erica said enthusiastically right as Jaxon sat down at the table across from me. Anger flashed in my eyes but I tried to keep it under control which was very challenging.

I ate with my eyes and head down, avoiding eye contact with everyone. Uncomfortable, awkward silence filled the air, making butterflies dance around in my stomach. I picked at my mac and cheese without making a noise but everyone jumped when a new voice came from behind me.

“This silence is very awkward,” I turned to see Cole standing behind me with a grin on his face, “So, I thought I’d drop in and brighten everyone’s day up.” I laughed excitedly and leapt up from the table, wrapping my arms around Cole’s neck tightly. He hugged me back, lifting my feet off the ground. “What? No hat?”

“I don’t always wear a baseball hat, Cole.” I laughed, patting his cheek playfully and pulled him over to sit between Blake and me.

“Well, every time I’ve seen you, you were wearing a hat.” He told me with his usual charming smile but I just rolled my eyes at him, suddenly aware of everyone’s eyes on me.

Before I could introduce him, Khione appeared behind Jaxon with a smile on her face. She pointed at Cole and said, “Hey, you’re that kid from the bar. I saw you last week or something." She sat beside Erica, glaring at Jaxon for a brief second.

"Yeah, I remember you." Cole said with a friendly smile and I looked over to see Blake nearly melting at the sight of my werewolf friend. I was pretty sure that she was still dating Chase, though.

"So," Jaxon said crossly, "Who are you?" It looked like he had to struggle intensely to keep from punching Cole. I smiled on the inside.

"I'm Cole," He said with narrowed eyes, "I'm guessing you're the jerk who broke her heart." Blake and Miles snickered beside him but Jaxon looked like he was going to kill Cole.Jaxon's murderous gaze found mine for half a second before pushing violently away from the table. I watched him trudge down the hallway, every step filling me with vicious pain. I wanted to go after him and maybe even yell at him a little more for hurting me. To be bluntly honest, I wanted to turn into a wolf and attack him but that would be illegal so instead, I pushed away from the table and ran after him.

"Jaxon!" I yelled my voice echoing through the empty hallways.

His shoulders tensed and he stopped, turning around, "Why would you do that to me?"

"Do what?" I asked him as we stood a couple of feet away from each other.

"Bringing some new guy in here to rub in my face," Jaxon said pointing to his chest angrily, "Are you trying to make me feel even worse for breaking up with you? Allie, it's killing me. It kills me every day because I still love you but I don't trust you." His hands clenched and unclenched at his sides, shaking violently.

Anger surged through me, "Listen to me," I yelled at him, "Cole is not my boyfriend. In fact, I turned him down yesterday because I knew you would be upset if I came in here flaunting a new werewolf boyfriend." Tears threatened to spill over but I forced them back. I was not going to cry. "And just so you know, I think I hate you. I think I hate you for not trusting me after I gave you my heart." Now, I didn't care that the tears flowed down my face because I knew he hated it when I cried in front of him.

Jaxon's face turned as white as a sheet when the words left my mouth but I didn't feel even a shred of guilt in the pit of my stomach. Tears fell down my cheeks as I stared down at him with all the hate I could conjure up which wasn't very much. He didn't say anything as his jaw dropped open. With one last sad look, he turned and walked out the front door of the high school. I fought back the urge to scream and slam my fist into a locker as tears flowed down my cheeks.

"Hey," Cole said appearing behind me. "You okay?"

I wiped the tears away before turning around and plastering on a fake smile, "Yeah, just some last minute things we needed to clear up."

Cole moved closer to me and dropped his voice to a whisper, "Is he a werewolf because he smells different?" I looked up at him with wide eyes before pressing my lips together and nodding slightly.

"But he doesn't know that I am one." I told him.

"How can he not know?"

"Because…" I swallowed, "I'm not really one anymore."

Saturday rolled around which meant multiple days without hearing Jaxon's familiar voice. I wanted to say that I was over him but that would be a total lie. Not being able to touch him or hear his voice made my heart throb painfully in my chest. My life became miserable faster than Khione could shift into a wolf. The sickness returned at nights again and I prayed that Spencer would come up with the test results. I just wanted to get better. I wanted this heartbreak to go away and I wanted… I wanted to be me again. But, the only way to do that was to become a better version of the werewolf I once was.

I awoke early to the sound of someone grunting loudly outside my window. Confused, I yawned tiredly before I peeled open my window to see Dallas lying on the ground, breathing heavily and sweating. My eyebrows pulled together in confusion but then I saw my mom standing a few feet away from him and everything clicked into place.

"No, oh God, no," I whispered as I hurried to get dressed into presentable clothing.

Khione startled awake, "What are you doing this early?" She groggily rubbed her eyes until she could see me clearly, struggling to get into my jeans.

"Mom is teaching Dallas," I grunted when I nearly tripped, "To fight werewolves." At that Khione jolted awake and joined me in getting dressed.

"She's teaching him that we are the bad guys?" Khione asked as she pulled a sweatshirt over her full head of messy hair.

"Yeah, because she doesn't know that there are two perfectly nice ones living in her house." I said swinging open my door as fast as I could and running down the stairs two at a time with Khione right on my heels.

"Are you ever going to tell her?" Khione asked breathlessly but I covered her mouth with my hand when I opened the door.

“Shut up,” I whispered to her as I stepped out on the porch. Mom threw a punch at Dallas but lucky for him, he ducked as fast as he could. “What are y’all doing?” I asked trying to hide the fear from my voice as I made my way onto the grass.

“I am training Dallas,” Mom said breathlessly and bending down with her hands on her knees, “Like Oliver has been training you.” Dallas looked up at me with confusion in his eyes. Mom continued, “These werewolves are dangerous and we need as many people as we can get to stop them.” I glanced back at Khione who seemed to be struggling with her anger at the moment.

I was looking at Dallas when I said, “How do you know that all werewolves are bad? I don’t get it. What did they ever do to you?” My brother glanced back and forth from Khione, to me, to mom with wide, confused eyes that made my heart clench.

Her green eyes clouded with storms of pure anger when she said, “They destroyed my career. That boy nearly killed me even after I tried to save them.” She squeezed her eyes shut and a single tear fell down her cheek.

“Who? Who did that?” Dallas made the mistake of asking her the one question I had wanted to avoid.

Her eyes snapped open at the question and mom looked at Dal, “The Lochlans. Jaxon Lochlan tried to kill me after I set him free.”

The look on Dal’s face was even worse than it was when I told him I was a werewolf. Hurt, betrayal, anger, and a thousand other negative emotions swirled in his eyes and I knew I had to get him out of there unless I wanted the Lochlans whereabouts known. I shot a look back at Khione but the way her hands shook told me she was otherwise occupied at the moment. So, instead I thought of a way to get out of there.

“I have training with Oliver in a few minutes,” I said quietly but Dal’s eyes stared straight ahead, “Dallas, come with me.” When he didn’t move, I grabbed his arm and dragged him over to the truck, shoving him into the back with Khione beside me.

We drove in complete silence the whole way there, none of us saying what we were thinking. I looked back every once in a while to see a tear streak down my little brother’s face as the horrible reality finally reached him. Life sucked most of the time. I gripped the steering wheel tighter until my knuckles turned white and pain lanced through them. I pulled into the driveway furiously and leapt out of the truck before it even came to a stop. Dallas and Khione were right behind me, an angry trail on my heels. I jammed my key in the door and slammed it open as hard as I could, making Oliver run out of the kitchen but I couldn’t focus on him because all I could smell was the Lochlan family. In a trailing blaze of anger, the three of us stormed into the living room to see the family spread around on different couches talking and laughing loudly. I stopped in the doorway, my arms crossed and fury flaring through me. None of them turned and saw us yet so my eyes found Jaxon, the guy who tried to kill my mother, where he was leaning against the window sill. His eyes found mine.

I couldn’t take it anymore. The anger was too great. In a flash, I flew across the room and slammed into him with all my strength. He grunted as he fell against the blinds but I wrapped my hand around his throat, lightly but I just wanted him to know I was seriously unhappy.

“You tried to kill her?” I asked through gritted teeth as I willed my eyes to stay blue which was a lot harder to do than I thought.

“What,” he gagged, “Are you talking about?” Jaxon grabbed my wrist and in a second wrenched my hand off of his throat, and had pinned me against the wall.

“Dallas knows,” I glanced at Kate who was watching Dallas with wide brown eyes, “And my mother said you tried to kill her.” I knew he could’ve been gripping my throat harder than he was but I had faith in him that he would never hurt me, no matter how angry I made him.

“Both of you stop!” Terrence roared over our voices and Jaxon’s body snapped to attention at the sound of his alpha. Slowly, my ex-boyfriend backed away from me a little reluctantly but not before I saw him take in my scent. I smiled inside.

“Dallas,” Kate said quietly standing up as a tear fell down her cheek, “I’m so sorry you had to find out like this. I wanted to tell you for so long but it wasn’t my secret to tell.” My brother just looked at her with sad eyes that showed too much pain for me to handle. “Say something.”

Dal hesitated before sighing, “I don’t know what to say. All of this just happened so fast.” He looked to me and I knew he was thinking of the secret I had told him. I bowed my head in shame.

“What happened so fast? Why is everyone so upset?” Erica asked in a confused voice, standing up and throwing her hands up in the air.

I fought back the urge to snarl at her, “Dallas found out about werewolves and now my mother is trying to train him to kill you guys because she wants revenge. So, excuse my lack of hospitality.” I shot at her with a death glare in my eyes. I realized my hands clenched and unclenched, shaking violently.

Erica’s lip curled up in a snarl and at that moment, my wolf howled with anger. I gritted my teeth until I thought they were going to shadow as the world in front of me literally spun in a circle. I squeezed my eyes shut, a small sound escaping from my lips as pain shot up my spine like a rocket. It calmed but I knew what was happening and I was out of the house in less than a second, leaving my car and sprinting towards Spencer's shop before the wolf could overtake me.

I stumbled blindly towards the glass doors of his shop as darkness threatened to swallow me completely. Something warm gushed from my nose and I lifted my hand to find that it was hot blood flowing down my chin. I pushed open the doors, tripping on the threshold, hitting my head on the concrete, and passing out before I could find Spencer.

"God, you are not making this easy," A girl grumbled through the darkness.

"Just hold her still," A male voice said in frustration right as something sharp went through my skin at the shoulder.

I didn't hear anything after that because I drifted back off to sleep. I didn't know how much time had passed before I came around again but I could feel cold metal wrapped around my wrists and more of the coldness on my back. I figured I was lying down on a metal bed? But, how had I gotten there? I tried to open my eyes or say something useful so that whoever was breathing at my bedside would know I was okay. I tried to move my fingers but that didn't work either. After a few minutes of struggling, my eyes finally blinked open, blurry at first.

I recognized the room immediately as Spencer's lair. Thank God, I thought to myself. My hands were still chained to the table which confused me and when I turned my head to the right I was met by two unfamiliar blue eyes. I squealed in surprise, trying to wrench my body away from her until I realized it was Eryn.

"Hey, sorry to scare you." She said standing up and holding her hands up in surrender.

I blinked rapidly and swallowed the metallic taste in my mouth, "It's okay. What happened?" I asked as she unlocked the chains and helped me sit up.

"You came in here, collapsed, and then went psycho when we tried to help you." Eryn laughed wiping some of the dried blood from my chin with a damp towel.

"Where's Spencer?" I asked looking down and realizing there was an IV stuck in my arm and hooked up to some complex machine. "And why do I have an IV in my arm?"

Eryn ran her fingers through her short hair, "He's asleep," She pointed to the mattress in the corner of the room where Spencer rested quietly. "And I'm going to let Spencer explain things to you. It's been a long two days." She was about to turn away but I grabbed her arm.

"Two days!?!" I half shouted at her in astonishment. There was no way I could've been asleep for two days. "Everyone probably thinks I ran away. I can't have my brother thinking I gave up on him." I tried to move the arm with the IV in it but it tugged on the skin painfully.

"I know but we had no idea what to do," Eryn said groaning in annoyance and then yelled, "Spencer, wake up!" He jolted awake with a surprised sound and walked over to where I was sitting.

"Hey, how are you feeling?" Spencer asked touching my arm lightly.

"Kind of crappy," I said pinching the bridge of my nose when a pounding headache pushed through my head all at once.

“Al,” Spencer said in a small voice as he came and sat on the metal bed beside me. Something in his voice made me anxious, “There is something you need to know. Promise me you won’t say anything until I’m completely done.” He grabbed my hand and held it tightly like he thought I was going to run away.

“I promise,” I whispered in a small voice that cracked as I spoke.

“So,” He said clearing his throat, “We have pushed the wolf back for so long but by doing that we messed with how your body functions.” He moved away to a table that was cluttered with notes and strange herbs. He brought over a page, filled with neat drawings of a wolf and a human girl. In other words, me. I still didn’t understand and I looked at him in a questioning gaze. He gave me a sad smile, climbing onto the metal table to sit side me again. “So, I’ve heard about the Lochlans from one of my friends. With her being a witch, she knew what they were instantly.” I rose my eyebrows in surprise but he kept going, “You and your friends are different types of werewolves. You were born and he was turned, therefore, you are more wolf than human. In other words, a wolf turned human. Jaxon and his family are humans turned to wolves.”

Comprehension now played across my face as the pieces came together. The headaches, the pains in my stomach, and the reason the wolf keeps breaking through during an adrenaline rush aren’t solely because of Jaxon. The wolf is desperately trying to survive. Not being a werewolf isn’t the only thing killing the wolf, it’s also killing me.

“I’m dying?” I sobbed, my hands covering my face. Absolute, pure terror and despair washed over me as tears shook my body.

I didn’t want to die. I finally had a life. I had a brother, a mother, friends, and Jaxon who I loved with my heart and soul. I wasn’t ready to let them go, not yet, not ever. But I wasn’t afraid of death. I never had been. I was afraid that my time had come so early because I had people here that made me want to stay.

"So," I sniffled, "What do we do now?" I said my voice unable to go above a whisper.

"Oh, you're not dying on me, sweetheart." Spencer said hugging me close to him, smiling at Eryn who stood across from me.

"Yeah," Eryn said with a smile, "Even though you still scare me sometimes, I think we can work on being friends." She said with a shy smile.

As I looked down at my hands, an emotion I never thought possible welled up inside of me. It wasn't fear or angst. It was pure excitement and anticipation. I wanted to be a werewolf again. I want to be a werewolf again. My eyebrows pulled together as realization set in. I always thought that I was supposed to be human. I thought that was how I was supposed to make a difference in the world. But, as I sat there, wanting to be a better version of the old me, I realized that was what I was called to do. I was an alpha too and I was going to challenge Lydia and Marcus if it was the last thing I did. A true smile spread across my face.

"What are you thinking?" Spencer asked with hesitant anticipation in his deep voice.

"I am thinking," I said confidentially, "That I want to be a werewolf again." I yanked the IV out of my arm, wincing slightly, and then marched to the door. I said proudly with a smile, "I am an alpha and it's my job to do what's right for my pack." And with that, I pushed open the door and stepped into the bright morning light.

Jaxon

The house was oddly quiet when I woke up the next morning. Birds chirped quietly outside my window, threatening to lure me back to sleep. Bright light streamed in through my windows, blinding me as I made my way to the bathroom. I still hadn't fixed the bathroom mirror after Allie had smashed it with some weird, newfound strength that I still didn't understand. I dragged my toothbrush across my teeth and tried to fix my messy hair even though I couldn't see myself. The cellphone on my nightstand buzzed repeatedly until I pressed the answer button.

"Hello?" I asked tiredly though I had slept till eleven o'clock.

"Hey, it's me," Someone I didn't totally recognize said on the other line.

"Who?"

"It's Blake, idiot. Didn't you check your caller ID?"

"No, why are you being so snappy?" I asked as I made my way downstairs to find the house completely empty of my brother and sisters. I shrugged.

"Sorry," Blake sighed, "I'm freaking out. Is Allie with you?"

"Um, no," I told her awkwardly, "Don't you remember? We kind of broke up." I shifted the phone to the other ear, holding it between my head and shoulder as I made cereal.

"Correction, you broke up with her and now she's missing."

I nearly choked on my breakfast, "What?"

"She disappeared, right off the face of the earth. Dallas and Khione or that Cole guy hasn't seen her either." Blake groaned in frustration and fear.

I moved the bowl of cereal away and closed my eyes, trying to get rid of the angst that consumed me, "God, the last time I saw her she was really pissed but I didn't think she'd run away. That's not her style." There was a rustling on the other line and Blake grunted.

Khione's voice came on the line, "Well, then you don't know her half as well as you think you do. Things are hard for her and you just had to go and crush her heart completely." I flinched at her words and forced myself to stay on the phone.

"Give that back," Blake said and Khione disappeared.

"Where are Dallas and my family?" I asked as I rushed back upstairs to get changed into something besides pajamas.

"Dallas is here with Khione and me. He's a wreck." Blake sighed, "As for your family, I have no idea where they are." I imagined her shrugging.

"And Allie's mom?"

"Currently at the police station. If Al doesn't come home today, she is going to be declared a missing person."

I cursed as I rushed out the door fully clothed, "You and Khione stay with Dallas. I am going to find Allie."

"Wait..." Blake said but I had already hung up and was sprinting into the woods.

Allie

The first step I took into the woods seemed to ignite a firework of happiness inside me. I didn't know how I was going to make myself shift after swallowing a boatload of magic over the years. Before, it happened when I had a burst of adrenaline but how was I supposed to make that happen unless someone I loved was in danger. I chewed the inside of my lip as I scrolled through ideas in my mind to complete my mission. Shifting was only the first step. I flexed the muscles in my legs and arms as if testing them out when I would finally feel them stretch again. But, of course on the day I needed it, the wolf wasn't right under my skin. She was miles and miles deeper than that.

"How am I supposed to do this?" I whispered to myself as I ran my fingers through my hair.

Focus, Allie. You have wanted this for a long, long time; now's your chance to prove your mother wrong.

A tiny spark of movement.

I squeezed my eyes shut and gritted my teeth. My hands clenched and unclenched into fists and my toes curled inside of my sneakers. Come on, come on. Everything was deadly silent except for the blood whooshing in my ears. Then, I heard the click of the safety being released on a gun.

My eyes flew open to see Spencer standing in front of me, a shiny black gun clasped between his hands.

"Spencer?" I asked taking a step back with shaky knees. What was going on?

"I can't let you shift." He ground out between clenched teeth. His hand didn't waver.

"So you're going to shoot me?" My chest heaved up and down rapidly as I tried to put together what Spencer was about to do.

"If I have to," He swallowed, "Then, yes, I will."

I forced the tears to stay back because they would just blind me, "Why? After all these years of trying to help me, you are just going to betray me like that?" I wanted to scream at him but I willed my voice to stay level which was about as easy as trying to baptize a cat.

"Warlocks and werewolves have always been enemies." Spencer said softly, "This is me reinforcing that legend." And with that he fired a warning shot that zoomed right past my ear.

My sneakers pounded the leafy ground of the forest floor as fast as they could. The cold hair pierced my lungs until it hurt to breathe and I was forced to take tiny breaths. My calves burned as I dodged trees and leapt over ditches that ruptured my path. How long could I keep going? God, where was the wolf when I needed her? Didn't running from a crazy person with a gun count as an adrenaline rush? I groaned in agony when I leapt over a river, falling to my knees on the other side. I glanced behind me quickly, my heart pumping wildly in my chest. Eyes scanning the forest, I tried to find my opponent but Spencer being a warlock, I knew this was going to be a hundred times harder than fighting Aiden.

Where is he?

I am going to die.

BOOM! Two more bullets flew right past me and I saw Spencer charging at me from the complete opposite direction he had started. What the heck? My pulse jumped and I catapulted myself back over the river, sprinting in the direction I had originally come from as Spencer fired another round at me. I stumbled over a maze of roots that threatened to pull me under the ground with them. Bark exploded from a tree beside me as I realized another shot had hit it. I cursed loudly and put on as much extra speed as I could conjure up. At the next moment, the feeling was there. The feeling of my feet not touching the ground was there and I knew the wolf was going to help me out.

That was when I slammed head first with someone.

“Allie?” A blurry Jaxon asked as I sat dazed on the ground for a few seconds, looking up at him.

“Run, Jaxon, run.” I screamed at him, leaping up and grabbing his hand but not fast enough.

Faster than a cobra, Spencer appeared, sweaty but not out of breath, his arm wrapped around Jaxon’s neck and the gun pressed against his head. I stared, terrified and completely out of ideas. Jaxon’s face portrayed the same emotions as mine.

“Spencer, stop.” I told him in the biggest alpha voice I could conjure up.

“What are you going to do about it, wolf girl?”

And there it was. Pain shot up my spine, curling through my whole body with greedy fingers. Black ran through my veins until it reached my fingers where claws lengthened my nails. I fell to my knees with a scream as a sickening crack resonated through my body and my spine shifted back and forth. Then there was the bowing of my rib cage as everything in front of me turned blood red and my fangs lengthened. Suddenly, I was standing on four legs, covered in shining silver fur but instead of blue eyes they were finally red.

I looked up at Jaxon and Spencer; both guys looked like they were going to puke. But, then I saw Spencer smile in triumph right before disappearing with a snap of his fingers. The parts of his plan all fell into place. This was all a way to get me to shift again and I had to believe that he was going to kill the one person I loved. Oh crap, I thought as I realized Jaxon was staring at me in my wolf form.

“Allie?” He asked in a pained voice, bending down so that he was level with me. If I was human, I would’ve touched his face gently.

Instead, I took a tiny step forward and pressed my cold nose to his cheek. He dragged his fingers through my fur before standing up again. A thousand, indescribable, emotions flooded his eyes but the strongest one was betrayal and I knew it was going to take a long time for him to forgive me. He was right not to have trusted me. He wasn't the one that played with my heart, I played with his.

I backed away from him slowly and trotting a couple of yards away from him. I looked over my shoulder to see him again but, just like that day at his house, the forest was empty. My ears flattened against my head in sadness but, I turned and galloped away, disappearing into the trees.

The wind whipped through my fur as my claws propelled me forward. Trees blurred by me faster than I thought possible and I launched myself over the river Spencer had chased me across earlier. There was nothing like the feeling. Goodness, I didn't realize how much I had missed being a wolf again. I let out a giddy yip as I dodged in and out of the trees, testing my agility. A white wolf zipped out of the trees and Khione was suddenly running with me, nipping my shoulders playfully. I leapt over her and abruptly changed directions to go to the peaceful lake that held so much serenity.

I came to a bouncing halt at the edge and sat back on my haunches, lifting my head to the sky and watching the moon with a loving gaze. I opened my mouth and howled a song that had been welled up inside me for nine years. It was a song of love, sadness, and power. Khione joined in, our voices mixing perfectly together as if I had been a wolf my whole life.

When our song was finished, Khione said to me, *I never thought this day would come.*

I did, I thought back to her, *I've always known who I really was. It just took me a while to figure out that it was what I wanted to be. I have missed it so much it's not even funny. I would watch Jaxon and the others run as wolves and it would kill me inside, knowing that that could've been me.* I lay down at the edge of the lake, folding my paws and resting my head on them.

You know, Khione thought as she lay down beside me, *If I were human right now, I would be crying tears of joy.*

Yeah, me too.

I gazed one last time up at the moon, gave a short howl, and then Khione and I fell asleep together as if times had never changed.

Jaxon

Oh, God.

No, this isn't happening.

Oh, God yes it is.

Allie isn't a werewolf.

Oh, dear God she really is.

I paced back and forth in Oliver's living room with my hands clasped over my ears to keep my own thoughts out. I wanted to scream so badly but it would only add to the noise of my siblings, Dallas, and Blake yelling at me for more information. My patience was pulled tight and I was about to snap at any minute.

"I ALREADY TOLD YOU EVERYTHING!" I yelled at them viciously with gold eyes. The room went silent. I smashed my fist into the wall, cracking it with my strength.

"How is this even possible?" Blake asked as tears streaked her face. We had had to fill her in on everything werewolf. I gazed at

Cole and Oliver across the room who hadn't said a word since I got here.

"You knew who she was, didn't you?" I accused both of them, my whole body shaking with rage.

"I'm a werewolf too. Of course, I knew." Cole said calmly which really made me want to punch the crap out of him.

"You're a werewolf?" Blake asked with wide eyes. Cole just smiled with a devious twinkle in his blue eyes.

"I only knew because I'm a werewolf hunter. A werewolf is always a wolf even in human form." Oliver said with a little more enthusiasm than Cole but I didn't miss him moving away from my father.

"How did I not know?" I snarled going for another punch for the wall.

"Whoa," Erica said grabbing my fist, "Let's not destroy our future house." I turned my snarl to her and shook her off.

"What did she do to hide it?" I asked Oliver with the same intense glare I had had since I walked in the door.

"It was rather an extensive process." My father said with an impressed look on his face, "But, it's not my job to tell you. Everything that girl did was to hide her and everyone she loved from her past."

Dallas cleared his throat from where he stood in the corner next to Kate, "Allie told me that day she was hurt by that wolf. She said that her mom, dad, friends and she had to leave because they killed too many people." His face had gone noticeably pale but all I felt was the anger inside of me.

"She's rogue?" Terrence asked in an offended voice.

Cole spoke up, “No, she isn’t. She’s a runaway.”

Dallas took his hand out of Kate’s and moved forward, “She said she is an alpha.”

The room went dead. All I could hear were the rapid heartbeats of my pack and the others in the room. An alpha? No flippin’ way could that be true. But then I remembered one of the first times she had come to my house.

“You can leave now. We have this under control. Thanks.” Terrence had said to her and was about to close the front door when Allie held up a hand.

“Don’t you dare slam this door in my face,” She snarled staring right into Terrence’s eyes.

Allie Jennings was an alpha of a rival pack.

I woke up sprawled on the ground underneath Blake who had fallen asleep on the couch. The others were scattered around the room in strange places. Kate and Erica were somehow piled on a tiny chair together, Terrence was beside me, Cole was leaning up against the wall with his head drooped to the side, and I was pretty sure Oliver was the shadowy lump underneath the coffee table. How he had gotten there? I did not know but everyone was stressed last night and we had stayed up either crying or screaming at each other until 3am. As my eyes fluttered open, I couldn’t locate any of the fury I had been raging with last night. All that was left was a big slice of betrayal floating inside of me.

“Oliver! Oliver?” A new voice yelled from outside the door, jolting everyone awake.

Oliver grunted in pain when he hit his head on the underside of the table as he woke up. Multiple tired groans filled the air as everyone woke up to the sound of banging on the front door. I sat up, running my fingers through my crazy hair and yawning after getting about six hours of restless sleep. It took Oliver extra time to get to the door because of how groggy and sore he was. That was what sleeping under a table could do to you. The door opened and I froze as the person's scent filled my nostrils.

"Oliver, this is an emergency."

Allie entered the room to see all of us staring at her in fear.

Allie

The Lochlans, Dallas, Blake, and Cole were sprawled out in different places on the floor. I expected to feel fear when I was forced to face everyone but even that couldn't bring down the amazing mood I was in after running for hours with Khione. The adrenaline was pumping gallons and gallons of itself into my system and I was about ready to bounce off the walls. My eyes went immediately to Jaxon's and that was what triggered the sadness because every emotion I had been hoping to avoid was there. And then I found Blake's. Oh crap, what was she doing here?

I threw my hands up in exasperation, "Are you guys always here?" I shook my head and ran my fingers through my dirty hair.

Blake blinked at me in confusion, "Allie!" She exclaimed and ran over to me, tackling me in a big hug that I hadn't been expecting. I raised my eyebrows in surprise and hugged her back. "Where have you been for the past two days?"

"It's a long story," I said moving over to the couch with her and sitting down, "You guys might as well get comfortable.

I told them everything. I told them about Lydia and Marcus, Spencer and his magic, me not shifting and having to hide, the truth about how I killed Aiden and then the men in the church, and lastly, about how I almost died and had to shift to save me and my wolf's life. Everyone was silent through the whole thing which made me wish I hadn't come here. But, I knew I was going to have to face them eventually.

Jaxon said in a plain, damaged voice, "You forgot the part where you are an alpha."

I glanced down at him where he sat with his back to me on the ground and tried not to cry.

Cole spoke up, "I knew there was something different about you when you walked into the bar that day." He didn't seem at all affected by my story, probably because he had guessed most of it and I smiled gratefully at him.

"That's why I had to hide," I said quietly, "I think Lydia is afraid I am going to kill her and take over the pack. She wants to get to me first." My hands shook slightly but Blake laced her fingers through mine to calm me down. Tears pricked my eyes and I smiled at her.

"I don't think you understand what being an alpha really means." Terrence muttered from in front of Jaxon.

"Pardon me?" I asked with raised eyebrows, staring at the opposing alpha challengingly.

Terrence let out a breath as he stood up, leaning against the fire place, "Khione was a part of your old pack which was abusive but you left her behind to possibly get killed by this Lydia person." He crossed his arms over his chest.

"You really want to play the alpha card right now?" I stood up, moving around Jaxon so that I was standing in front of Terrence who didn't sound like himself at all. "Because darling, I'm more wolf than human and I could crush you in an instant." I made a pinching motion with my fingers.

Terrence's eyes faded to red like mine had a while ago and he growled underneath his breath. I bared my teeth, my canines lengthening into fangs that poked my gums as I clenched my teeth. I held his gaze but when neither of us submitted to the other, my jaw dropped to expose my fangs even better. I was still a few feet away from him but I let out a vicious snarl that echoed through the house. Everyone was up on their feet in an instant and right as I went for Terrence, Jaxon grabbed me around the waist and pulled me back against his body. As soon as he touched me, the fangs and red eyes went away and I was just Allie again, wishing I hadn't screwed up our relationship. We stood there in silence for a few seconds, our heartbeats racing rapidly and his scent turning my body to Jell-O. He moved away from me. I had to fight back the urge to turn back around and crush his lips to mine.

Dallas said, "You are officially considered a missing person, Allie. Mom is sick with worry trying to find you. You need to go home." I smiled at the sight of my little brother holding Kate's hand and acting like the mature one.

But, my smile faded and tears spilled over, "I can't go home." I sobbed, covering my face with my hands and standing awkwardly in the middle of the room with everyone's eyes on me. "I'm a werewolf and she is trying to hunt me. Now, that I've shifted again, it's going to be harder to keep that secret."

I didn't want everyone to watch me crying but my body seemed frozen where it was, my hands covering my face. Without knowing who, someone wrapped me in a hug that swallowed up my whole body. I closed my eyes and wrapped my arms around the person's neck. My body shook as I tried to take in a breath to calm myself down but when I realized who was hugging me, it just made me cry even harder. Jaxon's body pressed against mine and his arms locked me to him like the world's best seat belt. I heard shuffling in the background and muffled voices but all I could think was… God, it felt good to be in his arms after all this time.

Too soon, Jaxon moved away from me, scratching the back of his head awkwardly. I wiped my tears and mascara away and looked at the ground as I folded my arms across my chest. I suddenly realized that the room was completely empty. The others must've deserted the room either because I looked so ugly when I cried or because they wanted to give Jaxon and me some private time. I hoped for the latter. We both waited for the other to say something but words seemed to be caught in our throats.

Jaxon was the first one to speak. He ran his fingers through his hair before saying, "Look, I'm… really sorry about not trusting you. I guess I understand why you did what you did now that I know. But, I still don't get why being a werewolf had to be kept a secret?"

I closed my eyes and let out a breath before opening them again and saying, "Because I didn't want anyone to know who I was." I snarled at no one in particular, "I killed thousands of people just because my mom/alpha told me to. That first full moon when your siblings tried to attack me, I was prepared to kill them too. That's what Lydia did to me. She turned me into a killer and I will never ever forgive myself…" And then he kissed me just like that night in the alley.

I let him force my lips open as I combed my fingers through his hair. Every thought, regret, and sadness vanished from my mind and I felt like every part of me was shining like the sun. Jaxon's hands encircled my waist, pulling me closer to his body and I squeezed my eyes shut, imagining our first kiss with the rain drowning me.

Someone clapped from the doorway, "Well, it's about time."

I made a surprised noise in the back of my throat, jumping away from Jaxon to see Erica and everyone else standing in the doorway with big smiles lighting up their faces. Erica clapped and ran up to me, wrapping me in a huge hug that nearly knocked me over. We laughed when Jaxon had to rest his hand on my back to keep me from falling over. I pulled away from her with a smile and glanced back at Jaxon who was watching me with a grin. I giggled enthusiastically and wrapped my arm around Jaxon's waist, leaning my head against his chest.

Three days later

"Oh, Gosh, please don't go into the closet." Blake squealed at the TV screen, burying her face in Cole's shirt.

I nestled closer to Jaxon's side as the movie lit up our faces like a campfire. Khione and Erica rested their backs against the couch just below my feet, shoving handfuls of popcorn in their mouths. It was Saturday night and no one felt like going out after a crazy week of discovering who everyone really was on the inside. So, we decided a scary movie night was desperately in need. I smiled at Cole and Blake who were curled up together at the other end of the couch. Dallas and Kate were the only ones that felt like getting dressed up and going out to dinner and a movie.

Being a wolf again reminded me of how tiring it was. Running through the woods and hunting every night didn't give me very much time to sleep so I grabbed at moments like these. With my knees pulled up to my chest and my head resting against Jaxon's, I squeezed my eyes shut as everyone prepared for the murderer to leap out of the closet. Screams and squeals burst the silence as the loud music made the suspense even more intense. I cringed, burrowing my face into Jaxon's shirt while he and Cole laughed at the girls.

"Shut up, you guys. This is freaky." Khione looked back and threw popcorn at the boys.

I looked up at Jaxon, "Yeah, why are we watching this anyways?" My boyfriend laced his fingers through mine, rubbing his thumb over the back of my hand.

"Because it's funny…"

Their voices faded out all of the sudden and something told me I needed to focus on my surroundings. I blocked everything out and stared intensely at the front door as I tried to figure out what my wolf was trying to tell me. Then, I heard it. The slight creak of a floorboard underneath someone's or something's foot as it walked across the porch. I lifted my face in the air and flared my nostrils, letting the thing's scent float into my nostrils. It took all of my willpower not to scream when I labeled the scent as werewolf.

"Shut up," I whispered to everybody, leaping off of the couch and pressing my ear to the front door.

"What's wrong?" Jaxon asked as the others came to the door. I put my finger to my lips, my eyes turning bright red.

Snuffling came from the other side and I glanced back to see my friends' eyes change to yellow. They heard it too. My fingers wrapped around the cold doorknob and I counted to three before I flung open the door, the cold air rushing in.

The porch was empty.

"Crap!" I yelled when I burst out onto the porch, throwing my hands up in the air.

"I am so confused," Blake said coming to stand beside me as the suddenly cold air washed over us.

"Cole," I turned to look at him, "Stay with Blake. I'm going to go check this out."

“Wait,” Jaxon growled, grabbing my arm, “I’m coming with you.”

“Fine,” I sighed, “I’m staying human. I haven’t fought as a wolf in a while.” I twisted my brown curly hair up into a high ponytail and then hopped off the porch without bothering to put any shoes on.

“Me too, then.” Jaxon said before looking back at the others standing on the porch and then running into the woods beside me.

The only sounds in the dark woods were me and Jaxon’s feet crunching on the ground and our lungs taking in the frigid air. I gripped Jaxon’s hand like it was my life force as we picked our way slowly through the rocky terrain. The silence was almost painful and it only increased the feeling of puking from the nerves. I chewed the inside of my lip, flaring my nostrils over and over to try and take in the scents of my surroundings.

“I don’t think it’s out here anymore.” Jaxon whispered under his breath and pulled on my hand, forcing me to come to a stop.

“I swear it was out here.” I sighed scrubbing my hands over my face and plopping down on the ground, my back pressed against a tree.

“I heard it too.” Jaxon said coming to sit beside me, pulling his knees to his chest and resting his arms on them.

“My wolf told me there was something out there.” I sighed pinching the bridge of my nose and leaning my head on Jaxon’s shoulder.

He laughed quietly and shortly, “It still seems strange that you are a wolf too. I can’t really get used to it.”

I pressed my lips together, “Yeah, me neither. It feels so good, though.” I leaned my head back and breathed in the cold air.

Jaxon opened his mouth to say something but new scents flooded my nostrils like water breaking through a dam. Jaxon must’ve smelt it too because both of us leapt at the same time, immediately standing back to back, ready to fight. All at once, about seven men and women in black rushed forward, pointing various weapons at our chests. We were completely surrounded by werewolf hunters.

“Wait!” A familiar voice called out and my mother rushed forward to stand in front of me. She held the world’s largest assault rifle in her hands.

No words came to mind as I realized she was also staring at Jaxon, who I had tried so hard to keep hidden. I gripped Jaxon’s arm as hard as I could without hurting him. I gritted my teeth as I stared at my mother, quaking with trepidation.

“Who are you?” Mom asked with a sneer and I knew things were about to get ugly.

“Umm…” Jaxon stuttered scratching the back of his head and glancing behind us.

“Holy…” Mom started to say with wide eyes, “You’re Jaxon Lochlan.” Her hands shook slightly and suddenly the gun was aimed at my boyfriend’s head.

I leapt in front of him, “Mom, stop!”

We stood face to face, our gazes never wavering as mom finally got the chance she had been waiting for. She had finally gotten the chance to kill Jaxon Lochlan but, I was going to be the one to stop it. I didn’t know how far I was going to have to go to slap some sense into her but no matter what the cost, I was going to keep her from destroying Jaxon, me, and herself.

"Allie, get out of my way. You have no idea what he is capable of." Mom said through gritted teeth as she continued to stare right over my shoulder into Jaxon's wide, horrified eyes.

"I know what he is." I told her as her eyes widened, "I've known about werewolves my entire life. I can spot one when I see one. I used to live with werewolves. They might've been abusive but Jaxon and his pack aren't and they have saved me plenty of times." I wrapped my fingers around the barrel of the gun and lowered it until it pointed at the ground. "Now, it's my turn to save them."

"You've known all this time?" Mom asked and I warily glanced at the other hunters who still had their guns pointed at us.

"I've been dating Jaxon for the past few months and I know him well enough to know he would never ever hurt me." I said with a shaky voice, reaching behind me to grip Jaxon's fingers in mine.

Mom hesitated for what felt like years before she said, "I've never trusted werewolves," She raised the gun again, "And I am not about to start, I'm sorry Allie."

Before she could pull the trigger, rage poured over me and suddenly I had body slammed my own mother and pinned her against the nearest tree. My arm pressed against her throat, I bared my fangs in her face and snarled intimidatingly. I could see my red eyes reflected in her blue ones but all I could think about was protecting Jaxon and his pack. Pure shock and horror played across my mom's face as she stared back into my alpha eyes, probably not recognizing her own daughter.

"Allie," Jaxon's voice came firm and harsh from behind me and my mind snapped back into reality.

Letting out a breath, I quickly fell away from mom who stood frozen where she was, never taking her eyes off of me. The fangs, claws, and eyes had vanished and I was just plain Allie Jennings but I knew my mom would never get that image out of her mind. A tear fell down her cheek but she wiped it away quickly, anger and betrayal plaguing her features.

"You're… a werewolf? All these years you never told me. I know I wasn't really there for you after your father died but I thought I would've known you better to know who you really were. God, how could I have been so stupid." She cried as hot tears trailed down her cheeks, "You are not the daughter I used to know. I don't want to see you ever again and if I do, I swear on my life me or my hunters will kill you and your little pack. Please, get out of my sight."

I sobbed, my heart literally breaking inside. As she and the hunters walked away I angrily spat, "Don't bother calling Oliver! He's been on our side this whole time!"

I heard her yell a very loud curse, the wind carrying it back to me and into my ears. Then, she and the hunters were gone and it was just me, standing in the woods completely heartbroken and utterly alone. My breathing quickened but I couldn't seem to get enough air into my lungs as the world spun in circles around me. I crumpled to the ground with a sharp cry and that was when the pain from the past couple of days finally hit me. I screamed as loud as I possibly could until my throat hurt. Jaxon knelt down beside me and was saying something but I couldn't hear him, it was all just static in the background. Oh, what have I done? Jaxon wrapped his arms around me but comfort wasn't what I needed. I needed to run through the woods until the sun came up and would hopefully make my world bright again. I pushed away from Jaxon's arms and stumbled away from him, telling him to leave me alone right before falling to all fours and shifting into my wolf form.

I lifted my head and howled. It wasn't joyous like that first night with Khione. This one was low, bitter, and sorrowful. I glanced back at Jaxon one last time before I vanished into the woods to clear my head of everything and everyone.

Jaxon

"Crap, that girl is good," Cole snarled when he and I burst through my front door six days after Allie disappeared.

"It's been six days. She probably isn't coming home." Terrence growled slicing the knife through a tomato viciously. I slammed my fist down on the granite counter, cursing at the pain.

"She has to come home at some point." I told him as I sat my tired body down onto the stool. Cole and I smelled like we had just swum through the sewer.

"No, she doesn't." Khione said warily, suddenly appearing in our back door. Her bright blue eyes had dulled and she had dark circles underneath them. Everything about her seemed died down as if the loss of her alpha was going to kill her eventually. "That girl has been on the run for years. If you ask me, there is no chance of her coming home. Sorry, but it's the truth." She came to where I was sitting with my head in my hands and patted my back lightly.

"That's the problem." I sighed, "I know she can easily live out there alone but what about her other pack and the hunters. She can't kill them by herself." I removed my hands from my face and noticed that they were shaking slightly.

We sat there in silence for a few minutes before a buzzing sound made everyone jump halfway out of their seats. The knife fell out of Terrence's hand and clattered to the floor. Cole sighed and dug his cell phone out of his pocket, pressing the answer button.

"Wait, Pete, I can't hear you over the noise." Cole said covering his other ear and walking out of the room. I couldn't hear the voice on the other line because of all the music in the background.

"Oh, great." Cole sighed coming back into the room, "No, no keep her there. We are coming."

"What's going on?" Khione asked with wide, hopeful eyes.

"Allie's at the Midnight Hunter's Bar and not lookin' so hot according to Pete." Cole said as we bolted out the door with relief washing over me.

"Well, Pete doesn't need to think she's hot." I snarled protectively but Cole just chuckled as we leapt into his Jeep.

"Put your giant egos aside and drive." Khione said from the backseat, cuffing me on the back of the head. I snarled at her but she just laughed loudly as we drove away from the house to pick up my lost girlfriend who was harder to hold on to than a fish out of water.

As soon as Cole pulled into the parking spot of this well-known bar that was run and owned by werewolves, it took all of my willpower not to cover my nose from the smell. Yes, it smelt like werewolves but it also smelled like drunken werewolves. I leapt out of the Jeep as fast as I could and even though the smell was burning my nose, I plunged into the bar headfirst.

"Allie better not be drunk," Khione muttered under her breath when she and Cole caught up to me.

"She isn't allowed to drink until she's twenty one. Pete won't give her anything." Cole assured us but I wasn't so sure, Allie could be pretty convincing when she set her mind to it.

But, what I saw was even worse than a drunken Allie. Through a circle of rowdy werewolves, I could barely see the outline of her body, crouched down in a defensive position. A vicious string of growls clawed their way out of her throat as she faced off against a gigantic male wolf in human form that was about ten times her size. There were darkened spots on her clothes that revealed blood.

"Allie!" I yelled over the voices and as if I had zapped her, she straightened up and her eyes met mine.

But, as soon as she took her eyes off the wolf in front of her, he backhanded her across the face and she went flying.

"You get Allie." Cole said right before he dropped to his hands and knees in his wolf form with Khione right on his heels.

I followed Cole's instructions and darted over to where Allie was struggling to sit up, a dark bruise crawling across her cheekbone. I crouched behind her and held both her shoulders gently to keep her from getting up. When I put my hands on her, I realized just how much her muscles were quivering in fear. I pulled her back against my chest and glanced up at Cole and Khione who snarled at the burly werewolf threateningly.

"Come on, let's get out of here." I whispered in Allie's ear and helped her up, both of us stumbling towards the glass doors with two wolves galloping after us.

<u>Allie</u>

My hair was wet and plastered to my forehead from the rainstorm I had had to escape before I made it back to the bar. Every part of my body ached with pain and I wanted to curl up in my bed at home and go to sleep. I cursed myself. I didn't have a home anymore. Mom kicked me out and disowned me as her daughter. A tear fell down my cheek as I snuggled closer into the blanket that surrounded my shoulders. The Jeep hit a bump and I groaned as pain rocketed through me where the other wolf had sunk his teeth into me.

"Sorry," Cole said guiltily but I just gritted my teeth and nodded slightly to him, leaning my head on Jaxon's chest and letting him hold me tighter.

“I missed you,” He whispered into my ear, pressing his lips to my temple gently as if I were an expensive vase.

I smiled lifting my face to his, touching his nose with mine, “I’m sorry. I needed to clear my head.” His lips twitched slightly and he quickly touched his lips to mine.

“I understand. You will never have to apologize to me, okay?” Jaxon said looking at me in the eyes intensely.

A smile burst across my face and I lifted my hands out of the blanket to cup his face, “I love you.” Before he could answer, I pressed my lips to his, opening my mouth and accepting his warmth.

Khione snapped her fingers, “Hey! Let’s keep it PG you two.”

Jaxon smiled against my lips and I laughed, kissing him shortly one last time before snuggling back against his chest. His arm came around me, securing me to him. He pressed his lips to my wet hair and I smiled, tears welling up in my eyes as the car zoomed down the street towards the one place I could still call home…Oliver’s house.

When Cole parked his car in Oliver’s driveway, Jaxon wrapped his arm around my waist and helped me into the house where I plopped down onto the couch. I wanted to take a shower so badly and wipe away the dirt and blood from my body. Cole sat in a chair across from me, Jaxon disappearing for a second and returning with a cup of something steaming. I grasped it tightly between my cold hands and took a sip of the hot chocolate which warmed my insides up immediately. I leaned my head back, staring up at the ceiling and trying not to fall asleep. I wanted to stay awake and be with Jaxon after six days of getting lost somewhere in Washington and desperately trying to find my way home. I had only slept for a couple of hours every night because I was so afraid of Lydia or Marcus finding me that I couldn’t force my eyes shut.

Jaxon sat down on the couch beside me, the cushions bending underneath his weight. His hand stroked the back of my head and my eyes fluttered shut, the wolf purring at the electricity of his touch. I deemed myself insane for taking the time to "clear my head". Nothing was better than sitting here with Jaxon who lit up my world just by looking at me.

"Hey," He said quietly, my eyes fluttering open, "Dallas is bringing over your stuff. Oliver said you could stay here until we figure things out." I moved closer to him, tucking my head under his chin.

"Where's the shower in this house? I look and feel like crap," I smiled pushing away from Jaxon reluctantly and shrugging the blanket off my shoulders.

"Up the stairs and to the right," Cole said randomly, reminding me that he was still in the room. I glanced back and forth between him and Jaxon for a second before turning and following his instructions with a shrug.

After taking a much needed long shower, I stepped out of the steaming water, wrapping a towel around me. On the bed in the room I had stepped into, I found two suitcases loaded with all my clothes and some of my belongings I was guessing because I didn't own that many clothes. Numbly, I unzipped them and changed into one of my dad's old t shirts and some leggings that fit snuggly around my body. I sat down on the edge of the bed and scrubbed my hands over my face, wondering what I had done. How could I have destroyed my family like that? Dallas needed me and I needed him. How could my own mother say that I was no longer her daughter? She should've just shot me with the giant assault rifle instead. It would've caused a lot less pain than what I was feeling right then. I wanted to cry but no tears came and I decided that maybe this was going to make me ten times stronger when the time came to claim my place as alpha.

After a couple more minutes of wallowing in pain, I took my head out of my hands and looked around the room I was sitting in. I realized with a shock and a smile that I was in Jaxon's room to be. There wasn't much in it except a bed, dresser, and a desk in the corner by the tall window. I walked over to it, smiling at the pictures that covered the desk. One in particular caught my eye and I picked up the frame to see…me. It was a picture from that night when Jaxon had taken me out to look at the stars, both of us had been sitting on the hood of the car. I realized he must've taken it on his phone later in the night when I had dozed off. In the picture, I was lying on my back, my arms behind my head and my eyes lightly shut as the moonlight and starlight made my pale skin shine brightly. Tears pricked my eyes as I stood there, holding the tiny frame in my shaking hands and wondering how I had gotten so lucky.

"I saw that picture." Someone said from the doorway and I spun around, clutching the frame to my chest. Blake stood in the room with her arms crossed and a half happy half sad look on her face.

"I didn't even know he took this." I whispered looking back down at it in my hands. The smile never left my face.

Blake stood beside me, staring down at the picture, "Jaxon is literally everyone's dream guy."

I looked at her with a curious gaze, "What about Chase? I thought you really liked him." We moved to sit on the edge of the bed again. I still held the picture in my hands.

Blake shrugged, making a face, "Yeah, I kind of broke up with him yesterday." I raised my eyebrow and she rushed forward, "I mean, he was a good guy and everything but…" She dropped her voice so low I had to lean in to hear, "I think I might like Cole."

I squealed louder than I should have but Blake pounced on me, covering my mouth with her hand. I laughed loudly as we fell back on the bed, lying on our backs. Blake said after a few minutes, "It's good to have you back, Allie."

I smiled at her, "I'm sorry I've been so weird lately." I hesitated, "I guess now you know why."

Her chest rose and fell in a sigh, "Yeah, it's still strange to me, though and for the record I kind of wish it was you that would've told me." Blake looked pointedly at me and I laughed, turning my head away.

"Shut up, now you know. We are all good, right?" I smiled holding out my pinky for her. She glared at me but then twisted her finger around mine and both of us laughed like we had never laughed before.

Blake and I made our way downstairs to see Khione, Cole, Jaxon, and Oliver sitting around the coffee table, talking quietly. Jaxon's eyes found mine immediately and I smiled, reminded of the picture I had set back down on his desk. I practically skipped over to him, standing behind the couch and leaning over, wrapping my arms around his neck. Jaxon tilted his head back and pressed his lips gently to mine. I smiled against his mouth before moving away from him and walking into the kitchen.

After grabbing an apple from Oliver's overstocked fridge, I stood in the doorway and watched as Cole smiled at Blake before standing up and giving her his chair. Heat spread across her cheeks but she grinned gratefully and took the chair. Jaxon glanced back at me with a challenging gaze, beckoning me to come over to him. I rolled my eyes at him with a grin before I plopped down on the couch beside him, biting into my apple.

"Alright, boys!" Oliver came into the room and clapped his hands together once to get our attention. "It's late and everyone has had a long day. Go home," Jaxon and Cole growled under their breaths but obeyed Oliver after a few minutes.

Cole had already left but Blake decided to spend the night with Khione and me but I didn't miss the fact that Cole asked for a hug goodbye and she fit perfectly in his strong arms. Khione and she waved goodbye before disappearing back into the living room. Jaxon and I were left at the doorway alone. Finally.

"I wish you didn't have to go," I whispered, looking down at my hands but then Jaxon wrapped me in his arms. He held me close and I closed my eyes, breathing in his scent and trying to block all the shock from the past few days.

"I know. But you need some sleep." He whispered in my ear and I nodded my head slowly.

I pulled away and trailed my finger from his temple down to his jaw, "I'm definitely not going to be able to go to sleep after everything." A bitter laugh escaped my lips.

"Well," Jaxon smiled, pressing his forehead against mine, "I don't care what time it is, if you can't sleep, give me a call and we can talk, okay?" I smiled, tipping my chin forward to kiss him lightly.

"You're the best." I whispered brushing my lips against his again.

"So are you," Jaxon said before opening the front door and stepping out, "See you later," He smiled before I waved and closed the door tightly, locking it behind me.

My feet pounded the ground louder than they should have as the trees whipped past me. My breathing came out in white puffs as the cold air stung my lungs like a thousand angry bees. I didn't know where I was running to or what was chasing me but all I knew was that I had to get away. I sped around a corner and froze mid step because standing in front of me was my mom, once again holding an assault rifle in her hands.

I gasped.

"How many times do I have to tell you?" She said in a cold voice that sounded nothing like hers, "You are not my daughter anymore and I do not want to see you anymore."

"I have nowhere else to go," I sobbed as I stood before her shivering not only from the cold but from the fear. "What about the horses and Dallas?"

Her eyebrows lowered even more as her eyes glowed protectively, "You stay away from your brother before you destroy him like you destroy everything else." I quickly took a step back, stumbling over a tree root and falling to the ground on my butt.

I stared up at a woman who used to love me with all her heart but I had no idea who she was anymore. Tears fell down my cheeks but mom's face stayed stone cold as if she no longer cared about me at all. There she stood, telling me I wasn't her daughter and that I destroyed everything without even a shred of emotion. Then, she lifted the rifle, pointing it at my chest and before I could think to scream, she pulled the trigger.

I gasped, clutching my chest and sitting straight up in bed. I glanced around the room, expecting to see trees and the sky but all I saw was a dresser and a desk. My eyes found the picture and I knew where I was. Jaxon's soon to be room suddenly made me feel safer than I had been before. I looked down at my hands, realizing my claws had dug into the skin of my palm, drawing blood. Blake was asleep beside me, her ribcage moving up and down slowly. Khione sprawled at the end of the bed by our feet and the TV was still on, running through episodes of Glee. We must've fallen asleep before turning it off. I fished for the remote in the blankets, cradling my injured hand to my chest and then flicking off the bright light of the TV.

I made my way to the bathroom, wiping smeared blood off the cuts and letting them heal by themselves. They turned into three white lines across my palm. My cell started buzzing repeatedly where it lay on the desk and I dashed back into the room to get it before it woke Blake and Khione up. I pressed the answer button and held the phone to my ear.

"Hello?" I whispered sitting carefully on the chair that went with the desk.

"Hey, it's me," Jaxon said loudly on the other line. I winced because of my sensitive ears.

"Um, hi, what's up?" I asked with scrunched eyebrows, running my fingers through my hair. I tensed when Khione groaned and turned over but she stayed asleep.

"Come outside," he said and I made my way to the window, peeling it open to see Jaxon standing outside, looking up at me with a grin. I hung up and shook my head at him.

"What are you doing?" I half shouted to him, leaning out the window as my hair blew around my face in the wind. I pushed it away impatiently.

"Come down here, I want to show you something." He said beckoningly and I laughed quietly, rolling my eyes.

"Okay, hang on." I whispered holding up a finger before disappearing into the room again.

I quickly and quietly got dressed into jeans and a t-shirt, loving the fact that my wolf's body heat would keep me warm so that I didn't have to wear seven layers. I fixed my hair as best I could before glancing one more time over at Khione and Blake's sleeping forms but they were too tired to notice me leaving. I went back to the window, looking down and measuring the size of the jump.

"Back up," I whispered to Jaxon but he looked at me like I was insane.

"You're going to jump?" He asked.

"Yes, sir I am. I've done it plenty of times."

With that, Jaxon backed away very slowly and hesitantly as I stepped out onto the ledge. I took in a deep breath, sighing contentedly as the wind brushed my cheeks lightly. I leapt out and away from the house, flipping in midair, and landing softly on my feet in a crouched position to cushion my fall. Jaxon looked like he had just seen a ghost.

When I straightened up, I smiled, "See, piece of cake."

"You're insane."

"Thank you," I laughed as I followed him into the woods and away from the safety of the house. "So, what are we doing out here?" I asked after a few minutes of silence and Jaxon paused, turning to face me.

"I've never really seen you in your wolf form. Well, the first time I was too freaked out to notice but as cheesy as this may sound…want to run with me?" He asked but I was already smiling with excitement. It was my dream to run with Jaxon and now I was finally going to be able to do fulfill it.

"You don't even have to ask," I told him before I dropped to my hands and knees and traded my human skin for the sleek body of a silver wolf.

I looked up at Jaxon whose eyes were shining as he watched me closely. I flattened my ears and whined, waiting for him to shift with me. Every part of me ached to be with him in wolf form and as soon as he shifted, it was like confetti exploded inside of me. The brown wolf that stood beside me was about an inch or two taller and much broader whereas I was lean and fast. His gold eyes found my red ones and I yipped excitedly as if I were a puppy once again. Jaxon took off running and I leapt after him, my strides bouncy and playful as if I were running through three feet of snow. I took the entertaining way, climbing up a hill while he ran below me and I leapt down, intercepting him. Jaxon collided with me, unable to stop his momentum and both of us went tumbling down a hill. I laughed in my mind when we rolled to a stop at the bottom but when no one responded, I realized Jaxon and I were unable to communicate. I guessed it was because he was turned and I was born but it still felt strange.

Jaxon barked, bringing me out of my thoughts and I pricked my ears at him, my tongue lolling out to the side playfully. He moved closer to me and licked the underside of my jaw but I wasn't in the mood for affection. I wanted to run until I couldn't anymore. I yipped again and bounced away from him, trotting in the direction I wanted to go. I heard him following me and when he was close enough to touch me, I poured on an extra pound of speed. Jaxon growled in annoyance but he picked up his pace too and soon enough we were running side by side as if we had been pack mates our entire lives.

I finally came to a stop when I reached the lake that had become my safe haven over the past couple of weeks. Jaxon sat back on his haunches beside me, towering over me with all his muscle and height. The moon's reflection on the water made our red and gold eyes shine brighter. Something else caught my eyes when the light hit it. I glanced down to see a blue sapphire crystal resting right beside my paw. Jaxon noticed it too and I leaned down, using my nose to push it over to him as a gift. His tongue lolled out to the side playfully. The urge to howl was too great so I threw my head back and shared another song to the world. Jaxon hesitated as if he had never howled before just for the fun of it. After a few seconds, though, he joined me and I smiled inside at how well our voices blended together to form one.

Jaxon

Running with Allie had been amazing. No, more than amazing, it was everything. The feeling of her wolf's body next to mine made me feel ten times more alive than I already did. Things finally seemed to be working out for me. I no longer hated my wolf because Allie was one, we had gotten back together, and Oliver and Mary were keeping the hunters at bay. Oliver was doing it because he was protecting us but Mary was doing it because she couldn't kill her own daughter. I didn't doubt that she wouldn't hesitate to kill the rest of my family.

Allie and I had made our way back to our separate houses about an hour ago and now I was sitting in the kitchen watching Erica attempt to make pancakes. Surprisingly, I wasn't even tired after running around the woods with Allie last night. In fact, it just gave me ten times more energy. Kate and Terrence trudged downstairs after a few minutes but scrunched their noses up in disgust as soon as they entered the kitchen.

"What on earth are you making?" Terrence asked running his fingers through his hair that stuck straight up in different places.

"I'm making pancakes, okay?" Erica snapped looking up at us with a fake frown on her face.

Kate looked down at the burned breakfast, "That looks like something that came out the other end of a wolf."

Everyone groaned in disgust.

"Okay, now I've officially lost my appetite, thanks little sister," I patted Kate on the head before settling for an apple.

I made my way into the other room and flicked on the TV, the news channel automatically coming up. It was on mute for the first few seconds so when I saw the picture of a campground torn to shreds, I was very confused. I turned up the volume, calling my siblings in.

The news man said, "….and there was only one survivor, Mike Winter. According to Mr. Winter, the wolves snuck up on them in the middle of the night, quietly taking out tent after tent without making a single sound. Police are saying that they must've been rabid because there was no purpose for the killings. This is Kevin Walters reporting live from Moscow, Idaho." Terrence turned the TV off with shaky hands.

"Holy crap," Erica muttered from beside me, "Moscow is right on the border between Idaho and Oregon. They're close."

"We have to tell Allie." I said and all of us grabbed our sweatshirts before running to the car parked at the end of the street.

Allie

Blake, Khione, and I awoke around noon to the sound of someone pounding on the door. Khione groaned in annoyance, rolling off the bed with a thump.

"Ow," was all she said from the ground and I laughed quietly, hitting Blake with a pillow to wake her up.

“What?” She snapped at me, pulling the blankets over her head.

“Someone’s at the door.” I told her as I got up, realizing I was still wearing the jeans from when I went out with Jaxon.

“So, can’t you get it and let me sleep?” Blake said but I rolled my eyes and nudged her with my foot, hard enough to push her onto the floor. “Hey!”

“Come on, lazy.” I said walking around to the foot of the bed to see Khione curled up on the floor, falling asleep again. “You too,” I nudged her with my toes and she reluctantly stood up with a groan.

I pulled open the front door to see the Lochlans standing before me with concerned looks on their faces. My eyebrows pulled together in confusion but before I could ask what was wrong, the four werewolves burst into the house and made their way angrily into the living room. Blake, Khione, and I followed them into room quickly but with confused looks on our faces.

“Have you watched the news today?” Jaxon asked and I glanced at his hands, noticing with a shock that they were shaking slightly with anger.

“Hun, I haven’t even gotten dressed,” Khione snapped back, irritated that she was woken up so “early”.

“Stop with the smart-alecky comments for a few minutes, Khione and listen.” Terrence snarled, flashing his bright red eyes in a challenge. Khione growled quietly under her breath.

Jaxon said, “Lydia and Marcus’s pack is in Moscow, Idaho. They just devoured a whole campsite. Moscow is right on the border of Idaho and Oregon which means…” He drifted off, not wanting to say the words.

“That means they are coming here.” Khione said softly.

Time seemed to stop.

All I could hear was my shredded breathing.

In.

Out.

In.

Oh, crap I couldn’t breathe.

Panic rose in my chest as I tried to fight for more air in my lungs but it felt like none came. I needed to calm down. No, I couldn’t calm down. Lydia and Marcus were coming. The day I had been putting off for nine years was finally an inch away from my nose and I wasn’t prepared to face it. But, I had to do this. I was going to kill Lydia and Marcus and claim my place as alpha, saving the wolves from years of torture. It was time to wolf up and show my mother and father what Allie Brielle Jennings was truly made of.

The air whooshed into my lungs.

Time started again.

“Allie? You okay?” Jaxon asked and I was shocked when I realized he was standing much closer to me than before.

“Yeah, I’m fine.” I said in a voice that sounded much more confident than I felt on the inside.

“What are we going to do?” Khione asked her voice shaky from where she stood behind me.

“I am going to talk to my adopted mom and convince her to be on our side. Then, Khione you take Cole down to the bar, get as many wolves on your side as possible. Most of their alphas hate Lydia anyways. Terrence, pick up Oliver from work or wherever he went this morning. Blake, go home and protect Dallas. We will find you guys as soon as everything is safe and over." I looked around at the wolves that had become my pack, "It's time for this alpha to take back her throne."

The confidence that had surged through me when I told them about my plan vanished completely when I stepped onto the porch of my mom's house. It wasn't my house anymore. I stared at the closed front door like it was a snarling wolf, my fists clenching and unclenching with my nerves. Slowly, I lifted a fist, preparing to knock.

"No," I whispered, shaking my head and putting my hand down. "Ugh, come on, you can do this." I blew out a breath and then hesitantly, knocked on the door.

A few seconds went by before I watched the doorknob turn and my mom pulled open the front door.

She looked at me as if I were some sort of sales man before saying, "I thought I told you I never wanted to see you again." She folded her arms across her chest and I tried to keep the hurt out of my voice.

"Yeah, well, I'm not really big on giving up if you haven't noticed already." I told her, straightening my shoulders to make myself look bigger. "Can I come in for like five seconds? I really need to ask you something."

"Werewolves don't belong in this household."

"Please?"

"What does this have to do with?" She asked.

“Killing werewolves,” that seemed to have gotten her attention.

“Okay, fine come in.” She moved aside and I stepped across the threshold, “You have ten minutes.”

“Wow, how generous of you.” I said sarcastically but when I looked in front of me, I stopped dead in my tracks, “Oh…crap.”

Standing before me were seven hunters, dressed in all black but luckily they were only carrying small knives that hopefully would kill me right away. I watched them carefully, three women and four men standing stiff as if they were in the army. I swallowed the lump in my throat and said, “Did you watch the news today?”

Mom answered, “Yes,” she came to stand in front of her hunters.

“Well, then you know that the wolves weren’t rabid they were werewolves.” I said fingering the hem on the bottom of my shirt nervously.

“Of course, why are you telling us this?” one of the men asked but I just glared at him and he fell silent.

“Well, because the two alphas that are leading the raids are kind of… my real parents.” I confessed gritting my teeth and waiting for someone to yell at me. I looked at everyone but they were too shocked to even move. “Which means… I know what they are after.”

Complete silence.

“I finally figured it out!” I said loudly, making the hunters jump in surprise, “My parents are alphas which means they passed the gene to me. Oh my gosh, all these years I thought I had to kill an alpha to become one. That’s why Lydia is trying to kill me so that I don’t kill her first.” I ran my fingers through my hair and then turned to the hunters, “I need your help. The Lochlans aren’t the real threat, okay? Marcus and Lydia's pack are. You have seen what they can do and we need a strong army to take them down. That will only happen if the hunters and the werewolves can join together after all these years and save the people who aren't strong enough to protect themselves. We have the luxury of claws and weapons but they don't so we need to do something about this." I realized my hands were clenched tightly into fists, my fingernails digging into my palms.

Mom was silent for a few moments and I really thought she was going to agree to help us. I didn't know what else I could do to convince her. Threatening her would just make her not want to protect werewolves, even if we were the good ones. Mom and I watched each other for what seemed like eons and when she finally spoke, I felt like a bus had fallen on my head.

"No," She said and I didn't miss the look of surprise on the hunters' faces, "I will never be caught dead protecting werewolves. They are abominations and deserve to die." Her words dripped with poisonous venom and a sob rose in my throat.

"Fine, I'll go then," I said before I could either start crying or tear her to shreds.

"Wait!" Someone said and I spun around before I reached the door to see two hunters, Dale and his wife, the ones that were in the woods with me during the full moon. "We want to help you. I'm sick of listening to you," Dale and the woman glared at my mom, "Those wolves may have killed some of our people but they are much more loyal than this group. They are people too."

The two came to stand beside me with their weapons. I smiled triumphantly. As soon as the hunters saw Dale and his wife join me, they exchanged unsure looks and one by one more and more of them came to stand beside me until all seven were backing me up.

“You can decide if you want to join,” I told my mom, “We will be at the clearing in the woods later.”

And with that the hunters and I disappeared out of my old house.

Two hours later, my army stepped into the clearing with brave faces set on destroying the threat and reclaiming their safety. I stepped onto the grassy area with seven fierce hunters behind me. Across from the field came Jaxon with Erica and Kate behind him. Next, from my right came Oliver and Terrence followed by six more hunters dressed in all black. Lastly, Cole and Khione appeared out of the trees silently at first but then around sixteen werewolves in their wolf form surged forward into the center of the clearing, snarling and snapping at each other as adrenaline ran through their veins. Tears pricked my eyes as the hunters swallowed their prejudice and marched into the center, the alphas changing into human form to make amends with their lifelong former enemies.

I stood beside Jaxon and the Lochlans as I watched Oliver, Cole, and Khione greet the alphas and hunters. The feeling I got at the sight of the rivals coming together for once was unlike anything I had ever felt before in my entire life. It was the most beautiful sight in the world. It became even better when a familiar woman stepped in front of me.

“I never back down from a fight,” was all my mom had to say before I wrapped my arms around her, crushing her to me.

“Thank you so much,” I said into her hair as a tear rolled down my cheek.

She pulled away and gave me a puzzled look, “You ready to do this?” Her hands gripped my shoulders, firm but gentle.

"Heck yeah," I smiled as my blue eyes faded to red and my canines lengthened into fangs.

I moved into the center of the clearing, the wolves and hunters surrounding me and looking to me for the battle plans. Nerves and excitement swirled viciously inside my stomach and I plastered on a confident smile that seemed more real with red eyes. But the sight was beautiful. Werewolves and hunters paired up with each other, making an agreement to watch one another's backs during the battle. This was how it should've been our whole lives.

"Alright, everyone!" I said in a loud voice so that everyone could hear me, "I can't thank you enough for doing this. It is a great honor to fight with all of you at my side. I've never been very accepting of my wolf side but I got a taste of both sides when I started training with hunters. I found out that we all have the same purpose. We all want to protect the people who can't protect themselves. That's why we shouldn't be fighting each other. We should be fighting those who try and hurt those who don't have the luxury of crossbows and claws. This is truly a beautiful sight." I smiled at each and every one of the wolves and hunters.

The people around me burst into cheers and the wolves barked their agreement. I caught Jaxon's eye and they were filled with love and appreciation. A giddy laugh escaped my lips.

"Here's the thing," I told them once everyone was quiet; "We have to get Lydia and Marcus here. Don't let their pack know that we have hunters on our side so I just want the wolves to howl, signaling our position. Once they get here, wolves stay in wolf form and stay with your partner. I am going to be human so that I can talk to Lydia and Marcus. If she or he wants to challenge me, then no one can interfere, okay? No matter how bloody it gets, do not join unless their wolves do too." I raised my eyebrows at them to get my point across but the wolves whined, shifting from paw to paw nervously. The two alphas growled quietly, silencing the members of their packs.

I fell to my hands and knees becoming a wolf and I took in the other packs around me. Each wolf had a different quality about them that made them stand out from the rest and I greeted the closest ones with a wag of my tail. The Lochlans fell to the ground with us and shifted into their wolf forms. Jaxon pushed through the pack and made his way to me, rubbing his head underneath my chin. The born werewolves glanced at him curiously, noticing that he wasn't the same as us.

He smells different.

Yeah, definitely not one of us.

I think it's cool, an alpha and a beta.

Guys, I snarled in my head at the wolves from different packs, *he was turned into a werewolf. But, that's not the point right now. We need enough volume to reach Idaho, okay?*

Ooh, the California pack has volume under control, baby. A tawny male alpha thought, baring his teeth in a smile.

Let's hear it then, I thought challengingly and just like that, the afternoon air exploded with the sounds of wolves howling.

I joined in after a few seconds of shocked admiration. We sounded like a thousand wolves rather than twenty three. I added a snarl in the mix just for the fun of it and then added an extra pound of sound to our song. Voices being carried by the wind, I was positive Lydia and Marcus would hear it wherever they were.

An hour past and the nerves were finally starting to dawn on everyone. I heard glimpses of frightened conversation like, "We shouldn't have done this." And "What if this was a bad choice?". But, I also heard conversation from the wolves like, *Finally, Lydia is going to pay for what she has done all these years.* or… *I can't wait to see her face when she shows up here.* The wolves gave me hope more than the fearful hunters did but I had confidence in them that they wouldn't abandon us. I was about to call for another howl when a chorus of snarls filled our ears. Every muscle in my body tensed and I narrowed my eyes at the trees in front of me where I could see the eyes of the wolves stalking slowly towards us. Jaxon came up beside me and snarled but I placed my hand on him to keep him quiet. He looked questioningly up to where I stood in my human form. A low, feminine, devilish laugh bounced off the trees, making it sound like it was coming from seven different directions. My hands clenched and unclenched nervously and after a few extra seconds they appeared in front of us.

Over thirty wolves, over thirty of my friends, stood behind their two alphas, snarling quietly and salivating. My eyes grazed over the wolves, a sob rising in my throat when they landed on Monica and Rachel who stood behind Lydia and a little to her left. I also noticed that they were avoiding my gaze. I growled at the cowards that were once my friends. I scanned the others and was able to name almost every single one of them. Hunter, Jenson, Saxon, Kyle, and Lexie. There were so many hunters, trackers, fighters, mothers and fathers but they didn't realize they were using their talents for evil.

Slowly, I turned my angry gaze onto Lydia who was in her human form and Marcus who stood beside her as a russet brown wolf with red eyes. I was surprised when no more fear rose up in my chest. This time when I saw her face, all I felt was confidence that I could change the world of the werewolves. I took her in piece by piece. Lydia's dark brown hair flowed across her shoulders and down her back, shining in the sun. She had fierce green/gray eyes that seemed to burn holes into me as we stared at each other in silence. I was astonished how much she looked like me now that I was older.

"Well, well, hunters and werewolves finally joining together, huh?" Lydia said in an all too calm voice for my liking, "I bet my daughter had something to do with this." Her lips curled up in an evil smile, “Let’s just hope this immature little plan of hers blows up in her face.” Lydia’s eyes slid over the group behind me before finding mine. Her smiled widened.

“What do you want?” I spat the words in her face but stayed where I was a few feet away.

“What do I want?” Lydia asked in an innocent voice, placing her hand over her heart, “You’re the one who called me here. Quite loudly, I might add.” Her eyes flashed red and when she didn’t answer my question, I growled. Lydia’s laughter sounded like bells ringing, “Okay, okay. I’ll stop joking around. I think you are asking why I have been hunting you all this time. Well, my sweet girl, it’s because you have something I want.” Lydia paused and suddenly her canines lengthened into fangs and she snarled, “You have the powers of an alpha!”

I tried not to flinch at her voice like some of the hunters behind me did. As calmly as I could manage I said to her, “That’s not my fault, is it? I never killed another alpha. I was born an alpha. You can’t take this away from me.” Sensing a fight, claws extended my fingers and fangs appeared.

Marcus growled beside Lydia as she said, “But, my dear daughter, I can take that away from you. Want to know how?” when I didn’t respond she answered her own question with a deadly light in her red eyes, “By tearing you to pieces and making sure you never get back up.” When her fists unclenched, black claws lengthened from her nails.

Jaxon snarled and snapped his teeth threateningly.

Lydia looked at him like he was no bigger than an ant that she had crushed.

“I won’t let you.” I said straightening my shoulders, “I am what an alpha means, not you. I can protect your wolves and use their talents to help people instead of destroy them." I pointed angrily at the wolves behind her, "Those wolves will follow you to the ends of the earth and back not because they agree with you. It's because they are afraid of you. A pack should not be afraid of their alpha. They should be able to trust a leader, like me," I finished and kept my eyes on Monica and Rachel whose tails wagged slowly at my speech.

My eyes widened when I saw the two wolves glance back and forth between Lydia and me. One of them whined but I couldn't tell which one right before Monica's golden brown wolf stepped forward, ears pricked and chest puffed out with confidence. She bared her teeth at her alpha before walking slowly and calmly to where Jaxon was standing. Rachel was next, her dark grey fur glistening in the sun as she took a position next to her best friend. A small smile lifted at the corners of my lips as I glared back at Lydia who was trying to keep her composure. I waited for more to come over to our side but most of them quivered in fear, unable to disown their alpha like I did. I hid my annoyance as best as I could.

Lydia, being my mother, saw it, "Aw, did someone think trust would win out over fear?" She moved closer to me so that our faces were almost touching. The wolves and hunters tensed beside me as she said, "Well, let me tell you something, dearie…" her hand moved up to cup my cheek, her claws grazing my cheek, "Fear always wins." Then, faster than a cobra her other set of claws slashed me across the face and I was whipped to the side at the impact.

My body shook violently, the wolf and I ready to end this ongoing battle. Jaxon, Monica, and Rachel started to move forward to attack Lydia but I shook my head at them. "This is my fight," I whispered before my body was overpowered by the wolf and I was standing on four legs, blood dripping down my cheek. Lydia had shifted too and she snarled at Marcus to stand back; she wanted to kill me herself. The packs on either side of us took a couple of steps back to give us room as Lydia and I circled each other. I snarled, snapping my teeth threateningly as I watched practically my mirror image bare her teeth slowly. Lydia made a fake move to attack me and I countered, jumping backwards half a step. I knew I had to make the first move or Lydia was going to get the upper hand and she was ten times stronger than I was in her wolf form. So, I was the one that started the fight.

Like bullets out of a gun, Lydia and I charged each other, head on with our heads low and teeth snapping. Right before we collided, though, I bunched up my muscles and met my former alpha in the air, claws and teeth locking into each other as we fell like rocks onto the ground. All I could see was a blur of saliva, teeth, claws, and fur as we savagely tried to get a good hit in on one another. We came to a stop and I finally had Lydia pinned beneath me, my claws digging into her shoulders to keep her on her back. I went for her throat immediately but Lydia dodged my teeth, sending them biting the ground. Her fangs sunk into the flesh on the side of my neck and I thrashed, yelping wildly as her jaws closed tighter and tighter. Where she had gotten me wouldn't have killed me but it hurt like crap. I clawed at her face and chest as she held onto me as hard as she could, leaping up and pulling me to the ground in an instant. With my teeth rendered useless and Lydia pinning me to the ground, there was only one thing I realized was going to save me. My paws were trapped underneath her silver body that hovered over me. I squeezed my red eyes shut and did something I had never done before. I morphed my paw into a hand, nails lengthened with claws and while Lydia was busy trying to cut off my air, which was working, I jammed my claws into the flesh of her underbelly.

Lydia roared, releasing my neck as blood flowed from the wound I had caused. She opened her mouth and instead of growling, she coughed up crimson blood. My mother looked up at me through red eyes and for once in my life I saw fear. She coughed more blood and I knew it was my chance to end her miserable life right then. So, why did I hesitate? Why was I staring at her through my wolf eyes and seeing the wolf that took care of me? Lydia's legs shook and I knew she was going to die anyways as she collapsed, lying on her side and panting heavily.

Slowly, I stalked up to her, my claws digging into the dirt underneath me. A steady string of growls rolled from my throat and I stood above Lydia as she looked up at me. That was it. The moment I had been waiting for. Nine years planning how I was going to do it and there I stood hesitating. I whined before shifting back into my human form, blood covering my entire body and only some of it was mine. A sob rose in my throat as I crouched down beside Lydia's head, stroking her fur between her ears. She growled quietly and halfheartedly tried to bite my ankle.

"Please," she croaked when she shifted into her human form, bloodied and tired, "Please, don't do this. Allie it's me, your mommy." Lydia grabbed my hand but just as quickly I pulled away.

"No," I said as a tear fell down my cheek, "You may be my mother but, you will never ever be my mommy." I snarled as my claws grew back and I prepared to end her life right then. "Say goodbye to your horrible life, Lydia. I hate you so much." I said and saw the fear flash in her eyes right before I slashed my claws across her throat.

Blood leaked from the wounds that had cut her windpipe and a sob rose in my throat as her mouth dropped open slightly and then the life and fight drained from her red eyes that faded to gold and then back to grey. Lydia died on the grass where Jaxon had taken me to watch the stars. I sat there, staring down at my bloody hands with no emotions at all running through me. I wanted to scream but the alpha in me wanted to howl in triumph as my wolf gained more power. It felt like I sat there for years before I heard a roar behind me…Jaxon's roar.

I spun around in time to see my boyfriend in his wolf form charge my father who had been quietly sneaking up on me with his teeth bared. Marcus didn't even register quickly enough that Jaxon was strong enough to kill an alpha. Jaxon's dark brown body plowed into Marcus before I could scream and the two went tumbling into the trees, disappearing from sight.

"Jaxon?!?" I screamed desperately when everything went deadly silent and I no longer heard the wolves snarling. "Jaxon!?!" I yelled out again glancing back at the other Lochlans who stood at attention. I looked down one more time at Lydia's cold body before I leapt up and sprinted into the woods where I saw them disappear.

That was when I heard it. A low groan came from somewhere off to my right but the smell of blood was everywhere, nearly choking me to death. Tears streamed down my cheeks as a horrible image of Jaxon's wolf lying in a pool of blood flashed before my eyes.

He's not dead.

Jaxon.

What if he's dead?

Jaxon.

I love him.

I scrambled to a river bank and gripped the dirt edges, mud sliding under my fingernails. Panic rose in my chest when I saw two dark forms lying in the water. One was breathing; one wasn't. I leapt down into the river, water splashing up around me. I trudged through the current and when I finally saw the two figures, I fell to my knees with a gasp.

Jaxon

Power surged through me as Marcus and I tumbled over the edge and into the water. His claws ripped the skin of my shoulder and I howled in pain as water rushed up around us. We plunged deep into the river but before Marcus could drag me under, I paddled my way in a panic towards shallow waters with the alpha snapping at my tail. I couldn't let him go back there and kill Allie. I had to win that battle for her. I leapt up into the shallow part of the river and was immediately tackled by Marcus again, both of us going down. His teeth locked around my snout and I was at a complete loss of escape ideas but then, I fell silent and went limp in his grasp.

Marcus dropped me, thinking I had given up. I wanted to so badly. But then I heard *her* voice calling out my name and I knew she needed me to win.

I let my eyes fall shut, using my ears and nose to tell me that Marcus's teeth were about to close on my throat. My eyes flew open and I lunged forward, my teeth sinking into his throat and snapping his windpipe before he could think to dodge me. Marcus fell to the ground and the life drained out of his eyes like the red bled into blue.

My vision flickered as the world seemed to spin in a circle. A rush of strength and power surged through my veins forcing me to groan loudly. I gritted my teeth together tightly as I looked down at my hands which flexed when claws grew from my finger nails. Wait, claws? But then, they disappeared and my head whipped to my right when I heard a splash and someone gasp quietly.

Allie

Jaxon eyes met mine but they weren't brown or gold like they usually were. Instead, they were bright red, the color of the alpha and I realized Marcus was lying dead in front of him. Jaxon was an alpha like me and his brother, making me wonder how the Lochlans' futures would play out. My legs didn't seem to work so they wouldn't let me run to him like I wanted to.

“Jaxon,” I whispered in a cracked voice and was about to fall into the river from exhaustion when all of the sudden his arms were around me, lifting me off the ground.

I wrapped my arms around his neck tightly, burying my face in the crook of his neck and breathing in his scent. His arms lifted me higher off the ground and I wrapped my legs around his waist just to get closer to him and make sure he was real. I squeezed him tighter, feeling a tear splash onto my neck and I realized he was crying. I pulled away, dropping my legs to the ground so that I could see his face clearly. Another tear fell down his cheek and I smiled wiping it away with my thumb like he had done to me many times before.

“I thought you were dead,” I whispered to him in a voice that sounded nothing like the one I had challenged Lydia with.

Jaxon smiled, resting his forehead against mine before saying, “You can’t get rid of me that easily.” And then I kissed him with everything I had because I loved him so much.

One week ago, I had become an even stronger alpha than I was before by taking the power from Lydia. One week ago, Jaxon had also become an alpha with me. And one week ago, my life became perfect. I had my real mom back, the one that cared for me. When we told Blake the news right after everything she had gone straight to Cole and wrapped her arms around him. Lydia and Marcus’ pack was now my pack and Oliver had a company building houses for them on a big lot which meant my family got to move into a bigger house. The hunters and werewolves now joined together and tracked down rogues as an unstoppable team. And today was my birthday.

Oliver’s house was filled with tons of my friends from school who most likely just came for the food and the giant mansion.

Khione, Miles, and Erica were laughing together as if they had been friends since birth. Cole and Blake's hands were intertwined and he was whispering things into her ear that made her laugh. Terrence and Oliver chatted quietly, laughing like the father and son they were. Kate and Dallas stood together, both of them talking animatedly. Those were a few of the amazing things I saw as soon as I opened the front door with my mom beside me. My high heels clicked on the tile floor as I walked past many people who hugged me and wished me happy birthday. I wore a short sparkly black party dress with my brown hair curled into ringlets.

Mom stopped me in the corner and said to me with tears in her eyes, "You don't understand how proud I am of you. Your entire life you have done everything to protect the people you care about and I couldn't ask for a better daughter. Thank you for showing me what it really means to be a woman." A tear fell down my cheek as her words spread joy and sunshine through my whole body.

"I love you," I told her before throwing my arms around her neck and pulling her to me.

When I pulled away, my mom said to me, "Go have fun at your eighteenth birthday party. You only get one." And with that she squeezed my hand once and then disappeared into the crowd to go talk to Oliver and Terrence, most likely.

"Blake," I called out when I didn't see Jaxon anywhere.

"Hey! Happy birthday!" she said hugging me cheerfully, the light blue dress she was wearing making her eyes stand out.

"Thanks," I said back still glancing around I shouted over the music, "Have you seen Jaxon?"

Blake took a sip of her drink before nodding and pointing to the balcony that was above us on the second floor. "He's up there. He told me to tell you that, sorry, I kind of forgot." Heat spread across her cheeks when Cole squeezed her hand and I grinned.

"Okay, thanks, see you later." I told both of them before clicking up the stairs in my annoying black heels.

I made my way into the room that led out onto the balcony where sure enough I could see Jaxon's silhouette leaning over the railing. The stars and moon made him slightly visible and butterflies lurched around in my stomach as I pulled open the glass door. As soon as I stepped out, Jaxon turned around and his lips parted when he took me in. His chocolate brown eyes grazed me up and down before coming back to my eyes, his lips turning up in a smile.

"You… you look beautiful," He stuttered as if I had punched him in the gut.

I blushed big time, tucking a piece of hair behind my ear, "Thank you," I said quietly not wanting to disturb the peace as I stood by the railing beside him.

For a few moments, we looked out over the woods, our shoulders touching slightly but nothing else. I couldn't stop smiling for some reason and I realized how I had never felt like my life was perfect. For nine years, Lydia and Marcus dangled above my head, waiting to drop at any moment. But, now they were gone and I had everything I would ever need. Jaxon and I loved each other and now our connection was even stronger than it was before. He turned to look at me as if he had read my thoughts.

"I have something for you," He said breaking the silence and I turned to look at him curiously. He shoved his hand into his pocket and came out with a small box balanced on his palm. Looking up at him through narrowed eyes, I slowly took the velvet box from his hands. I opened it and a tiny gasp escaped from my lips.

Resting inside was a delicate silver necklace and dangling from the chain was the blue sapphire crystal that we had found by the lake the first night we ran together. I took it out and still unable to speak, I handed him the necklace, turning around. He placed it gently on my collarbone and hooked it together, pulling my hair out so that it flowed back around my shoulders. I looked down at the shining necklace and couldn't think of anything better to start off many good years to come.

I reached up and cupped his face in one hand saying, "Thank you, it's perfect." Jaxon beamed down at me and then slowly, I pressed my lips to his, letting the electricity flow through me like a soft current.

One hand pressed against my lower back and his other resting on the back of my neck, I moved closer to him until I felt like one person. I could feel the feather touch of my new necklace on my skin and knew it represented Jaxon perfectly, warm and always shining. We pulled away and I looped my arm through his as both of us leaned back on the railing. I rested my head on his shoulder and he glanced at me with a smile for a few seconds before turning his eyes back to the woods. There was nowhere else I would've rather been than standing there with Jaxon where I would always feel safe and protected.

Once upon a time I was a girl who was afraid to become a wolf. Then, there was a boy who embraced that part of himself. We fell in love, saved each other many times, and learned from our mistakes. Now, I'm not afraid to become a wolf because I know I won't lose myself anymore. He will always be there to make sure I always find my way back to his side where I belong forever.